FROM THIS DAY FORTH

To prevent the loss of his estate in a wager, Remy St Cyres agrees to abduct and wed the first woman who comes through the inn door. Fleur Russell is that woman. And, her reputation ruined, her brothers – who half kill her abductor – insist on marriage. The son of a Spaniard, Remy is recruited as a spy in England's war with Spain and thus begins a tale of betrayal, revenge and untimely love...

FROM THIS DAY FORTH

FROM THIS DAY FORTH

by

Janet Woods

Magna Large Print Books
Long Preston, North Yorkshire,
BD23 4ND, England.

British Library Cataloguing in Publication Data.

Woods, Janet
    From this day forth.

    A catalogue record of this book is
    available from the British Library

    ISBN   978-0-7505-3920-3

First published in Great Britain by Robert Hale Limited

Copyright © Janet Woods

Cover illustration © Malgorzata Maj by arrangement with
Arcangel Images

The moral right of the author has been asserted

Published in Large Print 2014 by arrangement with
Janet Woods, care of Kate Nash Literary Agency

Magna Large Print is an imprint of Library Magna Books Ltd.

Printed and bound in Great Britain by
T.J. (International) Ltd., Cornwall, PL28 8RW

ONE – 1778

The main parlour of the *Fox and Hound* was a broth of human ripeness, tobacco smoke and spilt ale.

Remy St Cyres gazed at the surface of his wine. A pair of dark eyes stared back at him, an inheritance from his Spanish-born mother. The expression in them was slightly reproachful.

Blowing a storm of ripples across the liquid, he pulled a smile on his face and looked to where one of his two companions sat. 'What's the time, Charles?'

The building shook and a gust of wind rattled the shutters. His lips thinning into a smile, Charles pulled a gold watch from his pocket. Once the possession of Remy's father, the timepiece had been lost on the turn of a card. Remy had the devil's foul luck when it was pitted against that of Charles.

'It's twenty minutes past the hour. You have until midnight.'

Remy smiled with false confidence. 'I live a charmed life, my friends. A maid of suitable birth is sure to come through that door. Once I'm wed I'll be back in my grandfather's favour and my allowance will be restored.'

Simon Ackland leaned forward, the expression in his eyes more challenging in inebriation than when he was sober. It was his birthday they were celebrating. 'Nothing was said about your bride being of suitable birth, just that she be of marriageable age.'

Remy stared at him, astonished. 'To marry unsuitably would defeat the object of this exercise. My grandfather would then disinherit me without compunction.'

Charles tapped a fingernail on the pocket watch, which lay face up on the table. Etched inside the hinged cover a ruby-eyed snake coiled inside a garland of Tudor roses. The St Cyres crest seemed to mock him.

Softly, Charles reminded him, 'There is more at stake than your allowance. If you do not carry off and wed the first unattached woman to walk through the door, I will call in your debts. The deeds to Rosehill estate should just about cover them.'

Remy blanched at the enormity of his debt to Charles. He gazed at the door, and then ran a palm over the ring on his little finger for luck. The ruby was his birthstone. The jewel in the ring glowed like fire in the lantern light. It had been a gift from his parents, one he'd sworn never to part with.

'The ruby is the lord of gems,' his mother had told him when he'd turned sixteen. 'Wear it on your left hand and it will protect you from misfortune.'

It had. Two months later his parents had been slain, their coach ambushed on the King's highway, on this, the Dorsetshire side of London. Nothing had been stolen, but there were rumours of a grudge slaying, for his father had held an important position as one of the King's advisers. Fate had given Remy a bout of dysentery, which had prevented him from being with them.

Now the ring was the only possession of value he had left. The thought of losing it at the gambling table along with his estate, made him sick at heart.

My home on the hill, Remy thought in desperation. That's what his mother had called Rosehill, the estate where he'd been born and raised. Now he looked set to lose it too.

He'd been too young to handle the responsibility attached to his father's estate and the title of Viscount which had been passed on to him. His grandfather, the Earl of Blessingham was an autocratic tyrant who'd disapproved of his mother's foreign blood. Recently, he'd withdrawn Remy's allowance, declaring his grandson a disgrace to the memory of his father, as well as to himself.

His lips tightened. Would his parents be proud of him now – a son who'd gambled away his birthright in eight short years? He doubted it. Whatever the outcome of tonight's drunken wager, Remy swore he'd never gamble again, especially with Charles, who was considerably skilled at cards and his senior by several years.

Head beginning to pound he gazed desperately at the hands of his father's watch, willing them to slow down – praying a woman suitable for his purpose would appear.

Charles wore a smug smile, as if he knew the outcome. Suspicion filled Remy's heart. Charles had the cunning of a fox. Had he arranged for his sister to be part of this wager?

Catherine Boney was not the type of woman Remy admired. She was too studied in her perfection. She made him feel uneasy, though he couldn't place a credit to his reasoning. What if it was arranged so she'd come through that door first? Charles would win either way.

He swore when the watch chimed half past the hour.

Charles' eyes were bland as he expertly shuffled the cards, but his knowing smile stayed in place.

Rain slanted against the roof. Rivulets found their way down the chimney to hiss against the glowing coals. Despite his bravado, Remy was pessimistic. No unmarried woman would be abroad in this weather unless she had a specific reason, he thought, his spirits plunging to a low level as Catherine came to mind again.

As he sloshed a measure of wine into his cup, the wager did not seem quite so funny to him now, and the wine had a bitter taste. He pushed it from him.

Due to the late hour, the road between Dorchester and the harbour town of Poole was almost deserted.

Fleur Russell drew a hood over her wind-whipped hair and surveyed her three brothers through narrowed eyes. 'I'm chilled to the marrow, as damp as a frog, and totally exhausted. The lights of the inn are visible up ahead. Please allow me go ahead and secure us some accommodation.'

Leland grunted as he and Macy put a shoulder to the coach, stuck axle deep in the mud. It would have been helpful if their uncle had helped lighten the load. Unaware of the misfortune that had befallen them, the bishop snored cozily in a corner.

The coachman's whip cracked over the horses heads, encouraging them to pull. They made a valiant effort. Steam snorted from their nostrils when they applied their over-worked muscles to the task. The poor beasts were beginning to lather.

Fleur sighed. 'You cannot allow those poor creatures to pull us on to Poole tonight, Leland. They need to rest. Stable them for the night and free the coach in the morning. A coin or two will get you all the help you need on the morrow.'

Straightening up, Leland eased the small of

his back with his hands. 'I think you're right. Go and secure us a couple of rooms then. Macy and I will unhitch the horses and wake the Bishop. He'll have to help carry the luggage.'

He jerked a red-thatched head at their younger brother. 'Take Cris to protect you,' he said, his expression clearly conveying something else. Crispen had just recovered from a lung infection and was labouring to breathe in the raw air without coughing.

Crispen was the one most like her with his green eyes and shock of sable curls. He wasn't as unpredictable as the dark-eyed physician, Macy, nor was he as straightforward as Leland. At eighteen, and her junior by one year, Crispen possessed a lively mind and an enigmatic charm.

Fleur loved all her brothers with a passionate intensity, but the youngest drew from her a motherly affection. Childhood playmates, Crispen's traumatic birth had been at the expense of their mother's life. Ten years later they'd clung together for comfort when their father's death had orphaned them.

Fleur had comforted her younger brother, and had attempted to shield him from the rough discipline their two elder half-brothers meted out as they grew. Despite her efforts, he'd managed to grow up with his fair share of the Russell fearlessness, which grew stronger with his journey into manhood.

The offspring of an earlier marriage, Leland and Macy had assumed guardianship and raised them. But the situation was changing. Leland had taken a wife a few months previously. At the same time, Macy had announced his intention to study surgery. As for herself, she was being packed off to live in the bishop's household.

It wasn't fair, she thought mutinously. She'd miss Cris, and she'd be bored witless.

There had been a ferocious argument before she left, of course, conducted out of earshot of the bishop in the stable yard. But Leland knew her too well and would not be moved by either temper or tears.

'Marguerite says you have hoydenish tendencies because I've neglected your female needs. I'm inclined to agree with her. You can't sing or play an instrument, or even dance. You've been educated in the wrong areas and are lacking the feminine virtues a man expects in a wife. Your Aunt Verity will rectify your faults, and a season in London will secure you a husband.'

She scowled at him. 'If Aunt Verity is so solicitous of my welfare, why didn't she offer to improve me before? Could it be because my spinster second cousin left me her fortune and Aunt Verity has a gibbering idiot of a nephew she wants to marry off?' She turned towards Macy for support. 'Can

13

you imagine me as wife to the Reverend Chalmers?'

Macy's lips twitched, but his hazel eyes remained flat and dangerous. 'To be honest with you, no, I can't. The man is a fat, lazy slug who left his brains in the cradle.' He took out his pistol and examined it. 'Rest assured, Fleur. The suitor who hopes to claim you, must prove his worth to me, first.'

Leland flicked him a grin. 'You've chased off every suitor who gets within a courting mile of her. It would take a fool to cross you.'

'He'll need to be fearless to cope with our sister.' Macy allowed an ironic smile to soften his mouth. 'Fleur needs a man with special qualities; don't you agree?' Macy didn't elaborate on those qualities but the look he exchanged with Leland was accompanied by a knowing grin.

Fleur snorted, knowing herself to be at a disadvantage when her brothers teamed up. 'Both of you can keep your counsel. Just be warned. I intend marrying the man I fall in love with, whether you think him suitable or not, Macy.'

'If you need assistance getting him to the altar, let me know,' Crispen offered, and the three of them began to punch each other on the shoulders and laugh.

Disgusted, because Crispen had united

with their brothers in teasing her, she gave them all a good earful before ascending into the coach after the bishop.

'They are ill-mannered brutes,' she tossed casually at him by way of explanation.

The bishop's sour expression spoke volumes and brought bright colour whipping to her cheeks. From that one look, she knew what her future held, and her heart sank. Anything would be better than living in this self-righteous bore's household.

As the coach carried her further away from her home, she grew more and more determined. If anyone expected her to become a weak-minded woman at the beck and call of some man they would soon learn different.

Conversation with her uncle proved difficult. Eventually her attempts became desultory, then ceased. She was relieved when his head lolled to one side, though he snored like a demented bullfrog.

As the horses ate the miles, her annoyance at being expelled from her home abated. Perhaps a few social graces wouldn't go amiss, she conceded. She would certainly like to learn how to dance.

Their sudden entry into the mud stopped her train of thought. The jolt propelled her forward onto the bishop's flabby stomach. He emitted a flatulent and deflating, 'frrr-rrumph!' then continued to snore.

'Just as well he's asleep,' she muttered, flapping her handkerchief in front of her nose and grinning when her brothers' heartfelt curses coloured the air.

That had been an hour ago. Now, bone-weary and hungry, the distant lights of the inn glinted a welcome.

Behind them, the sound of a carriage was heard.

'If we want a comfortable bed for the night we'd better be off, else someone else might get their first,' she said to Crispen.

The hands on the timepiece moved inexorably towards midnight. Remy and Charles stared at each other across a pack of cards. Simon staggered outside to relieve himself.

Without flickering an eyelid, Charles said, 'One last wager, Remy. Highest card. Your gambling notes against the ring.'

An even chance! Sweat pricked at Remy's forehead. It was as though the devil himself was tempting him. His palm circled over the ruby, reminding him it was a gift of love. He took a deep breath. 'I'm through with gambling.'

'How do you intend to retrieve the estate back from me then?' Charles sneered.

Remy tried not to sound as despairing as he felt. 'You haven't got Rosehill yet.'

'In exactly two minutes–'

The door crashed open. A draught set smoke billowing from the fireplace. Simon grinned as he swayed back and forth in the doorway. 'A woman and a youth on foot are approaching.'

Clearly startled, Charles shot to his feet, scattering cards in the process. 'A youth?' He recovered quickly. 'A peasant I imagine,' and he turned to Remy. 'I won't hold you to the wager if she's of unsuitable birth. No woman of quality would be afoot, especially at this hour.'

But he was talking to himself, for Remy had decided not to allow himself to be manipulated by Charles any longer. He would decide for himself if the woman was a suitable match. If he lost the wager he'd throw himself on the mercy of his grandfather.

Snatching up the watch Remy hastened to the door, slipped outside and snapped. 'Fetch my horse, Simon. Let's get this over with.'

The lantern they carried was extinguished by a gust of wind, but not before he caught a glimpse of them. Both were young, but the woman seemed well dressed and shapely. The lad was slight, and would be no bother.

It was surprisingly easy to take the woman. He tapped her on the shoulder, saying, 'Have you a husband?'

'No,' she spluttered and Remy caught the glimpse of a luscious mouth and a pair of large glittering eyes before she turned to the youth, who was suffering the onset of a sudden coughing fit.

As the lad bent double Remy pushed him to the ground. He grabbed the bottom of the woman's cloak, threw the garment over her head and bound her arms to her side with the noosed cord he'd brought with him.

Lifting her struggling form he threw her face down over his saddle and whooped triumphantly. It took but a moment to mount, and he turn his gelding towards Rosehill.

The youth sprang at his stirrup, managing to hold tight for a few seconds until he lost his grip. Remy put his foot in his chest and pushed, sending him reeling. He was doing him a favour. His mount was unsettled and ready to lash out at anyone who got within range.

Remy swiftly got the horse under control. A little while later he grinned when he heard muffled curses coming from the folds of the cloak. The wench had a lively turn of phrase. His glance slid along her length and he ran an assessing hand over her backside. She also had a form worth a second look.

An outraged shriek and her struggles to free herself were redoubled. The horse began to sidestep when she managed to disentangle a hand and grab its mane for support.

'Stop struggling, wench, or my horse will throw us and stomp all over you. He has no liking for strangers.'

'Keep your hands off me, you ... you gutless, hen-hearted bully. I'm not some brood mare you purchased at market,' she hissed, her fury muffled by the cloak.

An amusing truth under the circumstances, by God! He began to laugh until his horse smelt a warm stable ahead and went into a trot. His burden groaned. Aware her position was causing her discomfort, Remy slowed to a walk, rearranged her cloak and hauled her into a sitting position in front of him.

She jerked her leg back and heeled him in the shin.

He sucked in a deep breath, but managed to refrain from cussing. Had he been in her position, he'd have done the same.

The euphoria of the wine he'd consumed had worn off, and was swiftly being replaced by a headache. 'Calm down and just sit quietly. The sooner you do that, the sooner we'll be comfortable and I'll be able to explain the position you find yourself in. Do you understand?'

She said nothing. The power of her seething fury tensed her body. This was no wilting flower. Given the chance she'd uncoil like a spring, hurl herself from the horse and make a run for it. Half of him hoped she'd escape, the other half remembered Rosehill. He tightened the rope around her body.

Lightning flickered in the distance. A low grumble of thunder followed, like a warning growl from an unfriendly hound. He cursed when a sudden downpour of rain slanted down on them.

'Hah!' she spat out, 'A little cold water may cool your devil's blood.'

'Let's hope it cools yours,' he muttered, 'You're as prickly as a hedgehog in a pickle barrel.'

His burden hissed something intelligible, then relaxed a little as the horse plodded towards Rosehill. He tried not to think of the consequences of his action this night ... tried to ignore the tantalizing perfume lingering about her. He had other things to think about – mainly his own stupidity.

This girl he'd abducted was of good birth. He guessed her coach and escort had become mired back along the road, because she was not abroad on such a night by chance. Someone would look for her, and they'd find her without too much trouble.

The wind had increased in strength. The forest bent beneath its fury, the branches of the pines cracked and snapped above them, peppering them with bark and needles.

Then they were clear of the trees. Ahead were a long, sloping hill and the pale, flickering light of a solitary lantern to guide him home. As Remy urged the horse into a gentle canter his passenger showed her familiarity with horses by every unconscious movement of her body. They were too close for his comfort, he realized a few moments later, and he almost welcomed the icy deluge that fell from the sky too effectively take his mind from the carnal.

Fleur's ear pricked as the horse's hoof-beats changed. They were on a cobbled surface, probably a stable yard. There was a faint aroma of horse dung, the smell of the sea in the air and the faint, storm-tossed roar of breaking waves amongst the thunderclaps.

She was over her fright now, thinking clearly despite her discomfort. Her abductor was a man of quality judging from his speech and the feel of his clothes. He smelled strongly of wine. Had he learned of her inheritance? It was not uncommon for heiresses to be abducted by greedy and unscrupulous men, but she hadn't expected to become a victim, considering the reputation of her brothers.

Her mouth dried when her abductor lowered her into a pile of straw. Her cloak was a dripping shroud about her body, the cowl a forlorn droop about her face. Carefully, she eased some life back into her muscles.

A lantern was stood on a rough bench, creating a pool of light. Beyond that, darkness stretched. Her abductor was tall, lean, and well muscled. He'd lost his hat and his dark hair was slicked down by the rain.

He was seeing to the comfort of his horse, a fact that did nothing to reassure her. If the man was too impoverished to afford a stable hand, then he was definitely after her fortune. His preoccupation gave her the chance to rid herself of the noose and he didn't seem to notice when it dropped to the floor around her feet.

Lightning licked a bright square around a door at the end of the darkness. Whilst the man was occupied she edged silently back towards it. Her brothers would move heaven and earth to find her, she knew. She needed to find somewhere to hide until morning if she was to avoid the fate she imagined was waiting for her. She might be compromised now, but she'd not surrender to her captor willingly.

She'd nearly gained the door when a blast of wind blew it from its latch. It banged against the wall, the suddenness of it making her gasp.

He turned, his face illuminated by a prolonged flash of lightning. Dark eyes bored into hers. She snatched a riding crop from a nail when he strode towards her and turning, fled into the wildness of the night.

It was like running into hell. The rain was a frenzy of bruising, drenching slush. The wind tore at her clothes, forcing its way into her lungs to inflame them with soreness. The plants whipped at her, scoring her flesh with thorny fingers. The air was filled with the sound of fury as the unrelenting storm filled the boisterous night.

There was a lantern burning in a porch, someone in an open doorway. A woman! He wouldn't dare attack her with someone as witness. His footsteps echoed behind her. Heart pounding, breathless, she headed for the doorway.

'Is that you, sir?' the woman said in a high, quavering voice

A foot came down on the hem of Fleur's cloak, jerking her to a choking halt. 'Go to bed, Mrs Firkins,' her abductor said calmly, 'I'll see to my guest.'

'Yes, sir.' Mrs Firkins picked up a candle and it bobbed across the hall and up a curving flight of stairs.

The fact that the woman turned a blind eye to what was going on wasn't reassuring. Fleur loosened the clasp at her throat, stepped out of its folds then whirled round and slashed the riding crop back and forth across her attacker's face.

When he staggered back with a curse, she took the opportunity to follow after Mrs Firkins. She overtook the old woman on the stairs, took a left turn and traversed a maze of corridors before slipping through one of the many doors. There was a key in the lock. It turned with a satisfying clunk.

Lightning revealed a sleeping chamber of magnificent proportions. The furnishings were covered by dustsheets.

The storm was centred overhead now, the room illuminated by flashes of lightning as bright as day. The flickering light revealed a large dressing robe. She wrenched open the door. Inside, hung garments of every description. Everything a woman could need, in fact, though the style seemed a little dated.

Apparent from the unused smell of the room, the owner had not been here for a long time. The former occupant was probably dead, Fleur thought, but she was too cold to care, as long as they'd removed the body. And she was not too fussy to mind wearing the clothes of an unknown person who'd never need them again.

Shivering, she exchanged her sodden undergarments for a warm chemise, then pulled on a taffeta petticoat and a velvet overskirt and bodice. She crawled into the dusty centre of a four-poster bed and drifted into an exhausted sleep, oblivious to the shivers that racked her body.

Even the loud creak of the door opening from the adjoining room didn't wake her.

Remy held a candle on high and gazed down at his prize. Despite his throbbing head he smiled at the sight of her. Her hair was a gleaming tangle of tossed sable. She slept on her back, her breasts a soft swell against her bodice. One hand formed a loose fist in the shadowed cleft between them, the other curved against her cheek.

The outfit was Julia Cordova's, for this had been his mother's chamber when she'd been the mistress of Rosehill. His father had occupied the adjoining chamber.

Funny how his victim had chanced on this room, the one place she'd be safe from violation, if he'd been so inclined. If she hadn't left a trail of water to follow he doubted he'd have looked for her here, or found her so quickly.

She murmured something and turned on to her side when he plucked a couple of pine needles from her hair. The movement revealed a bare foot and an expanse of naked leg. Her foot was cold to his tentative touch and shivers swept over her body from time to time. Carefully, he eased a feather filled comforter over her.

Now he'd captured the girl he didn't quite know how to go about arranging the nuptials, for wed her he must if he was to retain the deeds to Rosehill. He wondered; Who was this beauty he'd captured?

There was an enamelled signature ring on her finger. He leaned forward, catching sight of an eagle with a rodent clutched in its talons before she moved her hand, hiding it from sight. Where had he seen the design before?

He closed his eyes for a second or two, recalling a vast hall, the design worked in marble on the floor. Taken aback, he paled. The Russell family!

When he'd been a child his father had bought a pair of matched greys from Earl Russell. They'd stayed the night, Remy joining the younger children in the nursery wing. A terrifying visitation by a couple of boisterous banshees at midnight had produced a disastrous effect on his bladder and had been the cause of recurring nightmares long after his bruises had healed.

Besides the childhood trauma, was the recollection of the reputation of the eldest two brothers. Neither backed down from a fight and Macy's reputation as a crack pistol shot was becoming legendary in sporting circles.

Remy managed a self-deprecating grin. Ah yes, he knew how he'd go about wedding the girl now, with the business end of a pistol in his back – providing her brothers allowed him to live long enough!

TWO

When Fleur opened her eyes it was to gaze at the underside of a blue brocade bed canopy. It was filthy. She inhaled the fusty stench of mice and there were droppings on

26

the pillow where her head rested

'Oh, God,' she whispered, shuddering when something moved stealthily in the web shrouded shadows above her. Pushing back a dirty covering she hastily scrambled to her feet and groaned. Her body ached all over from being thrown over the saddle.

The room was filled with the grey light of dawn. Rain tossed by the wind sent desultory splatterings against the window. A glance in the greasy dressing mirror reflected a muddy-faced, wild-haired stranger. Her clothes lay in a soiled heap where she'd dropped them.

There was a silver-backed brush amongst the bottles on the dressing table. Snatching it up she attacked her hair, wincing when it encountered knots and tangles. She wanted to scream when it went in all directions. She wished her maid was attending her, for she needed a hot bath and a tumbler of tea.

She spun around, holding her breath when someone rapped loudly at the door. 'Tis Mrs Firkins. Master told me to give you a hand making yourself presentable.'

The woman's master was a cowardly cur who needed to be soundly thrashed. 'Tell him he can throw himself off the cliff and drown himself,' Fleur shouted at her. And the sooner it happened, the better it would suit her.

'Best you do what he says, girl,' Mrs Firkins

27

said sharply. 'When you're ready I've got a nice bit of ham for your breakfast. Keeping it warm, I am. Master has gone without to feed you, he has, so you'd better appear grateful.'

'I don't want his damned breakfast,' she said, though her stomach rattled righteously at the lie.

There was silence. Creeping to the door, Fleur put her ear against the panel. Behind her something creaked. Heart thumping, she spun round. She hadn't noticed the door covered by the tapestry.

Black-garbed and bent, Mrs Firkins reminded Fleur of a crow. Her beady eyes battled for dominance with a jutting nose. The woman was well past her prime, and she sighed as she eased a water filled jug and a bowl on to the table.

Fleur asked her. 'How did you know which room I occupied?'

'Master Remy told me.' The old woman pulled a bar of gentlemens' soap and a sea sponge from the pocket of a voluminous apron, placing it next to the bowl.

Remy ... where had she heard that name before? Fleur crossed to the woman. 'How did he know?'

'I can't rightly say. The master was always a canny little lad.' Her eyes softened. The reminiscence had been stated with the comfortable familiarity of a long association, making it obvious to Fleur where the woman's loyalty would lie.

'I'll help tie back your hair, missy.' Her foot nudged against Fleur's clothes. 'Then you can change back into your own things, and be warned... I'll be checking your pockets before you leave. Master Remy is waiting to talk to you. Don't you expect no reward though, and you mind your manners. None of that rough talk.'

Fleur's face flamed at what she was inferring. 'You appear to be under some misapprehension about my status, Mrs Firkins. I'm the sister of The Earl of Stratton, and would prefer to be addressed accordingly. As for your Master Remy, you can take him this exact message, and manners be damned. Tell him he can wait for me until his donkey ears drop off,' she said as the woman deftly brought her hair under control.

Astute eyes engaged hers in the mirror, then deference came into them and a head bobbed. 'My pardon. I'll tell him, My Lady, but he won't like it. May I enquire if his action in bringing you here was questionable then?'

'Questionable? It was downright criminal.' At her request, Fleur's long curls were pulled into a braid. 'As for his likes and dislikes, I don't give a fig for them. The man abducted me, and when my brothers arrive he'll be killed for his trouble.'

She smiled at the thought, then scooping

water into her hands rinsed the sleep from her mouth. The remainder was splashed on her face and worked into a lather. The soap smelled pleasantly of sandalwood. The man had expensive tastes.

'Chamber pot's in the closet,' Mrs Firkins mumbled. 'I'll go and fetch your breakfast up.'

Drying her face on the small linen towel handed to her, Fleur warned. 'No tricks mind. Be sure, both doors shall be locked both behind you. And I prefer tea to chocolate.'

'I'll see what I can do, My Lady.'

She could find no key to the inner door. Finishing her toilette Fleur made good use of the soap and sponge to refresh herself all over. She hung the borrowed clothes back in the closet next to the soiled silks, taffetas and velvets and struggled back into her travelling clothes. They hung in damp, chilly folds against her body, making her shiver again.

The room she occupied overlooked a neglected garden. Gnarled and twisted, the limbs of rose bushes were being strangled by weeds. In the middle of an unkempt lawn and surrounded by overgrown lavender hedges she spied a fountain fashioned in the shape of a pair of naked, entwined lovers. Beneath her window arched the bare bones of a rose, which climbed through the ivy.

The room would have a heavenly fragrance

in the summer. She thrust open a window, and braving a cold blast of wind that sent the dust swirling, tipped the contents of the washing bowl on to the garden below.

Beyond the garden and separated by a low hedge, a lush meadow was divided by a path meandering towards the forest. Giant firs spiked upwards into a grey sky. Immersed in the scene, when the door opened behind her she murmured. 'Thank you, Mrs Firkins, leave it on the table, please.'

She thought she saw movement against the shadows of the trees, but even as she strained her eyes to see better, rain blotted the scene from her sight. Hastily, she pulled the window shut and turned.

'Oh!' She backed against the dressing table, momentarily unnerved by the unexpected presence of her abductor. He was tall. Black hair curled against his collar and matched the colour of his compelling dark eyes. He had presence, even in his shabby attire. His high cheekbones gave him a haughty, cruel look. Two livid welts traversed each cheek, a legacy of the whipping she'd inflicted on him.

He swept an arm across the table, sending flying the water jug, towel and soap. An overly dramatic and proud gesture for one about to be forcibly trounced from his own high opinion of himself by her brothers, she thought as he replaced them with a tray. His glance raked over her. 'I'm Remy, Viscount

31

St Cyres.'

She dealt him an equally insulting appraisal before her eyes blazed into his. 'You're nothing but a rogue of the first order, sir. You are an abductor of innocent women and your future is very short. My brothers will have your blood.'

'They might,' he said with careless bravado, 'But I imagine they'll display more sense.' He pulled back a chair. 'Come, sit and eat.'

Her fingers closed around a heavy scent bottle. Drawing it up she threw it with all her might.

He had the reflexes of a cat. One instant he ducked, the next the bottle smashed into shards against the wall. In a moment he was by her side, his fingers tight around her wrists. His eyes bored into hers, his voice was low with menace. 'I appreciate your annoyance, but throwing pots at me will not change your situation one little bit.'

He dragged her to the table and forcibly seated her. 'Stop being tedious and eat it before it cools. I'm attempting to make amends for my treatment of you. I asked the hen to lay that egg specially for you and she'll be disappointed if you do not eat it.'

He was being ridiculous.

'Also, you'll be pleased to hear that Mrs Firkins robbed me of the last of my tea supply on your behalf.'

Her stomach growled when she lifted the

cover from the platter and steam wafted upwards. She picked up the fork.

'Good,' he said with a sigh. 'I'll wait for you downstairs in the drawing room. But be warned ... I will not wait until my ears fall off.' His smile came as he backed towards the door. It was almost irresistible, that smile. It displayed a gesture of real warmth, of charm. It was a smile containing such a delicious intensity that it sent frissons of pleasure trembling along her spine. 'You certainly delight the eye,' he said as he reached the door, causing a blush to rise to her cheeks.

'And you rely to much on your silver tongue, My Lord,' Though she thought his voice sounded more like liquid amber than silver. 'Be assured, if my brothers do not kill you for this I intend to carry out the deed myself ... just like I wanted to when we were children.'

He relaxed against the doorjamb, an unconsciously assumed curve of male grace. There was a slight arch of his eyebrow. 'I feel flattered to be remembered after all this time.'

She didn't tell him it was his beautiful smile she remembered. 'Then you must have found some courage, for you gibbered and cringed like the coward you are at the first sign of danger.'

He bowed mockingly. 'The next time your brothers place a noose around my neck and attempt to hang me from the tree outside the nursery window, I'll try not to disappoint you by crying out.'

'My brothers were beaten for it,' she accused. 'Neither of them could sit down for a week.'

Liquid eyes melted against hers. 'If I recall, you were frantic on my behalf and begged your brothers to allow me to live. You ran through the house in the dark and fetched your father from his bed to rescue me, little Fleur. I owe you my life.'

She lowered her lashes, shielding her eyes from the intimacy of this shared memory. Used to the rough ways of her elder brothers, she'd sensed a gentleness in Remy the child, and had responded to it. Her brothers had interpreted it as weakness.

Remy wasn't gentle now, quite the opposite. He displayed a ruthless streak. 'I wouldn't fetch my father now. I'd cheer while they hanged you.'

'Your brothers deserved the thrashing they got,' he said dispassionately. 'As for you...' He touched one of the welts on his cheek, shrugged, and gave a grim little smile. 'Under the circumstances I can forgive you this.' He turned and strode away.

Fleur attacked her breakfast, smiling a little when she ate the coddled egg. She didn't want to disappoint the hen. The tea was lukewarm and weak. The water hadn't been brought to the boil so the flavour was still locked inside the leaves.

She poured the liquid back into the teapot. It was an old servant trick. Mrs Firkins would use it again for herself. Tempted to toss the remainder out of the window she was forestalled when the woman came in.

'The tea wasn't brewed correctly, Mrs Firkins.'

The woman looked rattled. 'It's all we have, My Lady, and Master Remy hasn't had his yet. I thought to use it again for him.'

Fleur felt ashamed off her earlier conclusion, especially since she'd consumed the man's breakfast. 'You should have informed me of this earlier. Brew it again then. I'll take mine with the viscount in the drawing room.'

The woman assumed a penitent pose. 'I urge you to forgive Master Remy, My Lady.'

'The reason?'

'My Lady, you can blame his grandparents for your predicament. They have plenty of money to spare, and are miserable, the pair of them. They wouldn't give the lad a home when his parents died on account of his mother being foreign, and they left him to struggle on as best he could. The old snipe says he ain't fit for nothing, him being a wastrel and all. They want him to wed and produce an heir before he'll get his allowance back.'

The abduction suddenly made sense to

Fleur. Somehow, Remy had found out about her journey and decided to intercept her. She frowned. He could have gone about it properly. He could have come to the house and asked for her hand. But then, perhaps he thought he had nothing to offer and her brothers would turn him away.

She warmed towards him a little. 'You plead his case convincingly, Mrs Firkins, but do him no favour by blaming his actions on others, who are not here to defend themselves.'

Mrs Firkins hung her head.

Fleur sighed. 'Your loyalty is admirable. You'd better tell me where the drawing room is situated, Mrs Firkins.'

'Along the corridor, down the staircase and second door on your left.' She hesitated for a moment. 'May I say something else, My Lady?'

'What is it, Mrs Firkins?'

'The master isn't as bad as he seems. When his parents died he was young and the earl expected too much of him. He's learned his lesson now, I reckon. Underneath, he has a heart of pure gold.'

'Thank you for your testimonial,' she said gently. 'I'll bear that in mind when my brothers take him to task for what he's done to me.'

'It could have been worse,' the woman called out when Fleur walked away, 'And would have been if he were a less honourable man than he is.'

That was true, and she pondered on the nature of Remy as she found her way to the drawing room. A short time later Fleur sat opposite her abductor, drinking tea from delicately translucent cups. At least the drawing room was halfway clean, she thought, gazing at the portrait of a woman hanging in pride of place over the fire place. A child was pressed against her knee, his dark eyes a mixture of innocence and mischief. It could only be Remy.

'Is that your mother?'

He nodded. 'Her name was Julia Cordova.'

His resemblance to her was uncanny, although his mother's face was softer and more rounded. She was certainly lovely with her dark shining hair and enormous black eyes.

'You could have worn her clothes. At least they were dry. Now you're cold and damp again.'

'I feel more comfortable in my own clothes.' Her eyes went from the pair of painted eyes to the identical living ones. 'How old were you when she died?'

'Sixteen.'

'You have her looks.'

'Yes.'

'I wonder what she'd have made of your behaviour last night.'

They sat in silence for a moment contemplating her remark. Then Remy stood, saying courteously, 'No doubt she would have condemned my behaviour but applauded my choice. Thank you for taking tea with me this morning.'

She didn't know whether to laugh or cry when she heard the sound of horses outside.

'Ah ... your brothers have arrived. Before I go outside to greet them I'd like to apologize for any distress I caused you. I'd prefer it if you stayed in here, but I realize I'm in no position to insist at the moment.'

He wanted to be left with his pride intact. She almost softened. But he hadn't considered her pride when he'd snatched her from under the noses of his pursuers. She was the victim, he the felon.

'The apology is accepted, your request is denied. I'll give you time to state your case with my brothers first.'

'So be it.' He smiled, bowed slightly then turned on his heel and strode off, leaving a pair of loaded pistols on the side table. He'd obviously changed his mind about going into the confrontation armed. Not a wise choice considering Macy's prowess, but Fleur was relieved, all the same. Her brothers would not shoot an unarmed man.

Picking up the pistols she balanced one in each hand before carefully disarming them.

They made a fearsome sight. The three

brothers formed a semi-circle. The largest was The Earl of Stratton. Leland Russell was heavy set and flame-haired like his father before him. To his right was the dark and menacing Macy. To his left the lad he'd pushed over, a handsome youth just coming into manhood. The youth slumped a little in the saddle. His cheeks were flushed from the cold and he was breathing harshly.

Behind them was a heavy carriage, piled high with luggage. The face at the window was that of an older man, and crabbed up with displeasure. The coachman was a burly fellow. Remy knew he'd made the right decision by not bringing the pistols. They would have been his death sentence.

Not one of the three Russell brothers spoke, and the silence unnerved him a little. Then the earl bawled out. 'Fleur ... show yourself.'

There was a rustle of clothing and the warmth of her passing behind him. She didn't run to her brothers, but stood to one side, leaving him alone with his shame – a prisoner in the dock.

The earl jerked a head in his direction. 'Did he touch you?'

'Yes.'

Remy opened his mouth to protest, then closed it again when he remembered running a hand over her. If the girl were still a maid she'd have no idea of the connotation of her brother's words. He shrugged.

There was a whistling noise and a whip coiled agonizingly about his shoulders. Fleur gave a faint gasp when blood seeped warmly against his skin. The whip was re-coiled. Noting that the lad who held the other end was trying to suppress a cough, he said quietly. 'At least allow me to state my case.'

'You've forfeited the right.' Leland Russell glanced at the youth. 'You've drawn first blood, Cris. Is your honour satisfied?'

When he nodded, Macy relieved him of the whip and expertly coiled it. Shoulders heaving, the lad gave in to his cough. Macy smacked the supple coil of leather against his palm.

Do they intend to whip me to death between them? Remy wondered, his blood running cold.

'State your case then, and be quick about it.'

'Your sister remains intact.'

The whip hissed delicately along his cheekbone, peeling the skin from a welt. 'How did you come by this, then?'

'A riding crop. Your sister might look like an angel but she has the disposition of a wasp.'

'And you have the disposition of the slithering snake on your family crest. You grovel along on your belly and spit venom when least expected.'

'I never grovel, as you will learn when we're wed.'

The two elder brothers exchanged a glance and grinned at each other. 'We will discover the truth of that statement for ourselves first,' said Macy, and Remy staggered backwards when the whip coiled around his ankles and jerked him off his feet. The next moment he was being jerked down the steps on his back.

For a moment Remy thought he was to be dragged behind Macy's horse. Instead, Macy leapt from his mount, fisted his jacket and hauled him upright. Flat, green-flecked eyes impaled him. 'Come on you pretty faced, mewling son of a maggot. Let's see what you're ma—'

Before Macy could finish his sentence Remy took the opportunity to hit him squarely on the nose. Blood sprayed before Macy caught him round the waist and swung him round. Using the man's own weight Remy threw him over his shoulder and took up a boxing stance. A kick below the knee caught him unawares, disabling him. Then Macy was upon him.

The weight difference gave his opponent the advantage, and punch after punch sent Remy reeling backwards. Though he managed to get a few in himself and used a wrestling hold to gain breathing space now and again, one of his ribs cracked under the pressure.

Head reeling from blow after blow he gave ground, all the while hearing the racking cough of the younger son. The lad should be in bed, he thought inconsequently as he fell.

Macy was waiting for him to get up. Painfully, Remy rose to one knee and shook his head to clear his vision. He caught a glimpse of Fleur's face, white and wide-eyed. Finding some strength he lurched forward and butted shoulder first into Macy's midriff. It was made of iron. Taken in a bear hug the breath was squeezed from his body before he was lifted from his feet and hurled backwards on to the ground. Gasping, he gazed up at the dimming sky.

'Get up you cur.'

He tried to grab Macy's leg and pull him down, but his arm had no strength in it. Macy kicked him in the ribs and he drew his knees up in agony.

There was a rustle of petticoat and the sight of a trim ankle below a muddied hem. 'Enough, Macy. His intent towards me was honourable enough even though his methods were not. I don't want to be a widow before the vows are said, and neither do I want a cripple for a husband.'

She found him acceptable then? She has no choice. Her reputation has been ruined now. He regretted the necessity of doing that to her.

Macy growled like an angry bear.

'Touch him again and I'll rip out your liver and feed it to your hound,' she warned.

Remy fought the urge to laugh. It was a ridiculous statement for a woman to make, especially to a man as big as Macy. Yet surprisingly, and looking decidedly sheepish, her brother shuffled meekly backwards.

Staggering to one knee, Remy gazed at him, and although it hurt like hell he began to laugh. Macy stared furiously at him for a moment, then his face cleared and he grinned. He held out a hand and helped him up. 'You always were a game little turkey cock.'

'*Men!*' Fleur said, looking disgusted.

Leland leapt down from his horse. 'Now we've sorted that out amicably, let's get out of this blasted wind and talk terms.'

Remy stared him straight in the eye. Were all the Russell family mad? 'Are you sure you don't want to take your turn at me?'

Casually, the earl backhanded him. Propelled backwards against the door jamb, Remy gripped it for support.

Leland gazed at him and smiled. 'Will that suffice?'

'I advise you to stay put,' Fleur hissed at him. 'My brother, The Earl of Stratton, is not normally aggressive, but he has a short fuse when pushed.'

Remy's pride told him to push it, common sense told him not to. Ignoring the latter he straightened up as best he could.

'Don't do it,' Leland warned softly.

Just then, Crispen gave a groan and slid from his horse to the ground. With a cry of alarm, Fleur hastened forward with her brothers.

Remy sagged back against his support, grateful for the intervention. The Russells were closely woven kin, he thought to himself, envying them a little. He'd have liked having a brother or two.

Mrs Firkins pulled at his sleeve. 'Come away in, Master Remy, I'll see to your injuries. You poor lad, look what those heathens have done to you.'

'They had the right, just be thankful they didn't kill me. Light a fire and make up the day bed in the sitting room off the hall. The young man will not be travelling on today by the looks of him.' He managed a painful smile. 'What do you make of the future mistress of Rosehill, then?'

'The lass has got a mind of her own, and there's no nonsense about her.'

'You approve then?'

Mrs Firkins gave a bit of a cackle. 'It ain't my place to approve or disapprove, but mind my words, the girl's no fool. You'll have your work cut out to win her round.'

'Win her round? A wife does as she's told.'

'Oh aye?' she said, grinning broadly as she walked away.

THREE

The bloodletting was over, honour was satisfied – everyone's honour but Fleur's! She glared at Leland. 'You're telling me he would have abducted any woman, that I was the unwitting victim of a ... *a wager!*'

'It was just bad luck it happened to be you.'

She'd have screamed if it would have made any difference to the eventual consequence of this farcical situation. Bad luck, was it? Remy St Cyres had yet to find out what that was!

She flung her arms wide. 'So, I was abducted and insulted to save this heap of crumbling stones from changing hands and its owner from starvation. Not that St Cyres looks hungry, in fact his appearance is...?' She forced herself to check the compliment she was about to pay him. 'He's tolerable, if one admires the dark intense look in a man, I suppose.' She remembered his smile and smiled herself.

Leland grinned. 'I've been looking round. The house is structurally sound. The furnishings need repair, but you'll soon work your way round that. As for his looks; a man of such appearance draws the envy of men and the admiration of women.'

'Do they indeed? I hadn't considered him that handsome.' Her eyes narrowed at the thought. 'What sum was reached for a dowry settlement?'

'The sum set aside by our father. St Cyres didn't ask for more. As you requested, the extent of your fortune was kept from him. In fact, he didn't seem all that interested in the financial aspect. He tells me he has expectations.' Leyland gazed at her, his expression troubled. 'You know he has right to your fortune when you're wed.'

'I know,' and she patted his cheek. 'But if he nearly lost this place on the turn of a card he may lose my fortune the same way. I have the option of leaving it in your hands until I reach the age of twenty-one. I intend to do that.'

Leland shuffled from one foot to the other. 'There's something I have to say to you, Fleur. If you had a mother she'd have prepared you on what to expect from the marriage union. It's about your wedding night.' His face mottled red and he cleared his throat several times. 'Men have certain expectations ... um ... rights, which you might like be made aware of and prepare for.'

She decided to spare him the details and

46

kissed his cheek. 'Pray, do not embarrass yourself further, dearest Leland. Marguerite has seen fit to educate me in certain areas.' And having grown up with brothers she couldn't have failed to notice the differences between them and herself.

Besides which, she thought, smiling inwardly at the relief of his expression ... spring burst forth rampantly in the country. Oh yes, she was aware of what was expected, which didn't mean those expectations had to be fulfilled. She was not a sheep to be impregnated at the first hint of spring, or a wilting maid who would meekly and uncomplainingly submit to the messy and painful process of male lusts.

Not that she believed Leland was as cruel and selfishly inconsiderate as Marguerite had so bitterly inferred.

She tried to smooth the creases from her skirt. Her trunk had been brought up by the coach driver, and the gown she'd selected for the ceremony was badly creased. It was a pretty gown, made of blue-tinted brocade with a laced bodice of soft velvet over it for warmth. Not that it mattered what she looked like for Remy St Cyres. He wouldn't care if she was a milkmaid as long as he won the wager.

She scowled as she threaded her arm through Leland's. 'Come, let's get this farce over and done with. Despite his shortcomings, Remy St Cyres is bound to be an improvement on the Reverend Chalmers, is he not?'

'Most definitely,' Leland drawled, 'And I hope he realizes how lucky he is to get you.'

'Be sure, I shall remind him of that every day of his life,' she said, then muttered, 'A wager, indeed...'

They were waiting in the drawing room, and a more disreputable looking bunch of men Fleur never seen. Macy had been to the inn to release Remy's companions. The pair had been given a thrashing for their part in the abduction and now looked the worst for wear after a day and night secured in a dank cellar.

Except for Macy's blackened eyes and a nose which flamed red, her brothers were unscathed. Fleur smiled sympathetically at Crispen, who although rested, looked far from well. He was supported on Macy's arm.

Leland gave a short, mirthless laugh when the bridegroom turned to gaze impatiently at them. 'Some prize you've got yourself, Fleur,' he whispered against her ear, giving her the urge to giggle.

Remy was indeed a sight. His face was a mass of bruises and swollen almost beyond recognition. One puffed hand protruded from a splint and he favoured his cracked ribs. The smile he gave her was slightly rueful, his eyes held a hint of an apology. She suppressed her snort of laughter. It was no time to relent.

Mrs Firkins' wide smile revealed a broad expanse of gum sprinkled with a few teeth. She bobbed a curtsy.

The bishop wore a sour, disapproving expression. 'This is most irregular,' he grumbled. 'I believe that marriage outside of a church is not recognized by the state. If one of the parties is unwilling...'

'Just say the words over them,' Leland roared. 'Through no fault of her own my sister's reputation is at stake.' He glared ferociously at his uncle. 'You're a bishop. Make it legal. We'll post the banns at the local church and have the vows said again if necessary.'

He turned to Remy. 'Do you agree to this marriage? And don't think too long about the answer, my friend.'

Remy didn't appear to think at all. He nodded.

'Do you agree, Fleur?'

'Yes.'

Face aggressive with impatience Leland turned to their uncle. 'You have your answer. Get on with it.'

'Very well,' The bishop opened a bible, saying unctuously. 'We will join together in the Lord's prayer.' When Macy's dagger pricked against his neck his eyes widened and he garbled. 'We are gathered together in the sight of God...'

Macy smiled and the weapon disappeared back into his sleeve.

Remy took her hand in his, caught her eye and smiled. Fleur avoided the smile, telling herself it was too much a study of charm to be genuine. Besides, it looked odd on a face battered beyond recognition.

Instead, she gazed down at the hand holding hers, trying not to feel guilt at his condition. She could have easily stopped Macy's punishment of him earlier if she'd but swallowed her anger. Not that Macy had emerged from the fracas unscathed. Remy's was a fine-boned hand with long fingers and a strong wrist. Macy had told her other wrist was badly sprained, but he didn't think any bones were broken.

The sound of a carriage driven at speed reached their ears.

'What now?' Leland growled as Mrs Firkins slipped from the room.

'Will you, Remy, Sebastian, William, Beresford, Christopher, Hernando...'

'Hernando?' she said, her eyes brightening with disbelief and laughter.

Remy stared stoically ahead. 'My Spanish godfather,' he whispered from the corner of his mouth, then said clearly, 'I will.'

'...from this day forth...'

She shivered. From this day forth she'd be the property of a man who was almost a stranger to her.

There came the sound of a woman's sharply raised voice, of Mrs Firkins' mumbled reply. Footsteps advanced in a determined trot across the marble flooring of hall and pattered up the stairs.

Remy smiled slightly as he slid a golden ring on to her finger. A ruby glinted at her. Remy's hand closed over it in possession of her. 'With this ring...'

'I pronounce you husband and wife in the eyes of God. You may kiss your bride.'

'He most certainly cannot,' Fleur said tartly.

Smoke puffed out of the chimney when the door was flung open. Calmly, she turned to greet her first guest as mistress of the house.

An old woman dressed in grey stood there. Sharp eyes gazed around the room, taking in the silent tableau. They filled with distaste when she observed Fleur's creased gown then settled ominously on Remy. 'What idiocy is this?'

Remy shrugged. 'It's the occasion of my wedding, My Lady.'

She scuttled across the room like a crab with a seagull after it. 'I have eyes in my head, and a bigger bunch of blackguards I've never seen.' She poked her stick in Macy's side. 'You, where are your manners? Escort me to a chair.'

'My pleasure,' said Macy, and one of his

51

hands closed under her elbow. She was almost carried across the room and lifted on to a seat. Her eyes sought out Fleur and she crooked an imperious finger. 'You, girl. Come here.'

Fleur crossed to where she sat, meeting her gaze without apology. 'I imagine you're Remy's grandmother.'

'You imagine right. Who are you and who is this band of cut-throats?'

Fleur bristled at her tone, but she managed to keep her temper in check. The woman's courage was admirable. 'My name is Fleur Amanada Russell ... *Viscountess St Cyres*. The cut-throats are my brothers and the viscount's wedding guests.'

Charles Boney's snigger earned him a blistering look from both of them. He fell silent.

'Don't bandy words with me, strumpet. What do you think you're gaining by marrying my grandson? If you have designs on his fortune I must tell you, he has squandered it all on loose living.'

She didn't bother sparing Remy's feelings. Her chin lifted. 'The deed is already done. I'm *married* to your grandson now, and I object to being called a strumpet when I was abducted on account of some irresponsible wager. It is my reputation which was at stake, and that which has been addressed today.'

'Is this true, Remy?'

Remy nodded. 'You wanted me to wed

and produce an heir. I'm now wed. The rest will follow.'

'Not if I have something to say about it,' Fleur whispered under her breath.

The woman's lips twitched as she flicked the bride a speculative look. 'Remy, do you expect your grandfather to support you in this folly?'

'This is neither the time nor place to discuss my expectations, Grandmother. This is my home and there are guests present.'

'Ah yes, Remy,' she said softly, 'I'd forgotten how filled with pride you are.' When the old woman held out a hand to her, Fleur assisted her to her feet. 'Let's see if pride keeps you warm at night, or if your expectations fill your belly when you are hungry.'

'The earl has no right to withhold my allowance,' Remy said stiffly.

'He has every right. It is our son's money and held in trust for you on his behalf.' Fleur's hand was squeezed. 'My apologies to you, young lady. Thank goodness he had the sense to abduct a woman of backbone instead of some whimpering miss. You are more than he deserves. Take me to my carriage, *Viscountess St Cyres*.'

As they left the room the silence behind them deepened. The sun had come out and the hall was a mass of dusty shifting sunbeams filtered through the painted glass as they descended the stairs.

Fleur said, almost to herself. 'Rosehill is a friendly house. I will set it to rights in time.'

When the old lady was seated in her carriage, she bestowed a smile on her. 'You are more than I expected. Do you come with a dowry?'

'Yes. My father provided for me long ago.'

'And you have a portion tucked away in case of emergencies, I trust?'

Fleur nodded. The amount was her business.

'Good. I'd not have you go without because my grandson has neither the means nor wit to support a wife. If you ever find yourself in the position of need you may call on me.'

The remark was more than patronising. Fleur fixed her with a glance designed to quell the most persistent of offenders. 'My brothers will not allow me to starve.'

The woman smiled. 'I do believe you and I will rub along splendidly.' She cocked her head to one side. 'Russell, you said your family name is?'

'My father was George Russell, Earl of Stratton, as is my eldest brother now.'

'Then your mother is Anne Goodsires. Old family, but impoverished. We thought she was set for spinsterhood until your father offered for her.'

The countess snorted. 'He took her without dowry and for love. Can't say I approve, but men surprise you, sometimes. Do you think

54

you can get the measure of your new husband?'

'He will not have things his own way.'

Fleur found her cheek being gently patted. 'You lack Anne's submissive nature, which isn't a bad thing. How is she?'

'She died giving birth to my brother. I was very young then, so cannot remember her.'

'She would have been proud of you, I'm sure.' A gloved hand rested on hers for a moment. 'You won't mind if I call you Fleur, will you? I'm too old to stand on ceremony. I admire your pluck and I wish you well of my rogue grandson. He has many good points but his behaviour is so reprehensible at the moment I find them difficult to recall. You have my permission to address me as grandmother.'

'You're very gracious, my ... uh ... Grandmother.'

'I'll speak favourably of you to my husband, but he's piqued at the moment so do not expect an invitation to call.' She sighed, saying almost inaudibly. 'A man's pride can be so very tedious, at times.'

Fleur smiled. 'I grew up with three brothers.'

'And ruled them with a velvet fist, no doubt. Was it your brothers who battered my poor Remy so?'

'It could have been worse for him. At least they allowed him to live.'

A tiny, ironic smile edged across the woman's mouth. 'Then please, you must thank them on my behalf for that small favour.'

At least the old lady hadn't been totally disapproving of her. 'I'll be sure to pass on your message, Grandmother.'

Fleur's hand was squeezed. 'Look after him. He's all I've got left to remind me of my son.'

Leaning forward, Fleur gently kissed her cheek. 'Next time you must stay and take refreshment with us.'

Out of the corner of her eye she watched Charles Boney and Simon Ackland slink off in the opposite direction. She didn't mind Simon but had disliked Charles on sight. Something about him struck a wrong note with her. She wasn't sorry to see them go.

'We'll see.' The countess rapped on the front of the carriage with her cane. 'Drive on, coachman.'

Bristling with footmen and outriders dressed in livery, and pulled by two shining black horses, the carriage rolled majestically away. Watching it disappear from view, Fleur wished the countess was staying. It would be nice to have another woman to talk to.

As she turned back towards the house she discovered Remy watching her from the step. Head held high she walked past him, beckoning to Mrs Firkins, who picked up her skirts and followed her through to the kitchen. When they arrived it was to find the place feeling cold and damp. The fire was out. Fleur sighed. 'Do we have any refreshments to serve?'

'Bread and cheese, ham bone broth with winter vegetables and barley, apples from the attic and wine. No doubt I could manage an apple pie as well, though it will empty the larder.'

'That will have to do, then. Tomorrow we'll rise early and see if we can buy some provisions from the nearby farms.'

''Tis market day in Dorchester. It's a long walk. The master has only the one horse and that one too fussy to carry any on its back but the master himself. I warn you though, the stall holders won't give us credit.'

'They won't need to. Don't leave without me. Now, let's get the fire lit, Mrs Firkins, then show me where the mops and buckets are kept. Two nights in that filthy chamber would be enough to give me nightmares and the adjoining room needs thoroughly scrubbing out.'

'Cleaning is no job for a lady.'

'Mrs Firkins, it's patently obvious you haven't got the strength or time to perform the multitude of tasks required to keep this house in order. Neither do I expect it of you. However, I refuse to sleep with spiders and rodents again. Until I can hire a servant or two I will clean the accommodations myself.'

Remy said from behind her. 'We don't have to sleep there. There is perfectly good accommodation elsewhere in the house.'

We! Bride or not, did he imagine she'd meekly share a bed with him? 'I like that chamber,' she said stiffly. 'Macy said Cris is unfit to travel so it will be handy to have him in the adjoining room where I can keep an eye on him at night.' And in case Remy got a notion in his head for a nocturnal visit, Crispen's presence would keep him out.

He gave her a steady look. 'I understand.'

'Good,' she said, feeling a little flustered by the depth of his regard. 'Also, the garden below the window will be fragrant in summer and I'll enjoy that. Once the personal chattels are disposed of and the chamber is thoroughly cleaned...' She became aware of the quality of his stillness. 'What is it?'

'The bedchamber you intend to occupy belonged to my mother, the adjoining one to my father. The chattels are theirs. The rooms have remained unused since their deaths.' He gave a faint smile. 'I come here sometimes to remember them.'

'Oh. I'm so sorry... I didn't realise.' Fleur was prepared to sacrifice her claim to such splendid quarters in the face of this display of fine feeling. A man who held his parents in such high regard deserved a little consideration.

He shrugged. 'You were not to know and one can't hold on to memories indefinitely. Perhaps it's about time the chambers *were* cleared out. Please use them, by all means. I'll fetch a couple of women from the estate cottages to help Mrs Firkins, who will know what to throw away and what to keep.

'Now, Macy had requested that you go and take a look at Crispen. He's of the opinion the local physician needs to have him under his care.'

It was obvious to Fleur that Crispen's lung infection had returned with a vengeance. His fever had returned and he was glassy-eyed and perspiring profusely. When she nodded to Macy, he and Leland followed her out. Leland was despatched to ferret out the local physician.

'I wish I could stay longer than today,' Macy said, 'but I don't think Cris is in any danger and if I don't get to London I'll lose my place to study surgery under John Hunter. What can I do to help in the mean-time?'

She drew a purse from under her skirt. 'He will need nourishment to build him up once his fever abates. Have a scout around the district. See if you can purchase a couple of laying hens and a cow or goat for milking. I noticed a cart in the stables, so a horse would come in handy. Nothing fancy, but strong enough to pull both carriage and plough.'

The purse was pushed back at her. 'It will be my wedding gift, sister.' He shook his head from side to side. 'This marriage isn't what we'd have chosen for you.'

'I'll have to make the best of it,' she said lightly.

'What do you think of your husband?'

Her head slanted to one side. 'Under the circumstances, how do you think I feel?'

'Flaming mad.' His grin was something evil. 'I could always despatch him to the devil for you.'

'Don't you dare,' she said, and more vehemently than she intended. 'If every fool was killed for a stupid act, there wouldn't be any men left.' She cuffed him playfully around the ear when he chuckled. 'Sometimes I wonder why I love you so much, Macy. Be off with you!'

His hug left her breathless. Macy's strength never failed to amaze her, yet he was as gentle as a lamb when required. She gave Remy credit for not only surviving the fight, but for gaining her brother's respect as well.

Remy arrived home with two robust looking women. A short time later the physician arrived. Leland stood patiently by whilst the man examined the patient, clucking his tongue all the time.

'Well?' Leland said when the man finished.

The doctor's advice was a repeat of Macy's and her own, which reassured Fleur as to his competence. 'He shouldn't be moved. Keep him warm, give him plenty of fluids to counteract the fever and nourishing food such as eggs in brandy and chicken broth. Make an infusion of willow bark and dose him at three hourly intervals. It will help relieve the temperature and loosen the phlegm.'

She ran a hand over Crispen's damp head when the physician had gone. 'You're staying here until you're completely better, Cris. However long it takes.'

He seemed relieved as he closed his eyes and drifted off to sleep. Fleur called the bishop from the library to watch over him whilst she investigated the progress of the cleaning. The man was churlish with her.

She left him and went to check on the cleaning progress. The women were sluggish until Fleur promised them a silver coin apiece, then they set to work with a will. By midday the rooms smelled freshly of soap and the bed linens were flapping in a furious wind on the line.

There came a commotion from outside and she rushed to investigate. Macy came into the yard, a bawling calf flung over his saddle. A leading rein was attached to a sturdy looking horse, which in turn was attached to a wagon. A black and white cow, udders swollen and leaking milk followed after them, lowing plaintively for her offspring every now and then.

The cart was piled high. There was hay and vegetables, atop of which was precariously balanced a sack of oats, flour and a flitch of bacon. Chickens squawked and fluttered in a crate and a sow was tied to the seat, captive to several squealing piglets jostling at her teats. Fleur wondered how many piglets had been lost on the way. Somewhere amongst it all, a puppy yelped. As for Macy, he was singing at the top of his voice and grinning from ear to ear.

Mrs Firkins placed a fist on each hip. 'Glory be, I haven't seen the likes since the Spanish captain came a calling. Shortly after master Remy was born, that was. He and the old viscount had a right old riot between them, I can tell you. I reckon that brother of yours has been sampling Blaggs' bran whisky.'

Fleur rushed from the kitchen to scoop up and cuddle the pup. Macy slid from his horse, his legs gave way and he sat heavily in a puddle, the calf cuddled on his lap. Urged on by the cow it scrambled to the safety of its mother's side and began to suckle.

'There was a milkmaid all forlorn,' Macy sang, and falling on to his back he crossed his arms on his chest and gazed up at the sky, still grinning. After a few moments his eyes closed and he began to snore.

'Oh, Macy, you fool, it's a wonder you found your way back,' Fleur said, laughing when she saw the bottle protruding from his pocket. 'Fetch my husband and brother, Mrs Firkins. They'd best put him to bed.'

Macy was moved inside to sleep it off. Crispen was installed in the upstairs room. Sour-faced, the bishop prowled the house, ate the lion's share of the available food and subjected them to a general diatribe about the inconvenience he'd been put to over this matter. He was then taken off to a destination known only to Mrs Firkins, who lit the way with the remains of a stinking tallow candle held aloft.

Wrinkling her nose, Fleur resolved to buy some decent candles as soon as possible.

Fleur retired herself shortly afterwards, leaving Leland and Remy to discuss business and make their own sleeping arrangements. Exhausted, she crawled into bed with the pup curled up at her feet for comfort. She'd expected to spend a restless night, but Crispen, though he tossed and turned in the next room, hardly coughed at all.

Morning brought a hasty departure. Fleur parted with her brothers and the bishop at the crossroads.

'I'll send over your maid, your horse and the rest of your belongings in a day or two,' Leland shouted.

Showing no signs of his recent excesses, Macy grinned and waved at her. 'I bought the pup from a gypsy. He's guaranteed to grow into a King Charles spaniel.'

'Not with those feet,' Remy muttered.

He'd insisted on accompanying her to market, leaving Mrs Firkins to watch over Crispen. After the Russell coach turned a bend in the road she set the cart in motion.

'The horse seems manageable,' Remy said. 'It was a generous gift, considering the circumstances.'

'Macy's a good judge of horse flesh.' She tossed him a careless smile. 'I expect he felt guilty about not guarding me well enough. Before he went foraging he offered to kill you on my behalf.'

Remy stiffened. 'What prevented you from taking him up on the offer?'

'I didn't want to see him hang over such a trivial offence.'

He chuckled. 'I think you're beginning to like me a little, Fleur.'

She didn't respond to his overture. Now they were alone together she felt shy and unsure of herself. Remy stared at the road ahead, silent, until the rooftops of the town came into view. 'I trust you enjoyed a restful night?'

'Yes, thank you. And you?'

His eyes were full of wry amusement when he looked her way. 'I've spent better. I didn't realize marriage was such a business. Not only did I get myself the responsibility of a wife, I got myself a dowry.'

Dismayed by the turn in the conversation she glanced sharply at him.

His amusement faded. 'You may, of course, do as you wish with the dowry.'

'Will it be enough to put Rosehill on a business basis and provide for us?'

He frowned. 'I'd have to take advice on that. I haven't paid much attention to estate matters in the past.'

'I've noticed the estate has slid into a decline. You should hire a steward.'

His lips tightened. 'One needs an income to hire staff.'

She frowned and pointed out. 'You have my dowry now.'

He sucked in a deep, annoyed breath. When he exhaled his nostrils flared proudly. 'I have no intention of living off your money, Fleur.'

'Then how do you intend to provide for us, by gambling?'

His voice sharpened. 'My gambling days are over. If necessary I'll grovel to my grandparents and beg them to allow me to take control of my inheritance.'

'You will lose their respect.'

'Ah, my dear Fleur, I lost that years ago.'

The set of his face told her to prod him no more. She ignored it. 'Pride will be your downfall, Remy. I understand that your immediate past leaves much to be desired, but you have the chance to redress that in the future. Some hard work will see Rosehill flourish.'

He offered her a slight frown. 'You would have me labouring in the fields like a peasant?'

'If necessary.'

'For what reason?'

She opened her mouth, and then shut it again.

'You cannot answer me, can you? A wife who has no intention of allowing her husband into her bed will never breed sons for him. Therefore, I have no need of a flourishing estate because there will be no heirs to pass it on to.'

Irritated beyond measure, she yelled at him. 'You're the most stubborn fool I've ever laid eyes on. Go to hell, then!'

'Perhaps I will,' he answered.

Flicking the reins she pushed the horse faster and faster until the hedgerows flew dangerously past at either side. Remy put his hand over hers to slacken the pace. 'Temper makes you reckless. Slow down.'

'Perhaps you should remember that, Remy.'

His hand gently closed around hers. 'Rest assured, wife. I most certainly will,' and the look he gave her warned her to beware.

FOUR

The market place was crowded. Trailing after Fleur's trim figure Remy began to feel more and more self-conscious. Word had obviously spread. The women looked down their noses at him or turned away and laughed politely behind their hands. Men elbowed each other in the ribs and guffawed.

Fleur came in for some speculative looks, too. She ignored them, nodding pleasantly at people and going about her business as if nothing untoward had happened. As she haggled with the stallholders and sent them scurrying to load her purchases on the wagon she gained their respect. He began to admire her strength.

Sensitive to the covert looks his injuries drew from the curious he was more curt than he intended to be. 'Will this take much longer?'

She stopped to dawdle in front of a pen containing a sorry-looking ewe. 'Am I to take it that you're embarrassed by the attention your appearance draws?'

'Certainly not,' he said stiffly. 'I hadn't noticed any untoward attention.'

Her smiled contained a touch of malice. 'Good, because I'm not ready to leave yet. Why don't you look over the labour on offer. We need a servant or two, a stable lad and someone for the kitchen. They will do for a start.'

'I can groom my own horse and Mrs Firkins manages in the kitchen.'

Her eyes glinted greenly at him. 'I daresay you can, but Mrs Firkins is old. She doesn't have the strength and skill to cater for guests. As for the stables, are you also prepared to groom and exercise the workhorse as well as both Crispen and my own mounts? A lad will not cost much to feed, and he can work in the garden as well.'

Remy opened his mouth to argue, and then clamped it shut again. A public argument would doubtless reach his grandmother's ears. Fleur had managed to make a good impression on her in the short time they'd spent together. Besides, he might as well admit it to himself. Fleur was right. However, knowing it didn't provide him with enough incentive to spend her dowry.

As if the matter was settled she ran her hands over the ewe then beckoned to a burly farmer. 'What price for the mutton?'

'That sheep be in its prime, My Lady.'

Her laughter contained an incredulous edge. 'It will be as tough as saddle leather. You should pay me to take it off your hands.

What's your name, farmer?'

'Blaggs, My Lady.'

'Blaggs, is it ... the same Blaggs who doubles as a purveyor of home-brewed whisky?'

The farmer's red-faced companion laughed. 'She's got you there, Bert.'

Blaggs grinned. 'I reckon. Beggin' your pardon for speaking plain, My Lady, but I heard you tellin' his lordship you need staff at Rosehill. You give my grandson and his mother a place and I'll throw the mutton in fer nuthin. Bessie's a right, fine cook when she's given her head. Trouble is, the missus won't give her the run of the kitchen unless it's to scour the dishes.'

Fleur might hold the purse strings at the moment, but Remy decided to make his presence known. 'Is the woman clean? I don't want a slattern and her brat foisted on to us.'

The farmer spat into the dirt. 'Bessie's no slattern, sir. She was married to my son proper, in a church with the bans called, all legal and decent like.'

There was a slant of green eyes his way and Fleur's lips twitched.

Witch! Remy thought.

'My William took the King's shilling and died on French soil. Bessie ain't much to look at, but she's an honest lass who'll give you a fair day's work for yer wage.'

69

'How old is your grandson?' Fleur asked him.

'Nigh on fourteen. Our Tom has a way with nags. Whispers to them, so even those gingered-up comes quiet to him.'

The farmer was referring to the practice of shoving ginger root into a horse's rear. Doctored thus, the tiredest nag appeared lively for the sale ring. Remy frowned. Such practices were an indelicate subject for a woman's ear.

Fleur just laughed. 'Send them up to the house, then. And with my *husband's* permission we will offer them a week's trial.' Her look of enquiry was a formality. When he gave a reluctant nod she turned back to Blaggs. 'The next time my brother comes calling don't feed him any of your bran whisky.'

'I didn't have much choice, my lady. Yer brother has a right persuasive way with 'im.' The farmer tipped his cap at her when they walked away.

Remy allowed his annoyance to show and her smile faded when she caught his expression. She raised an eyebrow, inviting comment.

He obliged. 'I'm surprised you allow such familiarity.'

'You are too proud, My Lord. If I do not establish a rapport with the local suppliers then we'll have rancid meat and mouldy flour to see us through winter.' When she hurried on ahead he caught her up.

'I'd prefer it if you didn't laugh at their vulgarity.'

'I grew up with brothers.'

'That's no excuse.'

She stopped suddenly, turning to face him, her eyes blazing. 'You were not so fussy when you abducted me. I could have been anyone. Perhaps you'd have preferred a milkmaid, or a ... a woman of no virtue.'

He sucked in a breath. With her mouth scornful and her witch-green eyes stormy, right at this moment he'd love it if she was a woman without virtue.

'When you make wagers with your friends, and especially wagers which amount to little more than a criminal act, you have no right to complain to the victim if she lacks measure to your self-perceived excellence.'

She was making a fool of him; and knowing he deserved it didn't make it any easier to swallow. 'Hush woman. If you don't lower your voice and assume some semblance of dignity I'll drag you back to the cart, throw you over my knee and beat some sense into you.'

'Hah!' she flung at him, but said nothing more. They resumed their walk through the stalls, the pair of them as stiff as couple of fighting cocks.

A couple of wealthy merchants doffed

their hats to him, men he owed money to. One of them bowed to Fleur with a fawning smile. Remy's mouth tightened. Although he had every intention of settling his debts he'd been trying to avoid Sedgeman for a little while longer.

'My Lord, I have a consignment of the latest patterns and fabrics just arrived from London.'

Thus he was reminded of his shabby coat, a coat he still owed the man for. 'I'm well-serviced at present.'

'Ah yes, of course you are. A dated style, but still serviceable, and one personally tailored for my special clients. I just won-dered if you might be attending the Duke of Warrington's annual ball.'

'I received an invitation, of course, Mr Sedgeman. The event brightens up what would otherwise be a dull winter in London.'

The man delicately coughed. 'My Lord, may I take the liberty of reminding you–'

Fleur interrupted then, her eyes sparkling. 'The ball will be such fun, Remy. Perhaps you should examine what Mr Sedgeman has to offer. Didn't you did tell me his work was on par with the finest ... or was that another gentleman's outfitter?'

He stared at her, agreeably surprised she'd seen fit to spare him further embarrass-ment. The message in her eyes, said, I offer a truce, so please respond.

'It was Mr Sedgeman, yes. I believe I mentioned that Mrs Sedgeman is a seamstress of the highest quality. Miss Catherine Boney is a client of hers, I believe.'

'An extremely valued client,' the man gushed.

'Really?' Fleur's eyes narrowed a fraction and her voice became honeyed. 'Then I doubt if your wife will have the time to cater for another client, especially as I will need a ball gown and several day gowns.'

'I'm sure my wife would be honoured to attend to you personally, My Lady,' he said, suddenly humble. 'She keeps herself informed of the very latest of fashions.'

'Then send her over to Rosehill on the morrow, if you please. I have a fancy for silk and my wardrobe needs replenishing for spring.' She placed a hand on his arm, keeping her voice at a discreet level. 'Do we have an account with you, Mr Sedgeman?'

'Yes, my lady.'

'Then please present it tomorrow. It's much easier to keep the books in order if accounts are presented regularly.'

Remy feigned boredom.

Sedgewick nearly fell over himself as he bowed several times then backed away with an oily smile on his face. Remy warmed to Fleur a little when she turned to him with a breathless giggle. 'He was easy to deal with.'

'He was not fooled by your play acting.'

'But too business-minded to risk losing a customer of your pedigree, even if you are a ragamuffin at present, Remy St Cyres.'

'It goes with the circumstances of my impoverished state. You will get used to it.'

'I will not. Being stubborn will not win you respect, especially if your seat is hanging immodestly out of your breeches. You have made no bones about how you are situated and I have no wish to be seen with so shabby a husband. Accept the dowry my father invested for me. Use it wisely and we will not mention it again.'

Her barbs were too accurate for his comfort. She smiled when he choked back a laugh, taking it for the silent agreement it was. 'Tell me of this ball, Remy.'

'It's held at the Duke of Warrington's London home to welcome in the New Year. It's usually a glittering affair.'

She placed a hand on his frayed sleeve. 'And will you escort me to this fine ball? I've never been to London. Are the streets paved with gold, as they say?'

He laughed at her enthusiasm. 'The streets are teeming with vermin and pickpockets, but we will go to the ball if that's your wish. I will try and secure accommodation for us.'

'We already have accommodation, a house I inherited from a relative. I've not had an occasion to use it yet.' She beamed him a smile. 'I'm so looking forward to going to the ball.'

Leland had forgotten to mention the London house to him, and his eyes narrowed. 'Then I'll endeavour to make sure you enjoy it.'

She gave a delicious shudder, then her face fell. 'There's one other little matter I should mention. I have never been taught to dance.'

'You cannot dance?' He admitted to astonishment. 'If we are to attend the ball you must learn some of the contredances, the allemande, and cotillion perhaps. And, of course, the minuet. As I recall, my mother had a manual containing the rules and figures. I will look for it.'

He stared at her for a moment. 'Mmmm, perhaps we will have a social supper or two. Charles can bring his sister, Catherine. And I'm sure Simon's three sisters would be only too pleased to make up an eightsome.'

'A ninesome. You have forgotten to include Cris.'

'No doubt we will need an extra one whilst the ladies take turns to provide us with music.'

Fleur shivered when a cold gust of wind blew through the market place.

'You are cold. If you've completed your purchases we'll return home,' he said. 'I believe it's going to rain before too long and I don't relish another drenching?'

'We need to pick up our sheep.'

75

He grinned. 'You might as well ask the farmer to butcher it first.'

'Oh no. She has a most beautiful fine fleece which can be spun into the softest of shawls. Besides, we'll need her to suckle her lamb before we turn her into broth.'

'Lamb? She looks too old and tired to give birth.'

'Then I'll assist her. I've helped Macy pull lambs from sheep on several occasions. He pulled a stuck calf from inside the cow once, using a rope tied to its legs. Despite his fearsome nature, Macy has a wonderful affinity with animals.'

Remy gave her a pained look. 'Animal husbandry is not a suitable subject to occupy the thoughts of a gentlewoman.'

'Oh, don't sound so nettled, Remy. Women have to think of something besides fashion, household affairs and the comfort of men.'

For the life of him, Remy couldn't think of a reply suitable to such a provocative statement – not without sounding more nettled.

Eyes brimming with innocence were turned on him, causing the breath to catch in his throat. 'Would you prefer to hear me prattle about embroidery?'

When he gave a small growl, she giggled, a delightful sound. He took her hand in his and smiled at her. 'I'd prefer you to drop the subject. I consider myself lucky it was you abroad on the road that night. I find you

76

quite enchanting at times.'

For a long moment her gaze touched against his. Then they widened fraction and her long lashes drooped to hide them. Much to his delight, delicate colour tinted her cheeks.

'Had you remembered my existence in the first place, you could have achieved the same result with much less effort, and without being beaten half to death,' she pointed out tartly.

'I was bored and the adventure appealed to me. I should have considered the victim's part in such an adventure, and although I cannot change the outcome I can tender my sincere apology for any fright or injury sustained by you.'

'I'm not afflicted by womanly vapours easily, and my bruises will heal.'

Fleur may have been brought up by her brothers, and might be able to assist a sheep give birth or cuss like a trooper if the occasion warranted, but she was naive. She knew nothing of the art of flirting, the looks, the touches and attentions that made the heart beat faster and brought mind and body into a slow, simmering passion. He decided to take things slowly, raise her awareness in that regard.

So when he helped her on to the cart he held her hand in his for a moment longer than necessary, then turned it over and traced his finger over the palm. She closed her eyes for a moment, allowing a revealing little tremor to pulse through her. Then the hand was snatched angrily away. Glaring at him, she rubbed her palm deliberately down her skirt.

It was obvious she hadn't fully appreciated the situation she was in, for she'd had no mother to advise her when she was growing. He hoped she wouldn't prove to be too difficult to bring round to her wifely obligations.

Having been raised by parents who'd displayed affection towards each other as well as him, it was the ideal union in his mind. He'd prefer a clutch of children rather than a single one, lonely and without playmates.

Fleur had called him stubborn. He preferred to think of himself as tenacious. Although he had regrets about the circumstances of this marriage, what was done was done. He was prepared to accommodate her feelings, but willing or not she would eventually provide him with ease and bear his children.

He gazed at Fleur's delicate profile. He could have come out of the wager with much worse. She had beauty as well as breeding, and the proud tilt of her head was softened by a sweet upturned nose and a sensuous mouth. He smiled to himself, contented with his prize as he relaxed in his seat. She would be as passionate in love as she was in anger.

Her face heated under his admiring scrutiny but she steadfastly refused to look at him again. When they reached the stables of Rosehill, the pup gained all of her attention with a wet and rapturous welcome.

'I wish I'd been born a pup,' he said lightly.

'What makes you think you weren't?' She picked up the animal, cuddled it against her and walked off towards the house without giving him so much as a backward glance. The sheep bleated forlornly at him as he lifted it down.

'I can wait, my fine lady,' he whispered as he set about unloading the rest of the cart and making the horse comfortable.

By evening, the new servants had arrived and he ate the best meal he'd had in years. Life was looking up.

A few days after she'd watched her elder brothers depart, Fleur's worldly possessions arrived, piled high on the coach and accompanied by her maid.

She gave Mary a welcoming hug before directing her to her chamber. At least she'd have another female for company beside the garrulous Mrs Firkins, even if Mary was several years older than herself.

The transference of her horse and belongings brought her no comfort. It was another reminder that her life and status had changed overnight. She no longer had her brothers to guide and comfort her, and be damned if she'd turn to her husband for advice. She intended to rely on her own will and wit, and keep an aloof distance from the man she neither admired, wanted nor respected.

To her delight Crispen shook off his fever, but the prolonged bout had left him weak. The slightest exertion produced spasms of coughing so the question of him returning home didn't arise. His presence provided a buffer between herself and Remy, so although they remained polite to each other, their relationship progressed no further.

Through good nursing and a constant supply of Bessie's nourishing food her brother's lungs began to improve and he strengthened in body.

To her chagrin, as he strengthened he changed. No longer did he seek only her company, but that of Remy as well. The pair spent most of their time in the library, poring over books, playing chess or speaking of the war. Although Crispen had often expressed an interest in buying himself a commission in the army, Fleur didn't take it seriously. Her brother was much too delicate for such a robust career.

She found it impossible not to resent the relationship he'd formed with Remy. It rankled her to be denied her brother's exclusive company and she spent most of her time in her chamber with the pup for company.

Still, she remained vigilant, locking her door each night. Thankfully, Remy didn't attempt to inflict any husbandly demands on her and she wondered why. One day she rose from her bath, stared upon her naked body in the long dressing mirror and said to her maid, 'Be truthful, Mary, am I beautiful?'

'Indeed, My Lady.'

Fleur sighed. 'You're my maid, you wouldn't tell me if I was ugly. How would I appear to a man?'

Mary smiled. 'The master is right taken with you, My Lady. He can't keep his eyes off you when you're together. Wait until he sets sight of you in that ball gown you're having made.'

Fleur gave her a sharp look and reached for her warm flannel petticoat. 'I was speaking generally, not personally. Help me into my riding habit, then go and tell Tom to saddle my horse.'

'You're never going out in the cold this soon after a bath? It's going to snow before too long. You'll catch your death.'

'Nonsense. I'll dress warmly.'

Fleur had second thoughts on her way to the stables. The wind had a sting to it that numbed her ears and fingers. The pup greeted her with rumbustious delight. She stopped to fondle its ears. 'How did you get out here?'

'He followed me out early this morning,'

81

Remy said quietly from the end stall. 'He's taken a liking to me.'

She spun round, her heart thumping erratically. Remy usually left earlier for his ride. 'I cannot see why.'

His eyes lit with amusement. 'That's because you're not a dog.'

She speared him a look. 'Tom, take him back to the kitchen and ask Bessie to find him something to eat.' She turned her eyes on Remy. 'He's my dog, Remy, and I'm trying to train him to obey me. You shouldn't encourage him.'

A nerve twitched in Remy's jaw and a struggle went on in his eyes. 'I should have asked your permission. Forgive me, I never thought to ask.' He smiled slightly. 'I like him, he's good company.'

A lump rose to her throat at this unexpected admission of loneliness. 'I didn't mean to be sharp,' she muttered, finding it hard to keep up a pretence of animosity as she fussed with her horse.

She didn't see of hear him close the gap before them and gasped when his fingers gently closed around her wrist. 'You afford the pup more attention than you do your husband. Why won't you look at me?'

Surprise brought her glance up to his. His eyes were dark and liquid, like the notes of a melancholy song. Fire burned at their core. Before she could turn away he pulled her against him and his mouth closed unerringly over hers in a kiss of infinite delight.

Too surprised to move and feeling too pleasured by the kiss to want to, she allowed him full advantage of the liberty he'd taken. Too soon he released her. He gazed at her, a half smile dancing on his lips. 'A sweet reward, wife, and worth the wait.'

The amusement in his eyes chased away any warmth she felt towards him. Furiously, she scrubbed the back of her hand across her mouth and scrambled from the mounting block on to her horse. His chuckle whipped fresh colour into her face.

Her horse was impatient to be off. As it surged out of the stable yard she allowed it to increase its pace and they headed towards the top of the hill. There, she reined it in and took stock of her surroundings.

She sucked in a breath at the beauty of the landscape stretching before her eyes. Below her the house nestled into the protective body of the hill. There was warmth in the rough hamstone of its walls, which supported the bones of a summer flowering vine and a lush patterning of ivy. The tall, diamond-paned windows were set into alcoves, those on the ground floor bearing a painted design of red tudor roses.

Compared to the home she'd grown up in the house was less imposing, but it possessed a great deal of charm. A thread of smoke coiled from one of the chimneys. She experienced a moment of sublime joy in her surroundings. In time, she would make the garden bloom and the house shine.

The air was so crisp it vibrated to its own music. Her breath was vapourous and the ground rimed with sparkling frost. She leaned forward in her saddle, her vantage point enabling her to trace the original layout of the overgrown gardens.

She smiled, remembering the expression on Remy's face after he'd kissed her. His eyes had been so soft and his smile ... she tried not to think of his smile. But there was more to being a man than having a handsome face and fine manners. She'd been brought up in a hard-working household, to which every-one was expected to contribute. It was a pity Remy's father had died before he'd passed on the skills necessary to maintain Rosehill estate.

When a horse and rider detached itself from the house her heart surged against her ribs. He sat his horse well as he moved slowly towards the path leading to the forest. He seemed to be looking at the ground.

When he stopped and turned to gaze at where she was outlined against the sky, she realised he'd been looking for marks made in the frost by her horse. She smiled to herself, wondering if he'd expected her to abscond from the estate.

Wanting no company but her own she wheeled around, moving down the other side of the hill. Ahead of her was another hill, and beyond that an expanse of sea churning winter grey towards the horizon. A path sloped gently downwards, and soon she and her horse were at a gallop. The buffeting wind tore the hat from her head and her hair unravelled and streamed out behind her.

She became aware of Remy beside her keeping pace. He grinned and pulled ahead. A laugh tore from her throat and she coaxed her horse to full stretch until they were racing neck and neck along the sand. A spit of loose scree, gouged from the cliff by the teeth of a storm, brought them to a halt.

Wheeling their horses around they cantered them back up the beach, laughing with the sheer exhilaration of the moment. Remy circled her hat, then grinning, turned his horse back up the beach a way, turned again and put the horse to the gallop. As he reached the hat he leapt to the ground, scooped it up and was back in the saddle before the horse realised it had been riderless.

As a feat of horsemanship it was an impressive display. 'Show-off,' she muttered taking off after him.

Both mounts were blowing hard when they got back to the stable.

Remy's hands spanned her waist and he lifted her down, setting her on her feet. He released her before she could murmur a protest. His glance touched on her dishevelled hair when he handed her the hat. His mouth twitched. 'I've never seen a woman ride astride like that. You handle a horse well.'

Her head slanted to one side. 'I prefer riding astride. I suppose you disapprove.'

One eyebrow lifted into a deliciously ironic arch. 'Why should you suppose that?'

'You're a man.'

'Ah, yes, I most certainly am.' His dark eyes met hers, candid in their admiration. The warmth of his expression made her uncomfortably aware of the meaning behind his words.

Flustered, she stalked rapidly towards the house, his soft chuckle caressing her ears.

FIVE

November, and they were unseasonably snowed in. Outside, all sound was deadened by the thick blanket of white whilst the sea swirled in a sluggish symphony.

In the drawing room of Rosehill logs flamed in the grate on a bed of red ashes. They swirled into grey flakes as they were sucked upwards into the chimney's maw.

Fleur was pleased by the snowfall. Reluctant to be left alone with Remy, the deep drifts prevented the imminent departure of Crispen. Nevertheless, she was anxious that it should thaw in time for the festivities and the New Year's Eve ball.

Her eyes lit up with excitement when she thought of the gown Mrs Sedgewick was fashioning for her. It was of the latest fashion, the petticoat just off the ground, the laced bodice and ruched overskirt decorated with a design of gold flowers embroidered on fine taffeta. The petticoat was a drift of translucent silk tinted a delicate shade of toasted almonds. With it, she intended to wear the necklet of pearls Leland had presented her with on her eighteenth birthday.

Fleur's dancing classes were progressing. She'd nearly mastered the intricate patterns and steps of the Allemande to Remy's satisfaction.

She enjoyed their social evenings. As a host Remy had a natural grace and warmth.

Simon Ackland and his three sisters were good company. They drew Fleur and Crispen into their circle with warmth and friendliness. The offspring of a wealthy merchant, unless the girls married well they would never rise any higher on the social scale, but were grateful for the attention the rare social evenings afforded them.

As with her brother Charles, Fleur could

not take to Catherine Boney. The woman was a little too perfect, her manner too superior, her actions too studied. She danced gracefully, played the harpsichord expertly and flirted unobtrusively. Catherine could read poetry with such exquisite enunciation and feeling it brought tears to the eyes of her audience – and she managed to monopolise the attention of everyone without even trying.

Beside her, Fleur felt clumsy, and although she told herself she didn't care, she felt a little envious of Catherine's self-assurance.

Just the evening before, Remy had been showing Fleur a step in the minuet when she'd tripped. Remy caught her before she fell. He blew gently in her ear before he stood her on her feet. A smile edged along his lips when she shivered.

'You must have taken too much wine tonight,' Catherine said, all breathless laughter and sweetness. Her grey eyes sparkled as she came between them and took possession of Remy's hand. 'Come, Remy will partner me and we'll show you how the steps are performed again. You are bound to learn them without falling over before to long.'

Remy and Catherine danced with exquisite elegance together, making Fleur feel at a complete disadvantage for the rest of the evening.

Ah yes, Catherine certainly knew how to

draw attention. The men couldn't keep their eyes off her. Crispen was smitten by her charms and was reduced to a stammering idiot in her presence. Not knowing if this was a symptom of his illness or puppy love, she wished Macy was here so she could discuss their brother's strange lapses with him.

Macy was now living in the house she'd inherited from her distant relative. Not only was she looking forward to seeing the house, at last, but also to seeing Macy again. Parting from her brothers had left a gaping hole in her heart.

Thank goodness Crispen was fully recovered from his illness. His eyes sparkled when he said one evening to Remy, 'I've been contemplating my future of late. In the past I'd considered a career as a soldier, but I've come to the conclusion I'd prefer to go to sea.'

'A fine profession for a man if he hasn't been pressed. You're not too old to become a midshipman.'

Fleur put the gloves she was darning aside, gazing at him in consternation. 'Cris hasn't the stamina for the rigours of a life at sea.'

Crispen threw Remy a grin. 'Fleur should know, she spends her days either mothering me or doctoring me.'

She was the recipient of a teasing glance from Remy. 'Her medical knowledge was gained by watching Macy pull calves from the insides of cows, I believe.'

Trust him to remind her of the kiss he'd stolen that day. Her face heated. 'Macy's a good physician. He's gone to train as a surgeon under the eminent John Hunter, who he assures me is the finest surgeon of our time.'

'They should suit each other well then. From what I've heard, John Hunter is a rough country bumpkin at heart. It's his brother, William, who's the darling of society. Still, if nothing else, brother Macy can become a butcher, afterwards,' Crispen muttered, grinning widely at her.

Pleased she'd turned his mind away from the sea she drew a letter out of the pocket hanging at her waist. 'Marguerite writes that the baby looks just like Leland, and they're going to call him Godwin, after the first earl of Stratton. I'm glad their first child was a boy. She wants me to stand as Godmother at his christening.'

Remy's smile was a little too personal when he said, 'A man should have a son to inherit.'

She stiffened, willing to argue a point. 'A daughter could inherit just as well.'

His eyes stroked against hers. 'I should enjoy having a daughter as well. I should imagine she'd have a gentle, softening effect on her brothers.'

Fleur frowned at the use of the plural. Having several brothers was not all that easy, especially when they couldn't see eye to eye over something and they resembled a pack of dogs squabbling over a bone. She grinned. Trying to infuse sense into male heads on such occasions was an impossible task.

Crispen winked at her. 'It's obvious you didn't have any sisters. If Fleur didn't get her own way she used to stamp and holler. I was then obliged to sit on her stomach and pinch her nose until she ran out of wind.'

Remy chuckled. 'I'll remember that the next time she acts the fishwife.'

She grimaced when he gazed at her, laughter in his eyes. 'It's a well known fact, men resort to using force when they run out of wits.'

Remy stirred the embers with the toe of his boot, causing sparks to fly up the chimney. Refusing to rise to the bait as he turned once again to Crispen. 'Talking about life at sea, did I tell you about my Godfather? Hernando Cordova is an uncle from my mother's side. He's a sea captain?'

Crispen's eyes began to shine. 'Does he sail with the British Fleet?'

Remy gave a light laugh. 'Hardly. He's a Spaniard.'

'Then he's our enemy.'

'Yes, I suppose he is, though I can't imagine him as such. To me he is just my uncle.' Remy's eyes became distant. 'He visited here when I was young. He gave me an eyeglass and a book on the voyages of Marco Polo. He was a hero to me, with exciting tales to tell of mermaids and pirates. He almost inspired me to follow in his footsteps.'

'Do you still have the book and eyeglass?' Crispen said eagerly.

'I'm sure I can find them. Did you know Marco Polo became an aide to the Kublai Kahn and...'

Stifling a yawn, Fleur rose from her chair. 'I'm retiring for the night. Try not to put too many adventurous ideas in my brother's head, Remy.'

Dreamy-eyed now, Crispen gave her a vague smile. Remy's slight frown was accompanied by a dismissive nod. He seemed eager to get back to the conversation.

Remy had a knack of firing Crispen into enthusiasm over a given subject, and was inclined towards intelligent and lively debate. However, she'd noticed the heroic exploits he related were usually at the expense of poor, neglected wives, who waited faithfully at home whilst their husbands went about the errand of immortalisation by slaughtering fools of the same mind set.

When she called to her pup he lifted his head, then lowered it back on to Remy's feet and ignored her.

Picking up her skirts she snorted as she flounced through the door, candle held aloft. A draught sent the flame flickering and the shadows dancing on the wall. She shivered as she shielded the flame in her palm. It was chilly in the darkness of the hall after the well-lit drawing room. She hurried upstairs, disinclined to linger.

Mary had lit a fire in her chamber and was waiting to ready her for bed. Soon she was tucked under the covers. Dismissing the servant, she extinguished the candle.

Sleep eluded her. The reflection of the moon on the snow lent an eerie brightness to the room, except for the hellish red leap of flames. The shadows seemed darker by contrast, but not menacing.

She wondered if the presence of Julia Cordova lingered in the room. The beautiful and tragic mother of Remy had an approachable look in her portrait, and when Remy mentioned his parents his eyes glowed with affection.

It would be nice to be held in such esteem by one's child. She couldn't remember if she'd loved her own mother, or not. Her eyes prickled with tears. The fond memory retained by Remy of his mother would be a precious possession to have.

The hush of night pressed against her ears, so each nerve twitched at the slightest sound. Somewhere, an owl hooted. She imagined her mother, building a picture of Anne Goodsires seated in the chair by the fire, watching over her whilst she slept. The fire died down to a glow, the bars of the grate clicked as they began to cool. It was a long time before she experienced the drowsy state of lowered consciousness before sleep.

In the back of her mind was an awareness of sound, of movement, like the whisper of fabric. A mouse scratched in the wainscotting, there was the muted creak of a floorboard as if someone crept lightly across the floor. The settling noises of the house, or a wandering spirit perhaps?

She smiled when her nose was tantalized by an elusive drift of sandalwood fragrance as a kiss lightly brushed her forehead.

'Goodnight, mama,' she whispered.

As soft as a butterfly alighting on a flower, her mouth was claimed. The pleasure of it relaxed her. She sighed and sought the moist sweetness of the kiss with an intimate urgency as her body surged with a thousand sensations.

This was too real to be a dream! She stiffened, pushed out with her hands and encountered nothing but air. Her mouth still tingled from the encounter, her body was sweetly, but strangely aroused as she sat up in bed and asked the shadows in a quavering voice, 'Is somebody there?'

Receiving no answer she snuggled back into bed, pulling the covers up round her head in a childish attempt to ward off danger, and leaving only her nose uncovered for access to air. She felt foolish, wide-awake and too aware of herself.

As stealthily as a cat, Remy backed away from the bed and let himself out. Fleur hadn't locked the door tonight, but it wasn't an invitation, she'd simply forgotten. He smiled, stimulated by his close escape. She was feeling more at home, allowing herself to be lulled into a false sense of security.

Ruefully, he mused, *I should have known better than to kiss her, but what an unexpectedly fruitful response.* Some time had passed since he'd enjoyed a woman and he was now uncomfortably aware of his rampant state. He could take Fleur any time he wanted, he reminded himself. He was her husband and had the right to her.

But at whose expense? His father had once told him that because laws were made by men it didn't mean they were always just, only convenient to men. And what could have been more convenient for him than to kidnap a woman with a dowry and beauty when he needed one?

Justice had been denied Fleur, who'd had no say in the matter of her marriage. His superior strength, a convention that conveniently labelled women in the wrong, plus the might of her brothers, had taken precedence over any consideration of her wishes. He couldn't heap further indignity on her to satisfy his own comfort, however strong the urge. At least ... not at this time.

The snow cleared faster than Fleur expected and Crispen announced his intention of returning to Stratton House. Nothing she said would move him to change his mind.

'I need to discuss something urgently with Leland,' he said, and no amount of prodding would prise it from his lips.

Some secret brotherhood business she'd be excluded from, she supposed darkly. There was certainly something edgy about him, some hidden excitement he couldn't quite contain.

'Keep your top coat buttoned and wear the muffler over your mouth if it snows again. And don't forget to give Marguerite my letter, it's in your pocket.' She thrust a parcel in his saddlebag. 'Here's a flask of brandy and some food in case you get hungry. Stay overnight at Grundy's farmhouse so you don't tire yourself.'

'Enough, Fleur,' he said, his tone unexpectedly gruff. 'You're not my mother, and I'm not an infant. I'm perfectly capable of looking after myself.' His mount tossed its head and whinnied, impatient to be on its way.

His words were little knife wounds in her heart, for his recent illness had demonstrated quite clearly that he was not capable of looking after himself. She gazed at him, near to tears now. 'Cris...'

His eyes softened and his hug enveloped her. He seemed thin when compared to her other two brothers. 'I appreciate all you've done for me. Take care of yourself, Fleur. Just remember I love you. We all do.'

Then he was gone. Blinded by tears she rushed past Remy and dashed upstairs. From her window she watched Crispen grow smaller and smaller. He stopped once, to turn and lift his hand in farewell, as if sensing her watching him. Then he blended into the shadows of the forest and was gone, leaving her feeling lost and completely alone.

Only she wasn't alone. Remy was there when she turned, his proud face shadowed, his dark eyes reflecting the intensity of her pain. She knew his arms were ready to comfort her. He'd listen to her troubles, allow her to cry on his shoulder then take advantage of her weakness.

The hypocrite! He'd been the cause of this. How dare he play the comforter for his own ends? Blinking back her tears, she took a deep breath and gazed at him in disdain. 'Is there something you wanted?'

For a few long seconds he held her eyes to his, then his lips curled slightly and his nostrils flared. 'I thought you might need something from me. Obviously I was mistaken.'

'I'll never want anything from you.'

He gave a faint smile before turning away. 'The time will come when your mind will be changed, my captive little wife.'

For a week she avoided Remy, rising early to exercise her horse. The remainder of the day was spent embroidering silk handkerchiefs with her initials captured inside the St Cyres crest, or having fittings for the various gowns she'd ordered. They were boring female occupations.

If she'd been at Stratton House she'd have pit her wits against Leland in a game of chess, or ridden with him round the estate, or visited estate cottages with gifts for the new infants or the sick.

Rosehill had no estate village. The estate was too small, more like a large farm. It would draw its labourers from the open villages and towns ... if it ever reached the state of needing their support.

Needing an occupation with purpose, Fleur took it into her head to make an inventory of her new home. She called on Mrs Firkins to furnish her with the old one.

The woman scratched her head. 'Can't say I ever seen one. Best ask the master.'

Remy was found in the library, his head in a book. Her pup, who'd now been named Gruff, was growing rapidly into a shaggy, shambling creature. With a disposition as amiable as his parentage was uncertain,

Gruff had transferred his affections to Remy, as if he'd recognized him as master. He lay comfortably with his head on Remy's feet.

Seated at a table near the window, Remy seemed totally engrossed, his dark head tilted to one side. He was made aware of her presence when Gruff's tail thumped against the floor. He raised his head to gaze at her for a moment, then gave a faint smile and rose to his feet. 'Ah, a visit from my wife, an honour, indeed. Have you come to take refreshment with me?'

'I'd thought to inventory the contents of the house and wondered if there was an earlier list I could consult.'

'Ah ... it's domestic matters you're concerned with.'

'It will have to be if I'm to live here.'

'So it will. The mistress usually attends to such trivialities, I believe.' His smile broadened. 'And since you've ignored every opportunity to escape, it seems you do live here. Is there something else you'd rather be doing then? Are you bored?'

'A little,' she said cautiously, for she couldn't measure his mood. 'I had plenty to occupy me at home. I played chess with Leland, visited the sick with Macy and helped Marguerite prepare for the birth of her child. Cris and I competed against each other in archery tournaments, rode together and sometimes we fenced or shot pistols at targets.'

'You could do most of those things with me, if you wished. You only need ask. I need practise in all the manly virtues. In return, I could instruct you in the feminine arts, give you another dancing lesson, perhaps. With practice, we might end up a perfectly matched couple.'

He was mocking himself as well as her. The last time they'd danced he'd kissed her on the mouth in front of their guests and her brother. She'd blushed and they'd all laughed, except for the simpering Catherine. She'd appeared outraged by the action. Her mouth had pursed up like a dried fig and for the rest of the evening her manner had been exceedingly cool – almost unpleasantly so.

The churlishness had pleased Fleur because Cris had taken notice and his infatuation with the woman had fled as quickly as it arrived.

Her face heated at the thought of that kiss of his. 'You treated me like a tavern wench on the last occasion we danced together.'

'You have my utmost respect, Fleur, as do all tavern wenches.' He smiled gently at her. 'I'm not your brother. I don't respond to you in a brotherly manner so you cannot treat me in exactly the same way as you do them. As a result you avoid me. It will not help matters in the long run.'

The conversation had taken an uncomfortable turn. His astuteness and unpredictability was a little disconcerting, but she refused to be drawn into matters so personal. 'Where can I find the former inventory?'

A smile flirted at his lips. 'In the steward's quarters, I'd imagine.'

She couldn't keep the impatience from her voice. 'Where are they situated?'

Mrs Firkins came in bearing a porcelain teapot with a design of exotic birds. Two delicate matching cups jiggled against each other as she set the tray on the table. She beamed approvingly from one to the other. 'I've brought you some nice cheese wafers Bessie's made, and tea to wash them down with.'

Remy pulled out the other chair for her and raised an inquiring eyebrow. After a moment of hesitation Fleur settled herself. The warm caress of his breath against her ear before he straightened sent a delicate tremor through her, but he didn't seem to notice. She was nothing to him but a means to an end, but what was that end?

'What are your plans for the estate?' she asked him when Mrs Firkins finished pouring the tea and left.

The cup looked fragile, but perfectly safe in his elegant hands. He lowered it carefully on to the saucer. 'What would you suggest?'

'We need a steward, and you need to learn

how to manage the estate so it will provide us with an income in the future.'

'If we live carefully your dowry will provide us with enough until my expectations come into fruition. My inheritance will last for several lifetimes.'

Here was a man who lacked purpose in life. She was direct in her questioning. 'Have you always been so idle, Remy?'

His smile became slightly strained as he indicated the library shelves with a casual wave of his hand and protested. 'I'm never idle. I haven't read a quarter of the volumes in here yet.'

She snorted. 'So, you'd prefer to see the estate fall down around your ears rather than preserve it.'

'Preserve it for whom, exactly?' he purred.

She wasn't about to let the conversation take that direction. 'Others are less fortunate, assets should be made to work for you.'

'Rosehill is primarily my home. If it's allowed to fall into disrepair it will still last longer than my lifetime.'

'But what about–' She bit her lip.

'Go on...' he purred.

She stood, saying icily, 'Perhaps you'd be good enough to direct me to the steward's quarters.'

'I'll do better than that, I'll escort you there myself and give you a tour of the house on the way. That way you can see what you so suddenly became mistress of. Drink your tea first. You can fetch yourself a shawl on the way. It will be chilly in the corridors.'

She was thankful for her warm wrapping as she followed Remy. The absence of mould indicated the place was free of damp, though mice scuttled away at their approach. 'We should get ourselves a cat or two,' she muttered.

The house was a comfortable open-sided square of three small wings. It was three storeys tall. Three barns and a smokehouse were set a little way off at the back. The front of the house had a long carriageway overgrown with weeds, that led to the road. There was a lake choked with lilies, and set in a garden so neglected she wanted to weep just looking at it.

The furniture was shrouded by grimy dustsheets. Rodents had taken up residence in some of the chair seats and the window hangings were dusty. Sun damage had been prevented on the west side by the use of shutters, and the ceilings were free of damp stains.

She liked the house. All it needed was some redecoration and a thorough clean to bring out its beauty. And perhaps a little refurbishment of the furniture might be in order. 'How long has Rosehill been in your family?'

'The original title was conferred by Henry

Tudor,' Remy told her. 'Rosehill is not part of the earl's estate, over which my grandfather holds the title. It was originally owned by a son of a remote branch of my grandmother's family, and run as a farm. From there, it took a torturous route, passing through a succession of female lines directly into the hands of my father when he was but an infant.'

It was an intriguing story. 'So, the earl is your heir and you are his.'

Remy chuckled. 'It's a situation that annoys him no end. Had I not been born, Rosehill would have gone to Elmira and become part of the earl's estate through marriage. And had you not been in the right place at the right time that night, I'd have lost it to Charles.'

He'd deserved to, but Fleur decided to keep her counsel, murmuring instead, 'My family's sympathies were with the Yorkists. Stratton House came as a dowry with one of the countesses, who was related to the royal house.'

Remy chuckled. 'Then we're natural enemies.'

'Except for one small fact. Henry Tudor wed the daughter of his enemy, Edward, and united the opposing forces into one.'

'Thus, a dynasty was founded.' He took her hand, leading her though a corridor to a set of rooms. It was a nursery, the windows barred. It overlooked the neglected fields, already walled and ready for the modern system of rotation farming. All the land lay fallow and the weeds had taken a firm hold.

The day was fine so Tom had put their livestock out to grass. There ewe, the milk cow, calf and horses, were coloured shapes munching on the tussocky grass in the same field, where, weather allowing, they were set free in daylight hours.

Blagg's farm was a shining jewel in the distance where it bordered on the earl's estate.

'Blaggs keeps an eye on me,' Remy murmured. 'There's not much going on here that my grandfather doesn't hear of.'

'Do you mind?'

'Perhaps I'm deluding myself, but I like to think he asks Blaggs to spy on me because he cares.'

'You're his grandson. I imagine he does.'

Abruptly, Remy pulled a sheet from a rocking horse, setting it in motion. 'In these rooms I spent most of my early childhood and learned my lessons. When I grew older I loved going out with my father, because I usually met other children.' His eyes were on her now. 'I remember you quite clearly. You were wearing a white gown with green flowers embroidered on it. When I first saw you the sun was behind you. Your hair was lighter then. It shone so brightly it reflected the light and I thought it was a halo, and you were an angel.'

Reaching out, he curled a tendril around his finger and gave a tender smile. 'Your nurse came after you with a hairbrush, and you leapt on the bannister and spiralled to the bottom to escape her. I was filled with awe and admiration at such a dangerous feat.'

'I expect I was showing off for your benefit,' she said, laughing at the memory he had of her.

'Curiously, you haven't changed much. You still shine, and still have a spirit of defiance and adventure.' His expression became quizzical. 'It's the angel image which puzzles me now. I think I may have been mistaken there.'

She laughed, at ease with his teasing. 'Never tell my brothers you associate me with such a vision. They'll make a nonsense of such a theory.'

He took her hand in his, leading her out and down a twisting staircase to the steward's quarters. It was a sizeable suite of rooms set between the stables and servants' quarters, with an office attached. As well as inner access, there was a separate entrance leading into the yard.

Remy searched through the ledgers and drawers, eventually blowing dust from a worn, leather-bound ledger. He placed it in her hands. Eight years had passed since the last purchase or sale had been recorded. Remy's lips tightened when she gazed at him, but all he did was shrug and say, 'Many items will have to be deleted.'

'Can you remember what they are?'

'No doubt the gaps will become evident to you when the inventory is completed. I expect Mrs Firkins will be of some help. She's probably hidden several pieces in the attic to prevent me disposing of them.' He gazed around with a sigh. 'What virtue does one look for in a steward?'

At least the tour had triggered an interest in the future of his inheritance, however vaguely expressed. 'Leland would probably be happy to advise you,' she offered, trying to salve his pride a little. 'He has more experience in such matters.'

He slid her a sideways look. 'There's no hurry. I'll consult with him when we're in London. You did say he'd be at the ball?'

'Marguerite is sure she'll be over the birth of Godwin by then, but they intend to leave him with his nurse. You won't mind if I ask Cris to stay with us in London, will you. I believe my ... *our* house in Hanover Square has plenty of room.'

'Hanover Square?' he said with the lift of an eyebrow. 'A fine address indeed.'

'Is it? I've never heard of it.'

For a moment his eyes were clouded with incredulity, then he shrugged. 'Arrange things as you will, Fleur. I quite enjoy the company of your brothers.'

'Thank you.' Even though Crispen had departed the previous week, the thought of seeing both he and Macy in the near future lifted her spirits.

He cupped her chin in his hand and gazed into her eyes. Smiling, he murmured, 'See how well we get along when we consider each other. I can think of a better way of saying thanks.'

'No doubt you can,' she murmured, her heart beating with erratic anticipation.

His fingers trailed gently down her cheek. 'I've never known a woman with softer skin.'

Her neck muscles tightened as panic set in. It was isolated in this part of the house. She wasn't ready to be a wife – and after what Marguerite had told her, might never be ready.

'How many women have you *known*, Remy?' she blurted out.

His eyes darkened with displeasure, his smile became slightly arrogant. 'No woman should ask her husband such a question. Do you require an answer?'

She shook her head.

'Good,' he purred, 'because I can't remember.' Releasing her, he strode off, leaving her feeling ashamed of herself and angered by his answer.

SIX

Fleur's relationship with Remy didn't improve, but neither did it deteriorate.

Although distantly pleasant, Remy showed very little interest in her unless she approached him. He spent his days riding, or entertaining the obnoxious Charles, or Simon Ackland.

Simon was the more likeable of the pair. His manner towards her was affable, though when they ran into each other and she tried to sustain a conversation he was awkward and attacked by shyness. He had penned her a note of apology for his part in the affair of her abduction, and begging her forgiveness had thanked her for her gracious acceptance of his sisters into her home. He also stated Remy to be the most decent man he'd ever met.

Not so Charles. The man had an overbearing, almost sneering attitude, and his manner towards her was either overly familiar or dismissive.

As for Charles' sister, Catherine hung on Remy's every word and agreed with everything he uttered. Softly spoken, but no longer in the flush of youth, her languid eyes were used artfully as she gazed at Remy, obviously besotted with him.

Catherine was civil, but amusingly patronising on the occasions they were together, as if Fleur was an idiot to be humoured. It was clear they'd never be friends.

Fleur's days were fully occupied with the inventory. She was thorough, as Leland had taught her to be with matters relating to estate expenditure. *It's the incumbent's duty to preserve and add to the estate for the next generation.*

Soon, the gaps in the ledger made it apparent that Remy had been more than lax. It was as if he didn't want to grasp the extent of his actions in squandering the valuables belonging to the estate. Very little of value remained in the main chambers. Disposal hadn't been recorded, and the large number of silver and porcelain pieces missing appalled her. Remy's gambling had stripped the house of practically everything but the furniture.

She sighed, saying to Mrs Firkins. 'What happened to the Meissen tea service?'

'It's safe and sound in the attic. It was a wedding present from the old earl. Lady Julia was right fond of it, and it troubled her that she might break it. Use the Lambeth Ware for everyday, Mrs Firkins, she says to me. It's much more practical. We'll keep the Meissen for when the King visits. Not that he ever did, of course. It was a little bit of humour between us, like.'

'Bring it down from the attic and put it in on show in that nice little glass fronted cabinet over there. Is there anything else in the attics I should know about?'

'I spirited lots of bits and pieces up there when Master Remy wasn't looking.' Mrs Firkins grinned suddenly. 'Things his mother was fond of, mostly. I knew he'd come to his senses one day and would regret his wild ways.' She sighed. 'I should have made a list. It will take a lifetime of Sunday sermons to go through it all.'

Mrs Firkins gazed around her. 'There used to be some real nice stuff in here, Venetian glass and the like. There was a set of miniatures in gold frames that disappeared. They were portraits of Master Remy's Spanish family. His mother brought them with her to the marriage.' She pointed to a series of hooks. 'They used to hang over there ... until that Sir Charles set his eyes on them.'

Fleur's eyes sharpened. 'He stole them?'

'Not exactly. He won them on the cut of the cards. Master Remy was seventeen at the time and had never gambled in his life. He was unworldly, eager to impress. He didn't realize the man was too sharp for him. That was the start of it. His parents would be right ashamed–'

Fleur closed the ledger with a decisive snap. 'Dwelling on the past will not help matters,

111

Mrs Firkins. I will not allow you to gossip to me about the viscount. You will treat him with respect however long you've been retained in his household. Is that understood?'

'Yes, My lady.'

But Fleur was glad of the information, and vowed that if Charles still had the miniatures, and if she was afforded the opportunity, she was going to retrieve them.

She found the opportunity after they'd been in London for a short while.

They'd journeyed there in surprisingly short a time. Boarding a small sailing ship in Poole, and with a strong wind at their tail to fill the sails, they were borne around the coast and into the mouth of the Thames River.

Remy did not take to the motion of the sea and looked pale and miserable. Fleur found the movement, bustle and creak of the ship exhilarating, the coarse shouts and sure lithe movement of the sailors as they moved about their business, exciting.

They docked in the congested upper pool of the Port of London. Macy was waiting for them and bellowed a greeting before the sails had been furled. He'd hired a couple of porters to carry their luggage, which was lifted on to a box slung by rope to two poles. Hoisting the poles on to their shoulders, the porters pushed their way through the crowded streets.

The air had an unpleasant odour after the freshness of the sea. Wide-eyed with wonder and fearful of being parted from the men in the crush of people, Fleur took a tight hold of Remy' s sleeve. As soon as they stepped ashore the colour had returned to his face and he looked much relieved to have solid ground under his feet.

He removed her hand, curling it into his, and smiled with genuine warmth. 'You will soon get used to it all.'

The house in Hanover Square was joined to its neighbours on either side. All had a solid, appearance and consisted of several storeys and a basement, with accommodation for servants in the attics.

A railing separated the houses from the wide public street and the square in the middle. There was much activity, with carriages and horses coming and going, and people parading the street in their fine clothes, despite the cold.

A footman in livery hastened to greet them and before too long the luggage was carried upstairs. Mary immediately went about establishing her superior position as the mistress's maid by issuing unnecessary directives to the under maids.

Macy called the staff together and introduced them as the new master and mistress. He then gave them a tour of the house before declaring his intention to go out. 'You won't see much of me, I'm sharing a friend's lodgings whilst you're in London,' he said, giving her a kiss.

She tried not to let her disappointment show. Now she was married the bond between her brothers and herself had subtly changed. 'How's Cris?' she asked, eager for news of him. 'Have you seen him? Did he travel up by road with Leland? Is he well?'

Macy picked up his hat, carefully plucking a piece of lint from the crown. 'Cris is fully recovered from his illness, thanks to you.' He jammed the hat on his head, nodded to Remy and headed out through the door.

The hall seemed much larger without his presence, but lost in her excitement Fleur didn't notice that Macy had not answered most of her questions. Overcome by the novelty of her London home she scurried from room to room again, exclaiming over the richness of the furnishings.

Fleur had a fine room overlooking the square. She didn't give much thought to where Remy was accommodated until the adjoining door swung open. Heart hammering, she turned and stared at him.

'Leave us,' he said to her maid. When Mary scurried away he engaged her eyes, saying directly, 'I had no idea your dowry stretched to support a household such as this.'

She couldn't quite meet his eye and fussed

with a hairbrush on the dressing table. 'It's grander than I expected.'

'How do you afford the luxury of retaining so many servants?'

'Oh, Leland sees to all that,' she said carelessly. 'You should hire yourself a personal manservant whilst you're here.'

'I'm perfectly capable of seeing to my own needs, Fleur.'

'Not with the fine wardrobe of clothes you have now.' Her smile was over-bright, forced. 'They will need to be cared for. I'll enquire if one of the footmen is capable of the task.'

'As you wish.' He joined her at the window, took a firm grip on her elbows and turned her to face him. 'You're being evasive.'

'Unhand me,' she said, beginning to lose her temper 'I have told you I've never been in the house before, so how do you expect me to know how it is run? Cease your inquisition, Spaniard.'

The molten liquid of his eyes contained enough heat to warn her not to go much further. 'I'd prefer it if you didn't use my mother's background as a personal insult to me. I'd also be obliged if you didn't shout at me like a fishwife, as you are doing now, but especially in front of the servants.'

She opened her mouth and shut it again. But it wouldn't stay shut. 'I was not shouting, but if you continue to ... to *bully* me I will shout as loud as I can and to hell with you! Now let me go. You will leave bruises on my arms.'

'Bully you?' His grin was touched by wickedness when he released her arms. 'Another man would throw you over his knee and spank you, it would teach you to respect your husband. Shout if you must then. I will tell the servants that you're afflicted by deafness.'

She giggled at the thought, but mostly at the amusement in his eyes. She loved the look of his eyes when he was pleased with life, loved the soft curve to his mouth and his smile. He was a fine looking man and she was glad his face had healed rapidly from the beating he'd taken.

Gently, she pressed a finger against the tiny scar remaining on his face, understanding his need to stand high amongst his peers whilst they were here. 'You needn't worry. My behaviour towards you will not give you cause for embarrassment. I will act the respectful wife to perfection. In fact, I will imitate the elegant Catherine.'

'I would prefer it if you didn't. There can only be one Catherine.'

'I'm uncertain. Should I be offended by that remark, or not?'

His eyes caught and held hers. His laughter had a rueful edge to it. 'You are uncomfortably perceptive at times, but my thanks for the reminder. I should not have brought the woman into the conversation.'

'Are you involved with her?'

'Judas priest!' He looked as startled as he sounded. 'What a strange question to ask your husband.'

'You are not annoyed?'

'I certainly should be.' He managed a tight little smile. 'Have I given you cause to believe such a thing?'

'Catherine is too openly admiring of you. I thought I may have given you cause by not being what you expected in a wife.'

'Ah ... I see.' His smile made her blush. 'The situation between us will be resolved eventually.'

'I doubt it.'

'My dearest Fleur, you are only a woman. You are made of flesh and blood and are ripe for loving, however much you deny it to yourself.' He stooped to kiss her lingeringly on the mouth, setting out to prove it.

No matter how she tried to hang on to her senses she was robbed of them, his kiss setting her blood aflame. When she pushed him away he laughed. 'You need not feel jealous of Catherine.'

'Such a notion didn't enter my head. You have too high an opinion of yourself, Remy St Cyres.'

'And you have too low a one.'

'Remy?' she said when he turned to leave, then thought better of what she'd been about to say when he turned back. 'It's of no consequence.'

'What did you intend to say, Fleur?'

'I wondered if you had enough cash for your immediate needs whilst we're here.'

His face shuttered. 'My needs are few.'

'But there are places I'd like to see whilst we are here, such as the Vauxhall Pleasure Gardens, and I should like to go to the theatre. I've never seen a play ... would you also take me to see an opera, and could we go to a masquerade?'

He chuckled. 'It's midwinter and the gardens will be deserted, but we could go to the Ranelagh Rotunda to socialize, which is under cover and heated by central fires. There is often amusement to be found there, and an orchestra to entertain. If we get a fine Sunday I will take you to Hyde Park. I'll see if I can obtain tokens for the Drury Lane theatre and perhaps there will be a masquerade ball or two. You must look amongst your invitations.'

'What invitations?'

'The ones on your bureau over there.'

Her eyes widened when she saw the many envelopes addressed to Viscountess St Cyres. 'How can this be? I do not know anyone here?'

'Word has gone around and everyone will be eager to meet the new face.'

Without thinking she dashed across the

118

room and threw her arms around him in a hug. 'Life is going to be so exciting.'

His arms crept around her. 'I hope London lives up to your expectations.'

His body was a warm column against hers, and for the first time since she'd known him she admitted she enjoyed the closeness. But with the enjoyment came a tension she didn't know quite how to handle.

Undecided whether to push away or stay there, she sneaked a glance at him. His smile coaxed one from her, and when he took the opportunity to steal a kiss she made no protest, just enjoyed the soft warmth of his mouth against hers and the sensations which crept through her body to lodge in the most secret of places.

It was very pleasant to be kissed, thus, and it was Remy who pulled away from it first. He ran a finger down her nose then smiled at her and walked away without saying anything. She had a strong urge to call him back to be kissed all over again, which was very odd, all things considered.

He turned in the doorway and smiled. 'I saw a small reading room downstairs. I'm interested to see what books are on the shelves. I'll be there if you need me.'

As soon as she read the invitations Fleur knew her wardrobe was going to be inadequate. Seeking him out she explained. 'I have only one ball gown, and we've been invited to at least five balls.'

'We do not have to go to them all.' He took the squares of embossed and gilded cardboard from her hands, shuffling through them. 'These three are on the same night.'

'But which one shall we accept?' she wailed.

'None of them. They're being held on the night we're invited to dine with the Earl of Northhaven, who was a friend of my father. I've already accepted.' He held out the remaining card. 'See, here is a costume masquerade you might enjoy. It comes from Charles, and the costumes can be hired. He has booked an assembly hall for the event. Perhaps we should go as a devil and an angel.'

She ignored the connotation. 'And the other?'

'The invitation is from a woman of dubious reputation. You will refuse the invitation.' He flicked her an amused glance when she sighed. 'Do I sense you crave a little excitement.'

'I feel like a hungry child at a banquet,' she admitted. 'I don't know where to start. How will I know who is suitable and who is not?'

'Listen to the gossip. No doubt you'll soon sicken of it. London will educate you, but I doubt if its artificiality will suit you for long. You'll miss the country too much.'

And it didn't take long. The round of social

visits soon assumed a similarity. Keeping her counsel and remaining pleasant at all times was a hardship when the women gossiped maliciously behind their fans. Confidential snippets of information were whispered from mouth to ear, until secrets became so twisted that, by the time they became common knowledge they no longer reflected the truth.

Behind the perfume and powders was the odour of decay, of rottenness. The more Fleur went abroad the more the sight of the poor, the homeless, the sick and infirm played on her conscience and affected her.

The men talked ceaselessly about the war with Spain and France, even the Earl of Northhaven, a rather plump man with a ruddy complexion – who, after a large dinner of salted pork with cabbage and stodgy dumplings, took Remy into his study for an hour or so, leaving Fleur with his worthy wife and her sister.

Fleur remained pleasant even though they prattled inanely about the regrettable lack of moral fortitude in the lower classes. Take away their comforts and how much moral fortitude would these two smug matrons be left with? But she held her tongue, and smiled and nodded, for they didn't seem interested in her as a person or require her to speak, just to act as an audience.

Remy found himself being interviewed by

the earl. 'I knew your father well. Such a pity he and your mother were killed in that ambush. He stood high in the King's favour and some thought Spanish spies were involved.' He smiled in reminiscence. 'Julia was a great beauty. Men would have died for just a smile from her lips.'

'I have fond memories of my mother,' Remy said stiffly, for he found the reference to her slightly distasteful.

Northhaven shrugged. 'My pardon, Remy. I did not mean to be disrespectful to her memory. Your mother attracted no gossip. Both she and your father hold a warm place in my memory.'

As he handed over a glass of wine a diamond twinkled on his finger. 'As you know I worked for your father up until his death. I was his trusted advisor and did all the paperwork necessary to the position he held. I also acted as an ambassador in the French Court from time to time.' Astute eyes came up to his. 'You do know what his job entailed, don't you?'

Remy's eyes hooded slightly. 'He advised the King on overseas affairs, I believe. He told me very little of what he did outside of Rosehill.'

'Yes ... well, he would have been discreet. That was only a small part of the position. Your father also ran a network of agents who brought back information to keep us abreast of foreign affairs.'

Remy tried to hide his surprise. 'I didn't realise... I think I understand.'

'Yes, I'm sure you do. I believe you're fluent in the Spanish language.'

'My mother saw to that. What are you suggesting, sir?'

'I know of your circumstances, Remy. When your father died freedom made you foolish. However, I feel I'd be doing your father a disservice if I did not help his heir to replace the fortune he lost to gambling.'

Remy's jaws tightened. 'I have learned my lesson, sir.'

'Of course you have. You come from fine stock ... which is why I'm offering you a position which will not only utilise your talents but will also provide you with adventure and an abundance of wealth. Are you interested?'

A little wealth of his own would not go amiss, Remy thought, leaning forward.

Fleur thought Remy seemed preoccupied when they took their leave.

'You were a long time with the earl,' she finally ventured to say. 'I thought I'd die of boredom waiting for you to finish.'

'He and I had some business to discuss.' He chuckled. 'I'm pleased I serve some purpose in your life, even if it's merely to relieve your boredom.'

'I never find you boring.'

He raised an eyebrow. 'I'll take that as a compliment. Actually, the countess and her sister were very taken with you. The earl said you were a fetching little piece who looked as though you might have a mind of your own.'

'Hah!'

He slanted her a sideways glance. 'I told him I beat you on a weekly basis to keep you obedient.'

When she made a face at him he slid an arm around her waist and pulled her gently against him. 'If you would like, we could go on to one of those balls we were invited to. It will help improve your dancing skills.'

Which immediately made her feel as though she didn't have any. She didn't feel like dancing after the heavy dinner she'd consumed, she felt like sleeping. 'You go out if you want. I'm full of dumplings and intend to retire.'

She hadn't expected him to go, but he did. She tossed and turned in her bed, imagining him dancing with the smiling Catherine. Just as she was about to drop off to sleep she imagined him kissing the woman and jerked awake. It was nearly dawn when he arrived home and she was short-tempered from lack of sleep the following day.

The next time he asked for her company she accepted.

One social event blurred into the other, and soon they became a chore rather than a pleasure. The preoccupation with appearances, the many changes of dress and the need to be on her guard against speaking her mind, took its toll on her.

She saw very little of Leland and Marguerite after the Christmas festivities, and even less of Macy, who had taken to his studies with singular passion.

Fleur began to crave the silence and solitude of the country.

Remy, more used to this kind of life, ignored the many games of chance on offer and accompanied her wherever she went. He paid her little attentions, whispered endearments in her ear and generally behaved like a man enamoured with his choice of wife. The languishing sighs and inviting looks he received from other women annoyed her a little, but were ignored by him.

Fleur found she drew the attention of many men, including Charles, who, rather unwisely as it turned out, expressed his admiration for her at the masquerade ball.

They had hired costumes. Remy was dressed as a Matador in a gaudy beaded costume that suited his dark looks to perfection. She was his counterpart in a red satin gown of many ruffles, her black mantilla held in place by a comb.

Charles had been partnering her in the Allemande when midnight struck. They unmasked themselves to a bevy of cheers and shouts. Charles was a little worse for drink, a state she'd often seen him in.

'I'll give you anything I possess for a kiss,' he slurred.

She gazed through the revellers towards Remy, who'd been partnering Catherine. Back towards her, he was gazing down at the woman. Fleur bit her lip when she slid her arms around his neck and kissed him.

'Come on,' Charles muttered. 'If Remy chooses to leave you intact you're fair game for the rest of us.' He took her hand and practically dragged her into a private ante-room, kicking the door shut behind them.

She gasped. 'You're insulting, sir.'

He laughed, whispering in her ear, 'I have most of what Remy ever owned. I intend to have you as well. It was my idea he snatched you off the highway, so I should get to share in his bounty.'

She would have slapped his face if she hadn't thought of the miniatures. 'I'll give you what you desire for the miniatures you won from him.'

Charles' eyes were cold, his voice strangely rough. 'That hardly seems a fair bargain. You think you're too good to kiss the likes of me, don't you? The frames alone are worth a fortune in gold.'

'Are you saying I'm worth less?'

'You certainly are, but everyone has a price,' he drawled. Fiddling with the ruffles at his cuff, his smile was loathsome as he removed a pack of cards from his waistcoat. 'The highest card takes all, then.'

Remy and Simon slid into the room. Remy gazed from one to the other. 'Explain this assignation with my wife, Charles?'

Charles shuffled the cards and slapped them face down on the table. He gave a light laugh. 'Fleur's wagered herself against your miniatures.'

Remy seemed carved from stone. 'Do you have any idea what you're doing?'

'It's only a kiss, Remy.'

Charles laughed as he shuffled the cards. 'I believe we agreed that the winner took all. Aces are high.'

She paled. 'I certainly did not agree to that. It was a kiss for the miniatures. I wanted Remy to have them back.'

'How sacrificial of you, Fleur. If you're able to fulfil the terms of the wager, go ahead,' Remy said coldly.

Charles had a predatory look on his face as his fingers drummed on the table. Fleur's quick glance towards Remy showed a face full of disdain, as if he didn't care what happened to her. Why should he? She'd been nothing but a means to an end in the first place. And he'd lied to her – he had Catherine to fill his needs.

Heart thumping, her hand hovered over the cards, then descended. She turned up a seven of hearts.

About to take the second cut, Charles' hand was gripped from behind and forced palm up. Concealed in his palm was an ace of spades.

Simon Ackland shrugged. 'I'm sorry, Charles, I couldn't let you do that to Fleur after enjoying Remy's hospitality so many times. Enough is enough. Send someone to your lodgings for the miniatures, for I know you have them there. I also advise you to return anything else of his you've *won* over the years.'

'Wait a minute,' Remy said, his fingers circling her wrist so she couldn't escape. 'Let him cut the cards.'

Simon stared at him. 'You can't mean it, Remy?'

Remy's glance touched on her, his smile a scimitar. He nodded. 'Cut, Charles. 'She has already cut the first card on my account. The rest is in the hands of fate. If you win the wager you can spend the night with her before I kill you.'

Closing her eyes Fleur bit back a sob. Surely he couldn't mean it?

'I don't think so,' Charles said shakily.

A knife pinned his sleeve to the table. 'Cut the damned cards before I slash your fingers off, you cheating bastard!'

Fleur's eyes shot open just as Charles' free hand descended. She exhaled a shaky breath

128

when she saw it was the five of diamonds. *Thank God!*

The miniatures were sent for. They were exquisitely painted and framed in gold, each one indented in a bed of red velvet.

Word had reached the rest of the revellers that Charles had been caught cheating at cards. A hubbub broke out, and angry growl went through the crowd.

'You'd better leave now,' Simon hissed. 'This might turn ugly.'

They joined the stream of guests hurrying from the premises. Remy kept a tight grip on her arm, and he dragged her through the streets so fast her feet barely had time to touch the ground. His anger was evident in his tense silence.

He dismissed the only servant on duty, and dragging her upstairs, threw her on the bed. 'How dare you make a fool of me,' he said through gritted teeth, his voice flaying her nerves to shreds.

'Remy, I–'

'So, you were willing to exchange yourself for these.' The box containing the miniatures was thrown on to a chair with a dull thud, raising a small cloud of dust. 'Well, here they are Fleur. They're yours.'

She struggled to get up but his hand found her middle and pushed her back down. He stared down at her for a moment, and then plucked the mantilla and comb from her head. 'What manner of woman are you?'

'Remy, I wanted the miniatures for you.'

His fingers went to her laces and he eased her bodice from her body. She protested when her skirt followed suit, leaving her in her chemise. 'Shut up,' he growled. 'The loss of the miniatures was none of your business.'

'Your business became mine when you abducted me.'

'So it did,' he said softly, 'And then you became my business.' His palms drifted lightly across her breasts. When her nubs hardened, he smiled. 'I'm about to make myself even more your business.'

Her mouth dried up and she whispered, 'What are you going to do?'

'You know very well, woman. You must pay me the penalty for that wager. Whether you chose to fight me is up to you, but the outcome will be the same. I can only promise you'll enjoy every moment, whether by force or submission.'

'I don't know what you're talking about,' she hissed, knowing exactly what he was saying, because this was a man who knew the depths of a woman.

'You will do when I'm through with you.'

When she tried to hit him, he laughed, and capturing her hands above her head took her mouth in a long, lingering kiss that put every other thought from her head. Afterwards he gazed down at her, his mouth sensual. You'll enjoy it much more if you don't fight me, Fleur.'

She couldn't meet his eyes, and dumbly nodded. Be damned if she'd give him the satisfaction of crying out or struggling. When he let go of her arms, she hissed. 'I've been informed that the act of union is painful, so I shall not make it any worse for myself by resisting.'

'I will not hurt you, Fleur,' he said against her ear, 'That, I promise.'

He stood to strip the clothes from his body. His form was a fluid, amber statue in the candle glow, and proud and unashamed in his manhood, she thought, trembling with nerves when he eased the chemise from her body and gazed at her nakedness.

When tears filled her eyes she squeezed them shut. Her body had tensed up so much with anticipation of pain that she was as rigid as a log of wood. Yet tremors racked through her and she trembled uncontrollably.

The tip of his tongue feathered away her tears. 'Look at me, Fleur,' he urged, and the expression in his eyes was as deep and mysterious as a summer lake. 'Don't be frightened.'

She gave a small sigh of surrender because she needed to trust him in this matter. Pleasure shot through her when he swiftly took possession of her mouth.

131

It was he who was perfection, she realized a little later, when any resistance she'd felt had been swept away by the delight of his caresses and the strength of his passion. He'd hurt her not at all, and now lay sleeping, half lying across her naked body, which craved for his touch again.

So she gently eased herself against him and sighed a little bit. Soon, he woke and his tongue curled around her breast. She ran her fingers through his hair, and she offered only encouragement when his mouth trailed kisses down her body. Only this time he didn't stop. Soon, ecstatic little cries left her lips, and she was transported to a peak of ecstasy.

'Ouch,' he whispered, 'Let me go, my love.' Prising her fingers from his hair, he turned her on to her stomach, lifted her to her knees, then slid deeply into her. How long they stayed like that she couldn't remember, but the long, slow thrust of him brought pleasures untold so she uttered little mewing noises of encouragement and her muscles refused to let him withdraw. It ended with a moist hot rush of thrusts. Filled with a surfeit of unbearable pleasure, she had to bury her face in the pillow to stop her ecstatic groan from waking the household.

Remy's chuckle ticked the inside of her ear. 'Tell me you're not enjoying my attention now, My Lady.'

'I will never let you leave this bed,' she vowed.

She lost count of how many times they made love, but each time seemed better than the time before. Eventually, she fell into a dream filled sleep.

When she woke, the sun was streaming through the window and her maid was shaking her from her lethargic and pleasure soaked dreams.

'What time is it, Mary?'

''Tis noon. I have your bath ready.'

When she sat up in bed the sheet fell from her body, leaving her naked. 'Where's my husband?'

'Gone out.' Mary drew a wrap around her shoulders. 'The earl is downstairs.'

When she lazily stretched, every muscle in her body begged for mercy. You will have to get used to it, she thought, smiling in utter contentment. 'Which earl is it? I've met so many lately.'

'The Earl of Stratton, My Lady.'

'Leland!' Scrambling out of bed she slipped into the bath, quickly drinking her tea whilst Mary soaped her.

'You have a bruise behind your knee, My Lady, and another at your waist. Shall I bathe them with witch hazel?'

She grinned slightly. Remy had known exactly where to nip her for maximum pleasure. 'Don't bother, Mary, they're nothing.'

It didn't take her long to ready herself. Dashing downstairs to the drawing room she smiled widely at Leland. 'I'm sorry you were kept waiting.' Her pleasure at seeing him was mixed with disappointment. 'Where's Cris, isn't he with you?'

Leland didn't spare her. 'Cris has gone to sea. He's now a midshipman on board the *Enterprise.*'

She paled. 'That's not possible. He's not strong enough for such a career.'

Leland took her hands in his. 'He didn't want to tell you himself, he knew you'd try and stop him.'

'Why didn't you stop him, Leland?'

'He had his heart set on it. Besides, he needs to make his own way in life. He's no longer a child.'

The exact words Cris had used when he'd left Rosehill.

She turned when the door opened. Remy came in, gazed from one to the other, his mouth curling in an intimate smile when he caught her eye. His smile faltered when he saw the fury in hers. 'Is something wrong?'

He'd brought this about. Remy had filled her brother's head full of romantic notions about life at sea – about his godfather, Hernando Cordova, the Spanish sea captain. If she ever ran into the man she'd fire a shot into his damned ship and sink it from under him.

'Just at this moment, I think I hate you,' she cried out. 'You filled my brother's head full of nonsense, and now he has run away to sea. I'll never forgive you, Remy.' Pushing past him, she fled to her chamber and began to weep.

SEVEN

Nothing Remy said or did would compensate Fleur for the loss of her brother's company.

Yet she put up no resistance when he took her into his arms, and she couldn't conceal her enjoyment of the act of union between them. He loved the feel and taste of her and every erotic shiver and wild cry she gave.

He enjoyed her charms as often as possible, not allowing her coolness towards him to drive a wedge between them at night. Each encounter was a pleasurable one for her, he made sure of that. He had to compete with the love she felt for her brothers – and it was the only thing he could give her that they could not. A loving and passionate union would bind them together in a unique relationship of their own – which would result in an infant if their lovemaking bore fruit.

Contrary to what she thought, Remy hadn't

deliberately set out to send Crispen to sea. He'd watered the seed of longing already inside the lad's mind. In time, she'd arrive at the fact that Cris was a man who thought for himself, and had a will greater than her own with regard to the course of his future.

He picked up his hat. He had an appointment with the Earl of Northhaven this morning, the last in a progression of such meetings after the approach made to him by the earl during their dinner engagement. Afterwards, he was meeting Leland at St James coffee house. There were urgent business matters relating to the estate he needed to discuss and he wasn't looking forward to dealing with them.

He grinned at his reflection. That he looked good in his pearl-grey brocade waistcoat and fine suit wasn't in dispute. He was immaculate, courtesy of an elderly gentleman who had once been a personal servant and who now opened the front door to callers and polished the silverware. His stock was blindingly white and his shoes silver-buckled to match the snakes-head cane Fleur had bought for him on a shopping excursion. It seemed an unwarranted extravagance to one who, due to his own foolishness, had never had much to spend on such fripperies.

Fleur's purse seemed to be bottomless. Every day, parcels arrived, from milliners, dressmakers and perfumers. They were pounced on with exclamations of delight. Her sleeping chamber was full of lace and satins, gloves of every fabric and colour, ribbons, hats, feathers and fans. It smelled like a bawdy house at times.

He grinned. Not that he had the need or inclination to visit one lately.

He shrugged as he made his way downstairs. Although the free spending alarmed him, it wasn't his money she was spending so he had no right to complain. If all went well though, soon he'd have the means to put Rosehill to rights for the future of his heirs. And if all *did not* go well...? He shrugged, it would not be through lack of effort on his part. He intended to drive a hard bargain today.

He smiled when Fleur came up the stairs, standing to one side so she could pass. She didn't even look at him, just lifted a haughty nose in the air to continue past him in a whisper of green silk and an aura of roses.

He didn't like being ignored. His fingers closed around her wrist to still her progress. 'No one would guess you spent half the night in my arms and begged for more.'

Blood rushed to her cheeks and for a moment the fire of their combined passion flared in the eyes that met his. He admired her spirit when she hissed at him, 'You could be any man. If you hadn't abducted me my brothers would have married me off to another. Your friend Charles, perhaps.'

She had the instincts of a gutter fighter.

'Unfortunately, it's a woman's lot to become a man's chattel. We have to make the best of it.'

'Ah … how delightful. You've assumed the classical martyred wife pose this morning.' He kissed her mouth, felt in its softness a need for him to be stronger than her will. 'You'll never be my chattel, Fleur, nor would I want you that way. As for Charles, he's no longer my friend, and if he makes another approach to you I'll challenge him to a duel.'

'Duelling is illegal, a fact of which you are well aware,' she scoffed.

He laughed at the notion of such a law being enforced. Matters of the heart involved the very pride and driving power of a man, something women didn't seem to understand. 'Anything worth keeping is worth fighting for.'

There was a flicker of interest in her eyes now. 'Are you saying you'd be willing to die for me?'

He placed a hand against his heart. 'Most certainly.'

Praise for such a selfless act was not forthcoming. 'You fool,' she said scornfully and snatched her arm away. 'If you want to die so badly, die in the service of your country not on my behalf. I don't want your death on my conscience and I happen to know you do not possess one chivalrous bone in your body.'

He grinned at the crushing reply. 'You're turning into a scold.'

'And you're turning into a–'

He kissed her again, keeping her to him until she began to respond. He let her go, and, laughing when she soundly cursed him, leapt down the remaining steps and out through the front door.

His laughter faded when he got outside. He just hoped her words didn't turn out to be prosaic.

Remy's meeting with the Earl of North-haven went as expected. The man was heavy handed with his flattery. His words, which made Remy squirm, were a means to an end as he compared Remy favourably to his father. That end was reached when they decided on a mutually acceptable reward for his services. Remy added his signature to that of the earl and slid a wad of papers into the pocket of his topcoat.

'Good luck, Remy,' Northhaven said after he rang for a servant to escort him out. 'Your father would be proud of you.'

The euphoria that had carried him through the meetings suddenly fled when the earl's door closed behind him. What had started as a way to fill the family coffers, was now assuming sinister aspects. It was possible he would not live to see his next birthday. Pulling his topcoat closer around him he shivered as he hurried towards the coffee house, where Leland waited.

The haze of smoke made his eyes water when he entered, but the place was pleasantly warm. Leland was seated in a secluded corner seat with a copy of the *London Magazine* spread in front of him. He glanced up to observe his advance, his eyes bland and a faintly derisive smile on his face.

He might have won over Crispen and been accepted by Macy, but Remy knew he still had to watch his step with Leland. The man had a faint air of menace about him, even when he smiled.

Leland inclined his head towards the bench opposite. 'You're late.'

'My apologies, I was detained by the Earl of Northhaven.'

Leland's eyes narrowed. 'You keep powerful company. He's one of the King's advisers and up to his ears in intrigue. They call him the spider.'

'It was a courtesy call,' Remy said blandly. 'Northhaven was a friend of my father. In fact, he stepped into his position at court.'

'Yes, there was talk at the time. But then, there is always talk and the perpetrators of the crime against your parents were arrested and executed.' The suspicion fled from Leland's eyes. 'You indicated there was business you needed to discuss.'

Remy nodded. 'Fleur seems to be living too extravagantly.'

There was a hint of amusement in Leland's eyes. 'She's never been to London before, what do you expect? It will wear off in time.'

Leaning forward, Remy stared at him. 'What I expect is an honest answer about where those means are coming from, not evasion. Her dowry couldn't maintain the Hanover Square House. She doesn't receive accounts, only receipts, and her purse seems to be bottomless.'

Leland shrugged. 'She's your responsibility now. Ask her.'

'I'm asking you.'

'And if I don't choose to answer?'

When Leland made a move to stand up Remy's face flamed with anger. Recklessly, he bunched Leland's coat in his fist and pushed him back down.

Remy suddenly found himself staring down the barrel of a pistol. Leland gave a great, booming laugh. 'Only a fool would do that to me.'

The weapon wasn't primed and Remy pushed it aside. 'Call me what you will but I intend to get to the bottom of it. If Fleur has means other than those stated it's my right to know the sum of them.'

Remy's remaining hand was brushed from Leland's coat like a troublesome fly. 'You snatch my sister from her family and think

141

you have the right to know her worth? You should have courted her in the proper manner, you strutting cockerel.'

'What I should or shouldn't have done is beside the point now. We are wed, and I want our union to be happy and fruitful. To encourage her to deceive her husband doesn't help her to accept her status. My rights to her and any property she brought to the marriage are unassailable, as are you to yours.'

'You'd better exercise some of those rights very carefully, my friend,' Leland said softly, 'Fleur has the ear of my wife and if any mistreatment occurs–'

'If Fleur feels the need to discuss personal matters with your wife I cannot stop her. As for me, I'd prefer to stick to business between us. The personal aspect of our marriage is none of your damned business.'

'I told her not to underestimate you,' Leland muttered. 'I will tell you then. Fleur was willed the house in Hanover Square and a healthy income by a distant relative on her mother's side. Fleur thought you might gamble it away, a sensible assumption when all things are considered. She asked me to continue managing her estate until you proved your worth as a man.'

Remy felt sick at being judged so unworthy, but thought he'd probably deserved it. He nodded. 'I'd be obliged if you'd keep managing it for the time being.'

Leland's eyes widened.

Remy gave a wry smile. 'I can see you hold no good opinion of me. I'm going away shortly and will be absent for some time. I'd be obliged if you'd escort Fleur safely back to Rosehill. The sooner she's out of London, the better.'

He took a wallet from his pocket and slid it across the table. 'Inside is a letter of credit to my bank. There should be enough on deposit to hire a good steward to get Rosehill Estate back on a working basis. Fleur can do as she will with the house. It will keep her busy and she will enjoy the challenge.'

At least Leland didn't ask where he'd acquired the money, but it seemed he'd already guessed. His eyes expressed his concern, but who that concern was for remained unclear when he said, 'I hope you know what you're doing. I wouldn't like to see Fleur widowed before she's properly a wife.'

The inquiry in Leland's eyes was met with a blank stare from him. The thought that Marguerite didn't attract the most intimate confidences from Fleur was reassuring. He didn't bother satisfying Leland's curiosity. The nature of his relationship with Fleur was not open for discussion. But hopefully it would soon become apparent – if nature decided to be kind to him.

'When are you leaving?' Leland said, rising reluctantly to his feet.

'Immediately after the duke's ball.'

'That soon? Does my sister know?'

'She does not, and nor will you tell her, for speculation will not be welcome in certain quarters.' Remy managed a faint grin, 'It seems to be my turn to deceive. No doubt Fleur will be glad to see the back of me.'

'I wouldn't count on it, she's a contrary creature.' Leland held out his hand and a grudging respect dawned on his face. 'Watch your back. You'll need to if you're involved in the spider's schemes. Be careful you don't get your damned fool head knocked off.'

Which was quite likely, Remy thought soberly as they parted outside the coffee house, so he'd better make the most of the time he had left. But first he had to set Fleur straight about a few things.

She had been on yet another shopping spree and was surrounded by packages when he arrived at the house. She showed him a plate with a delicate design of roses. 'Look, isn't this pretty? I've ordered some settings, and have asked a silversmith to design us some cutlery with the St Cyres crest.'

Didn't it occur to her that he must wonder where the money to pay for all these goods came from?

'How is this to be paid for?' he said, keeping his voice deceptively soft.

He was saddened when she gazed into his eyes and blatantly lied, for he'd thought they'd progressed beyond deceit. 'I have a little put aside for such things.'

'I'm not as stupid as you imagine me to be, Fleur. You have more than a little, as I learned from Leland today.'

Her mouth tightened mutinously. 'He told you?'

'I asked him. Honour dictated that he furnished me with the truth.'

'I don't see why you should object to me trying to make Rosehill comfortable. It was an inheritance, and all I'm doing is spending money on our home – a home you nearly gambled away.'

He sucked in a deep, steadying breath. 'Let me remind you of something, Fleur. We are joined in wedlock. Upon our marriage everything you owned became mine – the clothes you wear, this house, every guinea of your inheritance. I could throw you out on the street and you would have nothing.'

She opened her mouth, and then shut it again when he grasped her chin between his thumb and forefinger. 'I have no objection to your extravagance since it will pass. I do object most strongly to being lied to, though.'

'I didn't exactly lie,' she mumbled.

'Be quiet. I haven't finished. From now on you would be wise not to mention my past behaviour. What's gone before cannot be changed and I'd prefer it if you treated me with a little more respect than you've shown

145

me in the past. Do you understand, Fleur?'

Face flushed from the reprimand, she nodded. He let go of her chin. For a moment she stared at him, her eyes wounded, her mouth trembling with hurt.

He resisted the urge to ease her pain with kisses and soothing words. She'd grown up expecting it from her brothers. When she understood it wasn't going to be forthcoming from him she gathered her skirts together and walked slowly away from him, her back stiff.

The door closed gently behind her. Footsteps pattered across the hall and up the stairs. Her chamber door banged shut. He suffered an agony of remorse, imagining her broken-hearted and sobbing on the bed.

She was quite composed when she came down, her maid in attendance. She gave him an indifferent glance, playing the injured party to perfection. 'Do I have your permission to call on Lady Amelia, My Lord.'

He hardened his heart, saying curtly, because she might as well learn that he was no longer prepared to allow her to manipulate him. 'You don't need my permission.'

Her maid arranged a fur-lined hood on her head and Fleur slid her hands into a matching fur muff. She looked charming, but remote as they left.

Later, he found her chamber door locked against him. He didn't make a fuss. He knew there were times when women were indisposed. Although disappointed, he chose to suppose this was one of them.

A week later the door was unlocked again. He went to her bed and after a feigned reluctance on her part, found her eager and receptive. Her passion was easily aroused, as was his – and completely and exhaustively satisfied.

Fleur unbent enough to talk to him again, but her manner was aloof as she engaged him in endless discussions about what should be bought for Rosehill and what shouldn't. She was exacting her revenge the only way she knew how, and had as many barbs to bury in him as trees had leaves.

She didn't mention his gambling directly but posed provocatively worded questions. 'Can you remember what stood on that little table on the hall at Rosehill?' or 'I brought the Rosehill inventory up with me, shall we go through it and see if we can replace the missing ornaments?'

Christmas came and went in a flurry of rain. London lost its gloss completely. She stopped spending and began to complain about the acting at the playhouse, the noise, the dirt and the smells. She indicted most of the gossip, declaring what had once been a source of amusement to her to be malicious lies – the women who indulged in it, tedious.

She seemed out of sorts when she asked glumly, 'Will we be staying here much longer, Remy?'

'Only until the Duke of Warrington's ball. Are you missing Rosehill?'

She would not admit to it. 'I miss the country air. Everything is so stale here, and the night fogs are unhealthy and have a foul odour. Do we have to stay for the ball?'

Alarm stroked through him. He couldn't leave London now. 'It's only a few more days,' he coaxed. 'Leland and Marguerite will be there, and you've kept your gown a secret from me all these weeks. I've heard the King might attend.'

She brightened up at the thought. 'I should like to meet the King. I wonder what he's like.'

A few days later, when they were readying themselves for the ball, she exclaimed indignantly, 'Just imagine. The gossipmongers are talking treason, saying the King is insane.'

'There are times he acts strangely, I believe.'

She shrugged. 'He's the King and is bound to act differently. They're saying he provoked the war with America, and because of it the French and Spanish seized the opportunity to resume old hostilities.'

Her eyes grew so round at the thought of the King being so foolish that Remy was forced to hide his grin. Receiving no response she discarded the subject.

'I hope Crispen is safe. Macy told me he sailed for Gibraltar to help defend the garrison from the Spanish.' Her glance slanted towards him, slightly accusatory. 'Where do your sympathies lie, Remy?'

He frowned slightly. 'Has somebody questioned them?' Her eyes slid away from him, 'Fleur?'

She shrugged. 'It was nothing. Somebody mentioned your Spanish heritage.'

'Who?'

'Catherine.'

'She's causing mischief because of what has happened between her brother and myself. Bear her no mind.'

'She holds you in too high a regard not to be malicious in defeat. I think her heart was broken when you married me.'

He stifled a grin but encouraged the game along with, 'Does this imagined high regard for me bother you?'

'Why should it? It's her heart that's breaking.' Her eyes gently closed and her lashes swept her perfect skin before she opened them again.

She was in her chemise and robe. The tip of a pink tongue moistened her lips. 'There is something odd about Catherine, I feel. I have wondered why she has no suitors and why you seem to treat her with indifference.

Do you not consider her to be an attractive woman?'

'She has a certain style,' he said carelessly, wondering where she was leading him, 'But no dowry to speak of. Catherine is ... *mature* and I think she's aiming too high. She could easily find herself a husband amongst the merchant classes.'

The tragic expression in her eyes stabbed him to the core. 'It's being said you and she were once lovers. And I saw you kissing her at the masquerade.'

His heart took a giant leap. 'She kissed me before I realized her intention. Is that why you indulged in that stupid wager with her brother?'

'A wager you insisted I would keep, whatever the outcome. The thought hurt my feelings – as if you'd discarded me. How could you do such a thing, Remy?'

'I would have killed Charles first.'

'I've heard whispers that you had promised to wed Catherine.'

He sucked in a breath, astounded by the allegation. Were such wild exaggerations common in women's gossip? 'All lies; a proposition was put to me by Charles once. I refused it.'

Her smile was ingenious now. 'Why?'

The notion of him being interested in another woman seemed to have put her out of countenance. 'Because I've always found her perfection slightly tedious.' When his smile gently flirted with her, her eyes began to shine.

'Do you not find me tedious, also?'

'You are not perfect,' he pointed out.

The little pout she gave enchanted him.

'I find you intriguing,' he said, impressed by her initiative and pandering to it. 'You think for yourself and your opinions are always fresh. You are not submissive and there's a touch of wickedness about you that I quite adore.'

'Really, Remy?' She pulled the combs from her hair and shook it free, allowing it to cascade down her back in a gleaming cloud. He sucked in a slow breath when she took a brush to it. The reflection of her eyes in the mirror held a cat-like radiance.

He crossed to where she sat. His arms circled around her and his hands cupped the fullness of her breasts. His thumbs grazed gently across the nubs, bringing them in a hard caress against his palms.

Giving a tiny shudder of pleasure she dropped the brush, leaned back into him and closed her eyes. He nuzzled through her hair, kissed the creamy soft rise of her throat then loosened her robe and took possession of her luscious mouth.

'Mary will be here to ready me for the ball soon,' she murmured against his mouth.

He was so ready to love her he was close to

bursting. Leaving her for a moment he locked the door and came back to her, fixing about her throat a small ruby set in gold filigree that he'd bought her. 'I thought you'd like this small token of my regard to wear to the ball.'

Her eyes filled with tears. 'It's exquisite, thank you, Remy.'

She twisted and came up against him, trembling and womanly in her need. He held her close, surging against the silken apex of her thighs, now flowering open, moist and receptive. Her sweet musky smell robbed him of coherent thought.

'Oh God, I can't wait.' He slid his hands under her buttocks to lift her up amongst the fripperies on the dressing table.

The soft, shapely columns of her legs circled him and trapped him against her. Just as eager, her hands slipped between them, loosening the flaps on his breeches. As if he'd given her the world on a chain, she rewarded him most ingeniously, so their lovemaking was plumbed with a new depth of passion.

They arrived slightly late at the ball. They were unable to tear their eyes from each other. She was gazing at him with such awareness. He caught his breath, knowing he'd fallen in love with her.

She looked like a fallen angel in her white and gold gown, her mouth dewy soft and slightly swollen from his kisses. Her eyes shone with the satisfaction of the outcome of her first seduction of him. Wig dressed high and decorated with white flowers and gold ribbon loops, the ruby burned at her throat, a muted flame against the glowing purity of a circle of pearls.

He danced nearly every dance with her, besotted by her appearance, her fragrance and the power and fascination she held for him. She seemed just as entranced by him, and he couldn't wait to get her home again.

Then he remembered he wasn't going home that night. 'I love you,' he whispered in her ear a little later, because he couldn't bear to leave her without her knowing how he truly felt about her.

Then he nodded to Leland, who obligingly partnered her in a dance whilst he slipped out the back way. He remembered the tender smile on her lips and the luminous expression in her eyes and was content that the memory he would carry with him would be a pleasant one. He prayed that expression would still be there on her face when he returned – *if he returned.*

Away from the warmth and glitter of the ball, the wind howled and moaned, driving the litter of the day before it through the dark lanes and streets.

The docks were a tangle of swaying masts, the shadows dense and dangerous. Feeling exposed, Remy pulled his cloak snugly around him and leaned against a post trying to be inconspicuous. Rats nosed at the rubbish, cats fought in alleys and each blank window seemed like a watching eye.

A tavern door opened and a group of sailors spilled out, laughing and shoving each other. One detached himself from the group, staggered past Remy and hissed his name. 'Follow me.'

Half an hour later a ship slipped out of the Port of London on the midnight tide. Remy was aboard her.

Behind him, the church bells of London began to ring in the New Year.

'He's gone ... gone! He didn't even have the courage to tell me, just left me a note.' Fleur crumpled it up and threw it furiously at the wall. *'The hare-brained Spanish cur, I hate him!'* She burst into tears. 'And just when I'd decided to like him.'

Macy grinned as he smoothed out the paper. It was tied with red ribbons. 'This is more than a note. Listen, the man has quite a turn of phrase. He calls you his red rose of love, the touch of moonlight on water. He says your mouth–'

The letter was snatched from his hand. 'That's private, and if you reveal one word of what it contains to Leyland I'll tear your tongue out and feed it to the London rats.' She turned pale at the thought. Stuffing the missive inside her bodice, she clapped a hand over her mouth and rushed from the room and up the stairs.

A little while later she returned, smiling wanly at him. 'That's the second time I've felt nauseous this week. What's the matter with me? It can't be serious because there's no pain with it.'

'Don't you know?' Macy said, grinning broadly at her.

She stared at him. 'Have you suddenly gone deaf? I've just said so.'

'There's something of a personal nature I need to ask you, then,' he said, and without giving her time to think about it, asked, 'What is the nature of your relationship with Remy?'

She stared at him, blank-faced.

Macy sighed, deciding to use the language doctors reserved for recently initiated, but unaware brides. 'Have your courses arrived on time? Could it be possible that you are ... in a delicate condition.'

A blush crept under her skin and she gazed at him, her eyes wide with astonishment. 'You mean I may be...'

'With child?' he prompted, hastening to add, 'But of course I could well be wrong.'

A smile inched across her face as she grew used to the idea. Soon her face was illuminated with tenderness. 'I'll kill that man when he comes home from the war,' she said softly, leaving Macy in no doubt that the marriage was consummated, and in a manner totally agreeable to her.

'Well, my dear, it seems your infant, if there's to be one,' and he was damned sure there would be, 'will be birthed towards the end of August.'

'It cannot be born then,' she said, clearly aghast as she stared at him. 'I left instructions for a field to be ploughed in my absence and wheat obtained for planting. It will nearly be time to harvest it.'

He chuckled. 'Then your harvest will be more than you planned for.'

Suddenly, her face fell and she began to sob. Macy drew her into his arms and held her close, 'Fleur, don't be so upset.'

'You don't understand.' And if anything she sobbed even louder. 'I'm crying because I'm happy. I just wish I could tell Remy. What if he dies in the war without knowing?'

'Then, at least he'll have an heir to inherit Rosehill.'

Her eyes narrowed in sudden annoyance, her tears ceased to flow. 'He has planned this on purpose to get himself an heir for Rosehill.' She stamped her foot in fury. 'Damn his sweet lies; I had not thought him devious enough to plan for such an eventuality.'

Macy chuckled. 'It's not wise to underestimate any man. We're naturally devious by nature.'

'Men are all idiots. Why else would they go off to war and leave their wives and children to fend for themselves?'

Her glare boded ill for any unfortunate male child who might have the temerity to put in an appearance. 'I will pray for a daughter. Now, I must see Leland and make arrangements to get back home as soon as possible. Let's hope the roads are passable for I refuse to stay in London a moment longer.

EIGHT

Rosehill was a welcome sight after a nightmare journey over iron hard and rutted roads.

'I wonder if the duke's ball was worth the bother of the journey,' Fleur said crossly as the carriage wheel hit yet another pothole and almost tossed her from her seat. A memory of Remy's declaration of love stole into her mind. She smiled, his words evoking another memory, of a warm and secret caress inside of her.

Marguerite clung to the seat on for dear life. 'Of course it was, when we were honoured to be introduced to the King. Not everyone was lucky enough to be so blessed.'

'I didn't feel all that blessed by the event.

In fact, His Majesty turned out to be a disappointment,' Fleur murmured. 'I expected him to be frothing at the mouth like a rabid dog.'

The look Marguerite gave her was as sour as turned milk. 'He almost did when he saw that gown you had on. The fabric was far too sensuous for modesty. You could almost see through it.'

'But you couldn't, and that was the allure of it.'

Marguerite's mouth pursed. Her puritanical streak had been ignored when her fortune was taken into account. Well aware of her duties, she'd assumed her role as Leland's countess expecting nothing more from the union than to obey her husband and bear the Russell heirs. She had got exactly that.

Leland was often impatient with her, and Fleur, who wanted much more from her own marriage than to serve her husband with blind obedience, sometimes felt sorry for her – especially since her advice about the marriage act had been so misleading. She could have enjoyed Remy's attention much sooner if she hadn't been so frightened by the thought of intimacy with him.

'The gown was modest by London standards. Besides, Remy approved of it,' she said dreamily.

'Of course he did, he's a man. The pair of

you behaved quite brazenly at the duke's ball. As if you were ... *lovers*, instead of man and wife. I was personally embarrassed by it. To accept a kiss from a man on the mouth at a public gathering is outrageous.'

Fleur's eyes began to shine. 'At the ball Remy whispered in my ear that he loved me.'

'Men always use terms of endearment when they want their own way or are feeling guilty about something.' Sharp blue eyes stripped the dreams from Fleur's expression. 'It didn't stop him leaving you without notice, did it? Is that the action of a man who loves you?'

Marguerite's reasoning was too close to the bone for comfort, but rather than voice the uncomfortable thought that perhaps her own sharpness may have had something to do with driving Remy away, Fleur sought to excuse him. 'He wanted to serve his country.'

'And which country might that be?' Marguerite asked her tartly. The carriage suddenly picked up speed and bounced over a rut. 'What on earth has come over the coachman?' she exclaimed in annoyance as they were tossed sideways once again. 'I'll give him the sharp end of my tongue when we reach Rosehill.'

Fleur smiled, pleased to be presented with an opportunity to get her own back. 'I wouldn't if I were you. Leland has taken over the reins and I imagine he's been warming himself with the brandy he bought at the last inn.'

More likely, Leland had overheard Marguerite's mean remark and decided to punish her. However, Fleur's infant was being punished in the process and she had no intention of meekly submitting to Leland's moment of recklessness. Taking off her slipper, she rapped on the coach roof with the heel, casually shouting. 'Slow down, Leland, I'm not a sack of turnips to be tossed about.'

Marguerite's mouth was a tense line when the carriage eased to a slower pace. She said no more until they reached the house, then she had plenty to say, outraged over the condition of it, and the lack of servants.

'I hope the snow holds off so we only have to spend one night in this hovel.'

Leland threw her a warning look. 'Fleur might be my sister but I'd prefer it if you didn't insult her under her own roof. Perhaps a night in the stables with the horses would be more to your taste.' Marguerite's mouth clamped tightly shut and she said no more, just sat in a disagreeable atmosphere of her own making.

Followed closely by Gruff, whose tail whipped back and forth creating a draught and who seemed only too willing to transfer his affections back to her in Remy's absence – Fleur directed Bessie to light fires in the guest chambers, which were kept clean for unexpected guests.

After a meal of hearty beef stew and dumplings, Marguerite retired, much to her relief. Fleur, strangely contented to be back at Rosehill, talked about the future of the estate with Leland until they both began to yawn.

He left her at her chamber door and kissing her goodnight, said, 'Take no notice of Marguerite. She's been listening to gossip. We both know which side Remy is on. He may be a little hot headed, but he's no traitor and I've taken a liking to him. There is more depth to him than was first apparent.'

'My thanks, Leland, you have no idea how much it means to hear you say that.'

'Oh, I think I do.' He grazed his fist gently across her nose and smiled when she coloured. 'I'm so very pleased this turned out well and you're happy.'

She gave a contented smile. 'If he comes home safely to me, then I will be.'

Fleur's chamber was pleasantly warm. A fire crackled in the grate and Mary had heated her bed with a flat iron full of coals. Curled up as near to the fire as he could get without singeing his fur, Gruff opened one eye now and again as if to make sure all was well.

Fleur snuggled into the warm hollow her body had made in the bed and watched the shadows leap and dance about the room. It was good to be home. Before she fell into a deep and dreamless sleep she wondered where her husband was just at that moment.

'I am carrying your child, Remy,' she whispered into the shadows, and prayed he'd return safely.

Remy was part of a consignment of exchange prisoners being put ashore at Point Mala. His uniform smelled of another's blood and sweat, but the stench of vomit was his own.

Sea-sickness had been his constant companion since he'd left London, and the odour was offensive and inescapable. Lice had invaded his body, covering him in sores and scabs. He'd not eaten for two days and felt too weak to scratch himself. His stomach churned uneasily as he hung miserably over the side of the pinnace.

The boat scraped against the bottom. Thank God! At least they were on dry land now, not the unpredictable and uncontrollable shifting mass of water. With the other prisoners he sat in the sun for several hours, throat parched, watching the officers parley. Eventually, the exchange took place under a flag of truce.

Remy watched the boat pull away, low in the water and overcrowded with dull-eyed and emaciated British soldiers and seamen. Many showed every sign of being ill-used since they seemed in worse shape than himself.

A chill went through him when a twenty-four pounder opened fire. Grape shot exploded. He summoned up enough energy to dive for the shelter of a crate as shrapnel whistled around them.

'*Bastardos!*' the man beside him spat as shrapnel peppered around their crouching forms. The next moment the man was dead, his heart pierced through his back by a hot shard of metal.

Someone had given an order to fire prematurely, for the oarsmen began to curse as they rowed frantically and futilely towards the fleet. It wasn't long before the Spanish returned the fire. The boat containing the British prisoners took a direct hit, and was blown from the water. Observing the carnage, the war didn't seem quite so heroic to Remy now.

However, he had a task to carry out and there was no turning back. Inadequate as he felt himself to be he'd perform his duties to the best of his ability, despite how dangerous they might prove to be.

But he must endeavor to stay alive. Then he must pass himself off as a Spanish officer, collect information on the gun placements, or any other information that might be of use. Then he must seek out the contact Northhaven had provided him with. But first, he must learn to stop thinking in English, lest he give himself away.

So *Capitán Hernando Cordova* flattened himself to the ground. Pulling the Spaniard's body on top of himself for protection, Remy retched as warm blood soaked into his uniform. It seemed the truce was over.

In England, winter yielded to spring. The icing of frost on the ploughed field melted, leaving a friable crumble of earth to yield to the push of tender, young shoots.

There was a chaotic bluster to spring. Clouds raced across the sky on the breath of the wind. Hare chased hare. The air was fresh with spring scents. Wild creatures emerged from their burrows and lairs and their young tumbled, wrestled and sprang with the joy of just being alive.

The lamb had been born. Despite Bessie's urging, Fleur couldn't bring herself to kill and eat the pair. Tom cut the fleece from the ewe and Bessie washed and spun it, then wove it into a fine shawl for the baby.

Fleur's infant let its presence be known, the insidious flutters of movement disturbing her at quiet moments and strengthening as the days passed. One day she placed her hands over the gentle swell of her stomach, marvelling that this, the harvest of her body, would be born so soon. She felt well, the plague of morning sickness borne away on the back of winter.

She'd heard not a word of her husband.

Once her initial sense of abandonment evaporated and her anger waned she thought of Remy less, as if their marriage had been a dream. He'd left behind him a memory of his touch, his passion. Sometimes, the cravings of her body woke her at night and she'd reach out for the ease of his warm, supple flesh.

When spring softened into April, the Earl of Northhaven appeared on her doorstep. He was sympathetic, but matter of fact.

'The siege of Gibraltar ended in February. We've had no news of your husband and believe he was executed, along with some other prisoners.'

When she gave a cry of anguish the baby inside her jolted painfully, disturbed by her reaction. She realized then that she loved Remy. The thought of a future without him was painful to contemplate.

'Cannot enquiries be made?'

The Earl of Northhaven shrugged. 'For what reason when my sources of information are totally reliable?'

'But you said you'd had no news of him.

'All the more reason to believe he's dead. Had he not been he'd have turned up at the rendezvous point for his repatriation, or at least been amongst the exchange prisoners. No, my dear, either he was killed or he decided to stay in his mother's country amongst his Spanish relatives. The first is preferable, of course. It will save us the expense of an inquiry into his activities whilst he was abroad.

Fleur paled. She'd heard rumours of the earl's spy network. Still, she couldn't imagine someone who'd been so vital and alive as Remy as being dead. She resented the information – resented the fact that this man, once a friend of Remy's father, could think so little of her husband's disappearance. Indeed, he seemed to infer Remy had been a traitor to his country.

'My husband didn't tell me he was working for you. I thought he'd become an officer in the army.'

The earl's eyes narrowed slightly. 'Of course he wouldn't have told you. Your husband was in the King's service, and took an oath of silence. If it's any consolation, he was mentioned for his courage in despatches.'

'No consolation at all.' She bit down on her lip, keeping silent about the infant she carried inside her.

Finishing his glass of wine, the earl rose, frowning. 'The King does not bestow honour lightly. Your husband's bank has been credited with a sum compensatory to his duties. No doubt the Earl of Blessingham will provide for you, if required.'

He gazed around him, apparently liking what he saw because he smiled. 'When your mourning period is over, the countess has kindly offered to introduce you to suitable candidates. She has a cousin, a minor peer–'

'Thank you, My Lord,' Fleur said firmly. 'I realize the countess holds my welfare close to her heart, but I'd prefer it if the countess didn't put herself out on my account. My brother, The Earl of Stratton, acts as my adviser on such matters. He was charged by Remy to handle any estate matters in his absence.'

Another marriage for her was out of the question. The realization of her love for Remy had left her feeling quite bereft. She'd not replace him with another – not ever.

'As you will.' Losing further interest in her he took his leave.

The following few days were darkened by genuine grief for Remy. Then she began to remember the good things about him. Re-calling his parting words of love, the future without him seemed empty and bleak.

She wasn't entirely convinced he was gone though. Perhaps she was being fanciful, but she could feel him far away from her, like a faint pulse threaded to her heart. And if he were dead he'd live on through his child. Now she began to hope she carried his son. The thought snapped her out of her mourning. It was her duty to hand over Rosehill in good condition.

She sent word of Remy's disappearance to his grandparents. Then she sent a message to her brother, requesting that he hire a steward for her without delay.

Hamish McDuff arrived the following month. A thin, taciturn Scot, he brought with him a sturdy wife and a couple of lively children. They moved into the steward's quarters without delay. After a week it felt as if they'd always been living there.

Mrs McDuff was given a position in the house under Mrs Firkins, who'd been elevated to head housekeeper. 'I expect you to take instructions from Mrs Firkins and relieve her of the heavier duties. However, she must not be made to feel useless,' Fleur told the woman.

Tom had mastered Remy's horse in her absence, and although it was offered to McDuff to use, the animal bucked him off. 'A beasty is of no use if it cannot be trained or ridden, and it'll bring a few guineas at market,' McDuff told her.

Much to Tom's delight, Fleur refused to sell the horse. 'This is my husband's horse, Mr McDuff. He must *never* be sold, but kept in good condition in case my husband returns.'

She ignored his pitying look.

Two days later she was summoned to an audience with the Earl of Blessingham at Stragglemarsh Hall, the ancestral home of St Cyres.

Stragglemarsh was a three-hour ride away. Because she wanted to look her best, Fleur, with Tom at the reins, chose to take the cart rather than ride. It was a pretty May morning, soft with sunshine and alive with flying insects.

They stopped to rest at a stream, where she bathed her forehead and wrists with cool water. Tom handed her a napkin wrapped around some crusty bread, a slice of cheese and an apple. A tumbler of lemonade from an earthenware jug with a tightly fitted lid served to wash it down. She handed half her apple to the horse as reward for his labour and its velvety muzzle whuffled at her palm.

'Not far to go now,' Tom said, plumping her cushion before he assisted her back up on the cart. 'Stragglemarsh Hall be around that bend and up the road a ways.'

The grandeur of the place robbed Fleur of breath. They'd come into the grounds past a gatehouse. Round a bend, a long, wide avenue lined with spreading oaks led majestically to an imposing house silhouetted against the sky. Hamstone walls played host to creeping tracts of ivy. As they neared the house, Fleur became aware of a series of terraces, down through which a staircase of water cascaded into a lake.

So this was the inheritance Remy had spoken of. No wonder the Earl of Blessingham was annoyed so by his grandson's casual attitude towards his duties.

Tom slowed the horse to a walk as the carriageway gently incline upwards to a set

169

of magnificent oak doors carved with the St Cyres crest.

A servant in wig and grand livery strode out to greet them, a frown creasing his face. 'Be off with you. You can't bring that old cart to this entrance.'

Tom said grandly, 'Tell your master the Viscountess St Cyres has arrived, and be bloody quick about it, Numbskull.'

Fleur hid a smile. 'That's enough, Tom. Help me down then take the cart to the stables. You'll be called when you're needed.'

The earl was in the drawing room, a rug draped over his knees. Doors opened on to the terrace. The view went on forever, parkland and woodland merging into a mist of blue sky and sea. Stragglemarsh Hall was unashamedly and triumphantly, king of all it surveyed.

She turned her attention to the bewigged earl. He had the eyes of an ageing blood-hound and his hands shook with palsy. Old as he was, there was something of the dandy about the old man. His black brocaded waist-coat was threaded through with silver, his stock was of pearl-grey silk and his fingers supported intricately designed rings with gemstones of every hue. Amongst them was a ruby, twice as big as the one Remy had given her.

Fleur gently twisted her own ring around her finger and smiled at Elmira before dropping the earl a curtsy. 'I'm sorry I had to send you both such sad and depressing news.'

It was Elmira who answered. 'It came as a shock. Despite his faults, I loved my grandson. We both did.'

'The young fool,' the earl muttered. 'He was too proud to humble himself before me and request my help.'

'The very quality I liked about him,' Fleur said, her chin lifting a fraction as she engaged his eyes. 'Remy's reluctance to grovel to anyone was not pride, but the need to prove his worth to himself. He did not want my money either, preferring to put his life in danger to provide support for me.'

'You look well, my dear,' Elmira said hastily. 'Please be seated. My husband has something he wishes to say to you. Afterwards, we'll take some refreshment whilst you consider his offer.'

The earl's head nodded and his dry, old man's voice whispered about the room. 'I've consulted with an attorney, who believes the circumstances of the hasty marriage you made with my grandson might prove to be invalid, as might his last will and testement. I've decided it would be in your best interests to vacate Rosehill.'

He ignored her impatient intake of breath.

'Rosehill will be absorbed into the St Cyres estate, which will be duly passed on to a relative from a distant branch of the family when

171

I die. In deference to your rank, and the fact you were the wronged party, you will receive as recompense a generous amount of money as compensation. What do you say to that?'

Fleur exchanged a glance with Elmira, who'd been gazing at the gentle swell beneath her skirt with more than a little interest.

'What do I say, My Lord?' She took a deep breath to control her flaring temper, yet made it very plain. 'I say you are being presumptuous. Come harvest time the heir to Rosehill will be born. If you attempt to deny my infant his birthright, or try to force illegitimacy on my child, I will fight you tooth and nail.'

The earl's faded eyes narrowed in on her stomach then travelled upwards to rest on her face. 'You are outspoken, Madam.'

Fleur hoped her child didn't inherit his large, hooked nose. Her direct gaze never wavered from his. 'And will be more so, sir. My marriage was conducted by a bishop, and in front of several witnesses. It has been properly recorded in the parish register, and as you can see, consummated.'

Beautifully, wonderfully consummated, she thought dreamily, and thank God for the sweet reward. 'I guarantee my marriage to Remy will be held as a true marriage by any court in the land.'

Grandmother Elmira smiled complacently at the earl. 'There, Gerard, the matter seems

172

to have settled itself, and I couldn't be more pleased. A great-grandson. What could be better? I told you Fleur had a sensible head on her shoulders.'

The earl snorted. 'The matter shall not be settled until the infant is born. The child might be a female, or stillborn.'

'My infant will be born healthy and he'll live for his father,' Fleur said fiercely and shot to her feet. 'The matter is settled now, My Lord. Rosehill belongs to Remy. My capital is already invested for its restoration. A steward has been hired and eventually the estate will become productive and income producing. Rosehill will be passed on to Remy's child, whatever the gender. That is all I have to say on the matter. Good day to you, My Lord.'

'Wait,' he growled as she flounced towards the door. 'There's something I wish to ask you.'

She turned to gaze at him, haughtily indifferent. 'What is it?'

'I'm curious. You seem to think highly of your late husband. Why do you not show respect for your widowhood by mourning him?'

A wistful smile touched her mouth. It had never occurred to her. 'Call this fanciful if you wish, but I cannot believe Remy is dead until someone brings me proof. He reminds me of a cat, in that he always falls on his feet. Besides, he's unconventional in many ways. He would not expect me to mourn.'

'What would my grandson expect of you?'

'He'd expect me to restore Rosehill and raise his child with loving care. That's the legacy he received from his parents, whom he loved and respected above all. You said he would not humble himself before you. Perhaps you had nothing of value to make it worth his effort. If you had, shouldn't it have been offered freely?'

Elmira gave her husband a quick glance. Far from being annoyed, he was smiling when he said. 'Remy showed some rare sense when he married you.' When his glance touched against her breasts the tip of his tongue ran over his lips. 'So I'm to be a great-grandfather, eh?' The twinkle in his eye and the sly cackle he gave made the tips of her ears grow warm. 'Humour an old man. Stay for a day or two so we can become better acquainted.'

'Of course she'll stay.' Grandmother Elmira rose and embraced her, whispering in her ear, 'There, I knew you would impress him, my dear.'

Elmira thumped her cane on the floor, refreshments were brought and maids despatched to prepare a guest chamber. Much to his disgust, Tom was sent packing back to Rosehill.

And impress the earl Fleur did, for despite

his age and shrewdness he seemed to enjoy a debate on any subject, and was susceptible to female attention. Elmira bent to her embroidery with an indulgent smile, looking up now and again to throw in a tart observation to keep the pot of controversy boiling.

Fleur enjoyed the parry and thrust of the encounter. Despite his age, the man had a quick and lively mind, and the evening reminded her of similar evenings spent with her three brothers.

They spoke of Remy, 'I cannot believe Remy went to work for a man who hated his father so,' the earl observed.

Bewildered, she gazed at him. 'The Earl of Northhaven said they were friends.'

'He lied. There are those who still believe Northhaven was responsible for the murder of my son and his wife. The men they executed were known felons, but they denied the charges. When their belongings were searched, a couple of trinkets belonging to Julia were found in their saddle bags.'

Fleur shuddered at the thought of two innocent men being hanged. 'What would be Northhaven's motive?'

The earl gazed at her, saying heavily. 'Julia Cordova.'

Elmira put down her embroidery. 'Gerard, you swore we would never mention this to Remy.'

'If I had, he'd still be alive.' The earl shook

his head sadly from side to side. 'This is my fault.'

Fleur leaned forward. 'Tell me of Remy's mother. Was she and the Earl of Northhaven lovers?'

'Definitely not. He was besotted with her, but Julia despised him. He was persistent and wouldn't leave her alone. He sent her notes and gifts and started rumours about their relationship. It was said that my son was in league with the Spanish. My son was about to dismiss him from his post when they were ambushed and killed. William had the easier death with a bullet through the head. I understand Julia was ... violated before she was strangled. They were of different faiths and I did not approve of their marriage, but still–'

Fleur shuddered. 'We will talk no more of this,' Elmira said firmly. 'The Cordova family has sworn to avenge her death when they've gathered enough proof, however long it takes. In the meantime, Fleur, you must have nothing more to do with Northhaven. He cannot be trusted.'

Her hosts parted with her a little reluctantly when the time came, but with an invitation to visit as often as she wished. The earl kissed her forehead and pressed a jewellery box in her hand. 'We hope a fitting occasion to wear them will arise,' and he gently pressed a hand against her stomach.

'A celebration perhaps.'

She took the journey back to Rosehill in state, comfortably ensconced in the St Cyres carriage with armed outriders in attendance and pulled by four matching grey mares. Because she couldn't wait to try them on, around her neck glittered a necklace of emeralds interwoven with diamonds. Matching jewels dangled in her ears and a ring weighed down her finger.

Her grand arrival was met by a beaming smile of approval from Mrs Firkins. 'Better lock them fancy jewels away safe, My Lady. The workmen have arrived to see to the house. I've settled them all in the east wing.' Her hands went to her hips. 'That Mrs McDuff said they should be in the servant's quarters, said it would be too far to see to their meals. Let me bother about that, I said to her, for the mistress will want them to have room to spread out, and she won't want to listen to them all day. We all know how ribald that men's talk can get.'

'Enough, Mrs Firkins,' Fleur said with a laugh. 'You're quite right.'

'I told her to keep her Scottish nose out, that household arrangements were none of her business.'

'And you arrange things quite beautifully. Tell the architect I wish to consult with him as soon as convenient.'

The house transformation kept Fleur busy

as she chose new furnishings and linens. Simon Ackland and his sisters called on her to offer their condolences. The two eldest girls had become engaged, both to army officers. They were to be wed in the summer. Because of her condition, Fleur was obliged to decline the invitation to attend.

Taking Simon's advice she despatched a letter to Charles Boney offering him a fair price for return for the goods he'd cheated Remy out of. Fleur knew Remy would have been too proud to allow her to buy them back, but as far as she was concerned, they were heirlooms and belonged to the child she was carrying.

She received a curt note in reply saying he would consider her request. His spelling and lettering was of the most basic, and she wondered where he'd obtained his education.

Late spring turned into a golden summer. The workmen departed, leaving her with a home that was both welcoming and beautiful. There now was a full complement of staff to keep it that way.

Her belly became round and full, so she was sure it could stretch no more without splitting open. The child filled her like a kernel in a ripe peach, pushing against her bladder so she felt more and more uncomfortable. She placed her hands on the swell, feeling the life surge of the infant, imagining

178

what he would look like – for she was quite sure now that she'd give birth to a son.

She'd hired the services of a midwife, who prodded here and there, or sometimes she placed her ear against the mound and smiled reassuringly at her. 'Tis a big un, but you'll slip the bairn out easily enough, My Lady. You mark my words.'

The wheat ripened to rippling gold in the fields. It was harvested and tied in stooks. Thrown on to a cart, they were trundled away to the mill to be ground into flour. The stubble was ploughed in, but still her baby did not come. The heat lingered. A day passed, a week ... two weeks. Humidity filled the air and clouds massed on the horizon.

Fleur had no room left inside her – no room to stretch, to bend or even breathe properly. Her breasts surged heavy against her bodice. Her stomach was a lumpy, heaving mound under her skirt and her back ached intolerably from the weight of the infant. She felt ugly and bloated – as big and as clumsy as a cow.

Perspiration covered her face as she tried to arrange herself comfortably on the bed to rest one day. Just as she settled she needed to pee again and called to Mary to bring the chamber pot.

As thunder growled in the distance and she struggled to lift her misshapen body from the bed, a sudden rush of liquid gushed from between her thighs, soaking her through. The first contraction of her labour flowed and ebbed like the pull of the tide. Grunting at the relentless strength of the pain, her heart lightened and picked up speed. Excitement and joy bubbled up in her.

'Thank you, God,' she whispered, 'for I doubt if I could have stood another day of this precious bounty you and Remy blessed me with.'

NINE

Despite the ferocious thunder and lighting flashes, Macy was humming to himself as he set out from the *Fox and Hound*.

He'd feasted like a king on a huge slab of roast beef cut straight from the spit and oozing with hot juices. The space remaining in his stomach had been claimed by a dish of potatoes, cabbage and turnips cooked in the drippings. He'd managed to distend his stomach a little further, accommodating a slice or two of apple pie and washing the lot down with a tankard of mead. He grinned in satisfaction. His gluttony had been despicable, but a necessity if Fleur's larder hadn't improved.

He'd contemplated staying the night at the

inn when the weather had begun to deteriorate, especially since the serving wench had given him the eye. His carnal appetite had been dampened somewhat by the meal, though, so he thought he might drop in on her on the way back instead.

His destination was Rosehill, where he intended to give Fleur news of Crispen. From his calculations, her infant should have been delivered three weeks previously. He was eager to see the child before travelling on to resume his former medical partnership, where he would add surgeon to his shingle.

He took the short cut through the forest at an amble, contemplating the feasibility of finding a wife. He could offer her a substantial house, which admittedly needed a woman's touch to turn it into a home. He had a comfortable amount of money put aside, courtesy of a legacy from his mother's family. Plus, his living in the years to come would be more than adequate.

He didn't want much, he mused. His wife need not be a beauty, though a woman with an agreeable face, form and manner would certainly be a bonus. He needed a woman of good sense, warmth and humour. If she could cook, and if she applied a little enthusiasm to the marriage bed, then so much the better.

He hunched into his collar to stop the rain trickling inside is coat. Above him, the branches of the trees whipped and soughed a lament. The branches creaked and cracked, the trunks groaned and swayed under their burden and pine needles speared his shoulders and head.

It was almost dark when he emerged on the other side, straight into a gale of stinging, salt-burdened rain that roared in with a banshee wail of furious intent from the sea. It snatched his hat from his head and carried it off up into the branches of a tree.

Far from being dismayed, Macy laughed with the exhilaration of it and urged his horse into a gallop. The rain pelted on his shoulders, flattened his hair against his scalp and streamed in rivulets under his collar.

He heard the long-drawn-out scream as he neared the house. 'Fleur,' he whispered, and riding into the stable yard, threw the reins to a worried looking Tom. Snatching up his bag he followed the sound of the groans, took the stairs three at a time and dashed into Fleur's chamber, shouting at the trio of women in attendance, 'How long has my sister been in this condition?'

'Two days and a night.' Mrs Firkins seemed relieved to see him. 'Thank God you're here Doctor Russell. I sent McDuff to fetch the doctor, but his housekeeper said he's away visiting relatives and won't be back for a week or so.'

'Which one of you is the midwife?'

The older woman spoke up. 'Me, sir. I've delivered all the babies hereabouts for nigh on forty years.'

Macy's heart sank. She was the village crone and trained on old wives tales, no doubt. Still, she'd have to do. 'What's the problem?'

'The babe ain't coming out, sir.'

'That's obvious. Do you have an opinion as to why?'

'She be too small to birth him, sir. I've seen it many a time with the first one. I told her the infant will likely die if her heart don't give out first. Let me crush his head and pull him out, then it'll all be over, I says to her. By all that's holy, she be a stubborn one, though.'

Fleur's hand closed around his wrist and she panted. 'You must save my infant, Macy.'

He smoothed the hair back from her forehead. 'Neither of you are going to die.'

The fright in her eyes made him want to murder the midwife. 'When have I ever lied to you?'

She didn't have time to think of one of the many occasions. She strained and grew red in the face as her body contorted with the effort of giving birth. The low animal groan she gave developed into a drawn-out scream. Macy's hair stood on end.

Mrs Firkins dabbed the sweat from her brow, saying ineffectually, 'There, there,

Doctor Russell will look after you.'

Macy shooed everyone out but the mid-wife, sending them for hot water and soap so he could wash his hands. He would have sent the midwife packing too, but he knew he'd need help.

He took off his wet coat, hung it on a chair and leaned over his sister.

Her hair was dark with sweat, and matted. She managed to smile before the next con-traction took her in its grip, then she began to groan.

'The infant's long overdue and too big for her to birth, sir.'

'That's supposition on your part. Please don't mention it in front of the patient again. Has there been any bleeding?'

'Not yet, but the waters broke first up and the birth's dry. Lady Fleur's tired out, poor soul.'

Fleur soundly cursed all men when the contraction subsided and she was immedi-ately caught up in the maelstrom of another. Macy smiled, judging by the grip she'd taken on his wrist and the breath she'd saved for cussing, she still had some fight left in her.

The midwife gazed at him and shrugged. 'No sign of the head yet. I think the infant has breeched.'

Macy inwardly cursed the midwife as alarm filled Fleur's eyes. He needed her as relaxed as possible, and he guessed she was now remembering Crispen's birth, an event that had caused the death of their mother.

He washed his hands, then waited for a lull in the contractions and said to her; 'I need to examine you? I might have to assist the baby into the world. If I do, then you must do exactly as I say.'

'Haven't I always?' she gasped out.

Her attempt to lighten the moment with levity brought a wry smile to his mouth. 'I have your permission, then?'

Her smile was almost a grimace. Her eyes were wild with pain, like an animal caught in a trap. She gave a slight nod, past caring about her modesty or dignity.

He examined her dispassionately and in as short a time as possible for her comfort. The midwife was wrong; the baby hadn't breeched. However, it was facing towards the back. Contrary to what he'd been led to expect, the head had presented itself as a slick of dark hair on a slice of paler forehead. Fleur's next contraction pushed it down a little, and then it moved back up again.

'The infant is not in the breech position, but it's facing the wrong way and your muscle contractions are not strong enough to push the head through. It means you'll have to stop being lazy and work much harder.'

Fleur's eyes glinted greenly at him, her expression bode him ill will. 'Hah!' she said, but her words had no fire.

185

'Next time, I want you to keep pushing after the pain eases.' He laid a hand lightly on her distended stomach and spoke clearly and calmly. 'There's nothing to worry about, Fleur. Keep your mouth closed if you can because it will help your labour pains to remain strong.' He placed a hand on her lower stomach. Now was not the time for niceties. 'Push with the force centred down here, as if you were straining into the chamber pot. You understand?'

She nodded.

'The midwife will assist you. When the next cramp comes along I'm going to pull you into a crouching position. You must keep pushing after the contraction has subsided. It will help the baby descend.' He glanced at the midwife. 'Are you familiar with this procedure?'

'Oh, aye,' she muttered. 'I didn't attempt it because I knew I wouldn't have the strength to manage it by mesself.' She seemed slightly affronted at having been reminded as she placed her hands either side of Fleur's stomach.

Fleur's eyes gazed trustingly into his and she grunted. She wasn't quite able to stop her scream, but it emerged through gritted teeth and the main force of her energy was directed downwards. Macy hauled her upright and nodded to the midwife.

For several minutes Fleur strained and

grunted in furious concentration. The strength of her pushes when combined with pressure from the hands of the midwife, nearly sent him reeling backwards. Each contraction was followed quickly by another, as if the baby sensed the end of his painful passage into the world and was in a hurry to emerge.

'Check the progress,' he grunted when there was a lull.

The midwife inserted a finger and felt for the cord. Fleur cursed her soundly for the interruption, but the midwife, used to such phrases, ignored it. Her smile said the cord was clear. With the next contraction she got a grip on the infant's head, and pulled down. It was followed by a shoulder. Hooking her finger under an armpit the midwife gently turned the child and another push saw the little body slither from between Fleur's thighs.

The infant was followed immediately by the placenta. Much to his relief it was intact, for a ruptured one would have meant trouble.

Macy gently lowered Fleur to the bed when she collapsed against him. Covered in sweat, face flushed, and panting from the effort of her hard labour and the sudden cessation of pain, her head craned from one side to the other to see what she'd produced.

'Here he be, my bonny,' the midwife

crooned, and held the infant aloft by his ankles. 'No one will ever mistake him for a girl.' A slap on the boy's wrinkled backside was followed by a lusty and indignant wail ... an ignominious start for the latest male of the species.

Fleur laughed and cried at the same time, then began to tremble. Macy, his grin stretching from ear to ear, gently cradled her against him as she took a first look at her son. The aching brilliance of her smile brought tears to his eyes.

'He's so beautiful and perfect,' she whispered, observing her son with a maternal eye, her pain already forgotten. Forlornly, she whispered, 'I wish Remy was here to see him. He'd be so proud of him.'

Now the infant had arrived the women took over, turning a solid wall of backs on Macy and fussing about Fleur's bed.

Macy felt superfluous when faced with this formidable barrier of efficiency. They were making it plain – childbirth was women's business. Helping his sister through the birth was acceptable under the circumstances. To linger while they performed the intimate services required to make her comfortable was another. Leaving Fleur gazing adoringly upon her son, he made his way to the stairs.

A huddle of Rosehill staff stood at the bottom, gazing hopefully up at him as he descended. He smiled widely at them. 'Your mistress has been delivered of a healthy son.'

'Glory be, and about time,' somebody whispered.

Macy silently echoed it. He, who'd dissected many a corpse, including those of children, and with scant regard for the fact that they were once alive, found himself humbled and trembling before the sight of a newly delivered infant. He'd never witnessed anything quite so beautiful as the look on Fleur's face after the tortuous time she'd been through.

Going into the drawing room he poured himself a stiff brandy, marvelling at the dogged endurance of women and the miracle of new life. He raised his glass to the child in the portrait. 'She's produced a fine son to remember you by, Remy.'

Later, when Fleur had rested a little, he visited her again. The infant was cuddled against her breast, asleep. She smiled palely at him, clearly exhausted. 'Thank God you were here, Macy. I was at the end of my strength.'

He kissed her forehead. 'You would have managed somehow. You've delivered a strong, healthy child and will soon recover from your ordeal.'

'He was worth the pain. He looks so much like his father,' she said. 'I'm going to name him Gerard, William, Remy, after his three St Cyres predecessors.' She smiled and taking his hand in hers, bore it to her cheek. 'He shall also be named Macy after his uncle. I want you to be his Godfather.'

A lump grew in his throat, threatening to choke him. 'I'd be honoured.' To hide his growing emotion he took a crumpled paper from his pocket. 'Before I left London I received a letter from Cris. He's well.'

Her reaction was not what he'd expected. It was obvious young Gerard was about to usurp Crispen in her affections, an event that would please Cris no end. Eyelids drooping, she murmured, 'Tell me of his news tomorrow because now I need to rest.'

He grinned from ear to ear at the thought of being Gerard's Godfather. 'I'd better start behaving myself and set him a good example,' he murmured and she gave a faint smile at the thought.

He sat and watched mother and son sleep for a while. Gerard's mouth was a scant inch from his food supply and, although he wouldn't have had time to sample it yet, one tiny fist clenched the fabric covering his mother's breast, as if in possession. As Macy watched, the child's mouth opened and his head nuzzled blindly from side to side like that of a kitten.

Without waking, Fleur loosened the laces at her breast and slipped her swollen teat into his mouth. The infant's lips closed around her and he began to suckle, his hands knead-

190

ing her breast like a kitten's paws. The sigh she gave was one of utter contentment as Macy stole away.

The old earl received the news of his namesake's birth with great delight.

He smiled at Elmira. 'Tell the coachman we'll be travelling to Rosehill the day after tomorrow. And prepare the second coach with delicacies from the kitchen, a selection of wine from the cellars and gifts for the child. We'll need to take our personal servants. We'd better send someone on ahead to announce our arrival.'

'What are you thinking of?' Elmira said sensibly. 'You have not left Stragglemarsh Hall for years. Think of your health.'

'I *am* thinking of my health. If I drop dead next week I will never see my great grandson and heir.' He gazed at her, his eyes sad. 'My conscience has been troubling me of late. If I'd taken Remy under my guidance he might be alive now. Instead, I blamed him for his mother's blood and the grief she brought to the family. I suppose she couldn't help being born a Spaniard.'

'Any more than you could help being English.' Elmira gazed at him in exasperation. 'Julia's pedigree was impeccable. I notice you didn't mention your pirate ancestors to her.'

'They were not pirates, they were privateers in the service of Queen Elizabeth,' he reminded her.

'And how much Spanish gold did you say they plundered from merchant ships, my dear? And how many innocent Spanish lives did they take in the process?'

The earl cackled with laughter. 'My dear, Elmira, you will not divert me by provoking an argument. I've been thinking of ways and means to help the girl, of late. Perhaps we should select some of our finest cattle to take as a gift.'

Elmira's head bobbed as she spoke her thoughts out loud. 'There are bound to be some kittens to take. Rosehill smelt of mice when I saw it last, though I expect Fleur has started the restoration. She doesn't appear to be one to idle when there's work to be done.'

'Quite, quite,' the earl said vaguely. 'I wonder if she has a bull.'

'What in heaven's name would Fleur do with a bull. Some gifts for the child, I think, though Rosehill had a fine nursery, as I recall. A silver rattle with the baby's name inscribed on it, perhaps.'

She smiled benevolently at her husband, feeding his vanity. 'It was fitting she named him after you,' and good strategy on Fleur's part. Elmira thought for a moment, her head cocked to one side like a songbird. 'I believe there's a teether which used to belong to you in the attic. I'll send a servant to look for it.'

'You most certainly will not. He shall have a new one, not something his ancestor's teeth have gnawed on. And we'll purchase a Welsh pony for him to ride.'

'A pony!' she exclaimed. 'Gerard is newly born. We'll buy him a songbird in a cage instead. That will keep him amused.'

When they looked at each other, Elmira's smile faded. 'We cannot make up for the loss of his father with worldly goods.'

The earl suddenly felt old and grey. 'I wonder if that pretty young woman still imagines Remy is alive.'

Sinking back into her chair, Elmira stared into space. 'The thought touches my heart. She has made the best of a bad start and would have been the making of Remy. Can it be possible she's right? Remy's body has not been found, so he *could* still be alive. I received a letter from London just the other day. Rumours abound that he may have defected to the other side.'

'Vicious lies. Would he have been mentioned in despatches if he'd been a traitor to his country? Would the king have given his widow a generous portion under such circumstances? Rather, he'd have confiscated the estate and turned her out.'

'You're right, as always,' she murmured, for she'd always gently flattered him to gain her own way. 'All the same, I would give everything I own to have him back. I wonder what happened to him?' Yearning filled her eyes. 'Do you think it's possible he survived the siege and blockade of Gibraltar? Perhaps he's been shipwrecked on a remote island, or imprisoned in some foreign gaol. A pity we cannot do something to clear the doubt from her mind.'

And yours, the earl thought, hiding his grin at her manipulations. 'Hmmm ... instead of wondering, perhaps it would be more practical to hire someone to investigate his disappearance, my dear. The fact that the spider is involved in his disappearance is a matter for suspicion in itself.'

'It is indeed. He does not forget a grudge.'

'Neither do I. He is not the only one with contacts abroad. I'm sure the Cordova family would assist us in this matter. What are your thoughts, Elmira?'

She crossed to where he sat and gently kissed his cheek. 'As always, I bow to your superior wisdom, Gerard.'

Elmira smiled at him, satisfied with the outcome of the conversation. She'd learned long ago, it was always better to allow such suggestions to come from her husband.

Remy was having the dream again. He had found the papers on the body of the Spaniard. Somebody else had killed him, cutting his throat silently and efficiently. The man's blood had still been warm, still seeping into the white sand.

The corpse was Spanish, and he was a traitor to his country. The gold coins he'd received for his trouble spilled from his pocket across the sand.

It was British gold, left there by Remy as an advance payment for these papers. It was a shame to waste it. He slipped it into his pocket.

There was no sign of the assassin now. The small rocky beach was littered with bodies and lit by bright moonlight. He felt exposed and vulnerable, his nerves screaming with the danger of the silence, as if someone was watching him.

Crouching behind a rock he quickly read the papers. He sucked in a shocked breath. They were damning words. He must get to his rendezvous point quickly and get this information back to England as soon as possible.

Who would have thought this of North-haven? But here in his hand was the letter, signed by Northhaven himself and accepting Spanish gold in return for information.

Hearing a faint creak of oars he stared out to sea. What if it was a Spanish boat? He gazed at the telescope in his hand and smiled. He was a sailor returning to his ship. But first he needed to take a small precaution...

Crouching low, a minute or so later Remy made his way through the moonlit bodies.

He was nearly at his destination when one of the bodies suddenly twisted upright.

'You!' he exclaimed, shocked to the core by the sight of the pistol in the man's hand. Something exploded in his head and he fell amongst the other bodies.

Remy could smell blood and his stomach was on fire. He jerked out of his terrible dream and stared at the grinning guards. One of them placed a burning taper against a small mound of gunpowder on his stomach.

'*Capitán Hernando Cordova*,' he yelled. He must be, because that was the name on the telescope.

The gunpowder exploded and his flesh began to burn. He didn't cry out. He was growing used to the pain.

TEN

Time passed quickly and soon Gerard was charming Fleur with a toothless replica of Remy's smile. Fleur's pride in her son was equalled by that of his great-grandfather, who seemed to take on a new lease of life during his visit.

'Gerard is the living image of his St Cyres grandfather,' he said, pointing out that the boy displayed the same sunny disposition as his son. Didn't she agree that the infant's ears were exactly like his own in shape? As were his feet, his hands and his nose!

'God forbid,' Elmira murmured under her breath, exchanging an amused glance with her.

Examined and dissected piece by piece, the Earl of Blessingham claimed every portion of Fleur's son as belonging solely to the St Cyres side of the family. When Leland visited he did exactly the same on behalf of the Russell family, which didn't endear him to the old earl one bit.

The pair glared at each other before appealing to her for arbitration.

Fleur just laughed. 'Gerard resembles his father – who, as you can see from the portrait, resembled his mother. So I think Gerard takes after the Cordova family – and I'll tolerate no more arguments on the matter.'

She adored her infant's tiny mouth tugging at her breast, the warmth of his body snuggling against hers, his dark puppy eyes and every soft strand of hair clinging to his head. Her love for him was deep and overwhelming.

The old earl's visit was prolonged for several weeks. Strong though she was, Fleur began to tire. Her baby's feeding regime and the tasks associated with the estate took up most of her time. She did her best to be social, but sometimes she caught herself nodding off in the middle of a conversation.

'You should get yourself a wet nurse,' Elmira advised. 'God didn't intend women of our class to suckle their offspring and Gerard will not thrive if your milk dries up.'

As if Elmira's words were an omen, the following week Fleur suffered a bout of fever and her abundant milk supply dried to a trickle. Gerard became fretful as he sucked in frustration on her near-empty breasts and kept her awake with his loud wails. Her nipples grew sore and cracked.

Tearfully, she consulted Elmira, who ordered the carriage to be brought around. 'Often there are women registered for hire at the almshouse, women who have recently lost their infants. One of them will be glad of the position.'

Infant mortality was common, it seemed. Ensconced in the almoner's office they interviewed several candidates before employing a young widow of pleasant manner and modest demeanour. Her face was quietly attractive, her eyes a sad, cornflower blue. Three days previously, Lucy Yates's son had died before he'd hardly drawn a breath. She was grateful to be given a chance to recover from her ordeal with a decent roof over her head.

Fleur had taken to her on sight and though saddened to learn she had also lost her husband a few months before her son was born, knew it gave them something in common.

When Lucy saw her charge, a tender smile crossed her face. She picked Gerard up, cradling him for a few moments before opening her bodice and putting him to her breast. Gerard stiffened and looked as if he was about to refuse, but hunger soon overcame his initial distrust. His mouth closed around the alien teat and he set about the substitute meal with such unseemly haste, the milk trickled from the sides of his mouth and into the folds of his neck. An ecstatic little shiver went through Lucy's body and she closed her eyes for a moment.

It seemed as if the needs of both mother and child would be met by this arrangement. Fleur's eyes filled with despairing tears. As if sensing the wrench Fleur felt at the sight of her son suckling from the breast of another, Lucy turned to her. 'Thank you for trusting your son's welfare to me, My Lady. Be assured, he will be in good hands.'

She was mindful of the fact the woman had recently given birth herself. 'Perhaps Gerard will help you recover from the loss of your own son. I'll ask Mrs Firkins to assign a maid to the nursery for part of the day. When you're fully recovered we'll work out a schedule, for I'll want to be with my son as often as is convenient.'

Gerard was soon a contented child again.

Elmira announced their intention to return to Stragglemarsh Hall. After she kissed Gerard good-bye, Elmira smiled sagely at her. 'See how contented he is and how much more energy you have. I told you so. It's always a mistake to go against nature's intent.'

But feeding Gerard herself hadn't been a mistake. She'd loved every moment of closeness with her son, and knew that if she had another she wouldn't hesitate to feed the infant, if only for a short time. She put it from her mind. Unless Remy came back, such an event was impossible, for she had no intention of marrying again.

Fleur didn't expect to have to make her intention clear so quickly, and certainly not to Charles Boney and his sister, who presented a petition three months after Gerard's birth.

She'd heard that he and Catherine were back in residence in the manor, but after the distasteful scene in London, she looked back on the incident with shame for the embarrassment it had caused Remy.

She hadn't expected the Boney brother and sister to call on her, and wondered what had motivated them. She certainly had no intention of returning the visit.

She was in Hamish McDuff's office when Mrs Firkins came scurrying to find her. Her expression was disapproving. 'That Sir Charles wants to see you, My Lady.'

In the middle of a discussion about whether to replace a former stand of trees, because the estate oaks had been claimed by the crown for shipbuilding, Fleur frowned. 'Tell them I'm out visiting.' She turned back to Hamish. 'I see no reason why we shouldn't replant the oaks for future generations to enjoy. Perhaps we could plant some yews along the front of the estate, as well.'

Mrs Firkins coughed. 'Excuse me, My Lady. Sir Charles has brought back one or two of the pieces of the china unaccounted for on the inventory.'

Fleur's eyes sharpened. 'Tell them I'll be in directly.' She stood, shaking the creases from the blue, flowered house gown she wore, and made her way to the drawing room.

Catherine was exquisitely dressed in a gown of striped burgundy silk, her wide-brimmed hat was trimmed with feathers and a bow to match the ribbon at her throat. It was a little flamboyant for the country. Catherine looked almost *too* perfect and Fleur knew she contrasted badly with her.

Gazing at the gold Cordova miniatures was Charles, handsomely attired in fawn breeches and a brown double-breasted cut-away coat over a striped waistcoat. She surprised an expression of avarice in his eyes, quickly masked when he turned and smiled.

His glance swept over her gown. 'My dear, Fleur, how well you look. The country air obviously suits you.'

Catherine's lips stretched into a smile, but her grey eyes remained cool. 'We have heard of Remy's unfortunate demise and are here to offer our sincere condolences.'

Catherine sounded as sincere as a hungry she-wolf. 'You're very kind,' Fleur said, keeping her manner as distant as possible.

Charles gently coughed as he spun a gold piece in the air. 'Of course, we realize the marriage was ... unusual?'

'Yes, I suppose it was.'

'I wish to offer my sincere apologies for my part in the affair.'

Surprised by the admission, she stammered, 'There is really no need,' and she smiled when Gerard came into her mind. 'All was resolved satisfactorily.'

'Quite. Death can be a convenient solution. Had Remy not been so very much in our debt, in due course he would have married Catherine. She has grieved him.'

Fleur's eyes narrowed but she kept her counsel.

Charles took up a stance at the window. The light shone directly on his face and his smile was a picture of studied sincerity. 'I have a proposition to put to you.'

Why was she not surprised? Impatiently she shifted from one foot to the other. 'I understood you came to return the artefacts belonging to Rosehill.'

'All in good time Fleur. First, I'd like to inform you of the reason for my visit. I've discussed this with Catherine and she totally approves. As you may have guessed, I have always held a certain fondness for you. I'm here to assure you of my continued affection and request your hand in marriage.'

Fleur tried to hide her shudder.

'I can see you're surprised,' Charles said pleasantly. 'I have heard Remy left the estate to you. Rosehill needs a master and I can provide you with heirs to inherit the estate. As this was once to be her home, Catherine has generously offered to forget the affront afforded to her, and move in as companion to you. She has exquisite taste, and can advise you on certain aspects of dress and behaviour.'

The tips of her ears heated. Charles was after the estate. Remy hadn't told Charles that his grandfather stood to inherit, and they obviously hadn't heard about Gerard. Thank God Simon had kept the news of her son's birth from him. It would be a delicious shock for these arrogant peacocks.

She had the urge to laugh when she crossed to the bell pull. Catherine was offering to advise her on dress and behaviour? The suggestion pricked at the core of her pride. This pair lived only to lie and cheat a livelihood out of the unsuspecting. If that was considered acceptable behaviour something was very wrong with them.

'Tell Mrs Yates to bring Gerard immediately to the drawing room, then ask Mr McDuff to attend me,' she said to the maid who appeared at her summons. She turned to Charles. 'Marriage between us is out of the question.'

He crossed to where she stood and took her hand in his. His eyes were cold and grey – predator's eyes. 'I expected some reluctance, of course, but when you've thought it over...'

She shivered at the thought of him touching her. 'I have no need to think it over. I dislike the pair of you intensely, and mistrust your motives. Rosehill is not mine even though a will was written in my favour.'

Catherine joined her brother. 'What exactly do you mean by that? Remy was a fool. He wouldn't have wed you if your brothers had not beaten him half to death. I doubt if the marriage would have been ... sanctioned.' She gave a tinkling laugh. 'He told me you did not attract him enough to act the part of a husband. Whatever the arrangement you came to with that doddering old grandfather of his – we could still get Rosehill back if you had Charles by your side. My brother knows many important people in London now – people who will assist him.'

With considerable effort Fleur managed

to remain calm, though the blood sang furiously in her ears and her nails dug into her palms. What could this cold-hearted bitch know of love?

There was a knock at the door. When bidden to enter, Lucy came to stand by her. Gerard was awake. He regarded the company solemnly. Recognizing her amongst the strangers he gave her a heart-wrenching imitation of Remy's bewitching smile, then belched ungraciously.

She turned to her unwelcome guests. 'Allow me to introduce you to Remy's son and heir. Gerard St Cyres.'

'What trickery is this?' Catherine was clearly astounded and cried out, 'We had not heard.'

Charles stared at the child, his lip curling. 'There's no mistaking the bastard's Spanish blood. Well well, your nature is more sluttish than it first seemed if you were prepared to fall in bed with a man who was stranger to you. Let's hope he hasn't got his father and grandfather's traitorous blood. I hear that the British army stood Remy in front of a firing squad and used him for shooting practice.'

Fleur was hanging on to the last shred of patience. So much for his continuing affection? 'A pity they don't do the same to you. Get out, Charles. If either of you set foot on Rosehill soil again I'll take a horsewhip to you.'

'Don't think this is the last you'll hear of me,' Charles hissed. 'You'd better guard that brat. Children can have all sorts of accidents if left unattended.'

Lucy took a step back. Fleur took one forward. Eyes blazing she lashed out at him, her hand raking down his face. 'Attempt to harm one hair on my son's head and if my brothers don't get to you first, I'll kill you myself.'

Charles raised his cane. Before it could descend Hamish McDuff appeared. Grabbing Charles' arm he twisted it up behind his back and propelled him out of the room and down the stairs. Catherine followed after, hurling insults at McDuff in as coarse an accent Fleur had ever heard.

'Shut your trap,' Charles snarled at his sister. He turned to sweep her a mocking bow. 'Remember what I said, My Fine Lady.'

'He deserves to be charged. Should I inform the magistrate?'

Shaking, Fleur watched the pair climb into their vehicle. 'No, Mr McDuff. I want no more dealings with them, and doubt if they'll bother me again.'

'Come away in,' Mrs Firkins said, offering her remedy for every ill. 'I'll bring you some tea to settle your nerves.'

What had happened to Catherine's impeccable manners? Fleur turned to the old woman. 'I've always considered Catherine

Boney not to be who she appears.'

'Aye, and neither is her brother. They turned up when the old squire died, as bold as you like. He said he was the squire's long-lost nephew and the girl was his sister. Old Blaggs said the squire had once told him his nephew died abroad from licentious living. He never mentioned having no niece, but he had a female cousin living with him who was weak in the head. There was talk she bore a child out of wedlock late in life. She was beside herself when they took it from her and the squire sent her to Bedlam.'

'What happened to the child?'

'Farmed out to a family, I shouldn't wonder. If it survived infancy it were probably sent to a foundling home when the squire died.'

'Perhaps the child *is* Sir Charles.'

'Never, he'd be too old. Besides, the child was called some funny biblical name. Tarshish, or some such thing.'

'Is the sister still alive?'

'I doubt it. I hear they don't last long in that place, poor things. Sarah Jane Boney her name was. God rest her poor soul.'

'Sir Charles must have been able to prove his claim.'

'Along come this army officer to vouch for the pair of them. Peer of the realm, he was, or so he said. According to him, the young squire had been in the army all along, and his sister, that Catherine woman, had been companion to the officer's wife. If you ask me she ain't his sister and that language is straight out of hell's kitchen. It's plain as the nose on your face that she's no lady.'

'Perhaps I should ask Leland to investigate them.'

'Don't be surprised if he discovers they're a pair of thieving impostors. I'm not one to gossip, but no matter how that Catherine tried to trap Master Remy into a proposal, she didn't fool him. I'm going to meet some-one special one of these days, Mrs Firkins he says to me, and I won't wed until I do. Bless his heart if he didn't.'

Fleur chuckled.

'You may well laugh, My lady. He had a nose for what was the genuine article and what wasn't. Quality is what he deserved, and that's what he got for hisself.'

Fleur grinned at the proud note in the housekeeper's voice, but didn't remind her it was more by luck than good judgement. 'Thank you, Mrs Firkins.'

As the woman wandered off Fleur thought about the threat Charles had made towards her son. Alarm filled her. Dashing up to the nursery she plucked Gerard from the cradle and cuddled him close.

'I'm going to have locks placed on the inside of the doors, and I'll ask one of the manservants to sleep in that room at the top of the stairs. He should hear the stairs creak if anyone tries to get up here,' she told Lucy.

Her heart gave a great wrench as she thought of Remy. 'Lord, please find it in your heart to let me know of my husband's fate,' she prayed. 'I may be a doubter, but I cannot mourn his death without proof. If he's alive then send him back to where he's needed.'

The prisoner was emaciated. A parchment of tanned leathery skin stretched over a framework of gaunt ribs. His eyes lacked lustre, his beard and hair were a matted, dusty nest.

From the man's body hung the shreds of a uniform, a shirt and breeches of unrecognisable hue. Sores scarred his body, lice fed from their host. They lived out their lives unhindered, for he no longer bothered to scratch.

He worked like an automaton, the sinewy arms lifting the mallet over his head and allowing it to fall with a resounding crash. Stone splintered around his ankles and rattled off the manacles that restricted his walk to a hobble. His feet were bloodied.

The sun was merciless, sapping him of his juices. He measured the rise and fall of the mallet. Soon it would be time to go back to his cell, to the kicks, the curses and the torture of the powder flash burns, which amused the more sadistic of the prison guards. He'd grown used to the diet, to the thin watery soup to which some cabbage and potatoes were added, if he was lucky.

He should have died long ago, from the rough treatment, the work and the disease of malnutrition. He looked forward to dying. No more thirst or pain, just a long rest and oblivion. No one would miss him.

But there was something he had to do first. His forehead wrinkled in an effort to remember what it was. A bell tolled in the distance, crows circled overhead. The quarry was a pit of heat, the rocks a glare of white. He narrowed his eyes against it, remembering his recurring dream of green hills with a house nestling in between. '*Mi casa en la colina*,' he muttered before it eluded him.

He flinched when a blow landed on his head, and hit the hate that sprang from his heart to flare in his eyes. Why didn't that heart stop beating? Rebellion might bring the death he longed for, but he knew he couldn't die without knowing ... *who the hell was he?*

'*Capitán Hernando Cordova*,' he muttered.

He'd repeated it time and time again, when they'd questioned him, when they'd beaten him. He didn't know why. It was the only name he could think off – a few of the words his thoughts would release. It was important they didn't find out his real name. Not that he could tell them – he couldn't remember what it was.

His brain released a faint memory of perfume, but when he tried to breath it in it somehow eluded him. Melancholy tears slid down his cheeks.

A few weeks later Remy was taken to the guards' block.

A man of middle years stared at him. Splendidly dressed in a navy uniform, his eyes held pity. He spoke in English with an accent.

'So, you are the man who tried to impersonate me.'

Remy shook his head, vehement. '*Capitán Hernando Cordova.*'

The captain turned to one of the guards. 'He doesn't appear to be English, and is Spanish in appearance. Didn't he have anything on him except the remnants of a British uniform when you found him?'

Opening a cupboard the guard pulled out an eyeglass and handed it over. 'It's not worth anything, the extension mechanism is broken. He only mentions a name and a house on a hill.'

The captain's eyes sharpened.

'We haven't been able to get anything else out of him. One of the prisoners told me he talks English in his sleep sometimes, which is suspicious. He asks Fleur to forgive him.'

'Some French maid he got into trouble by the sounds of it.'

The captain started when he gazed at the

eyeglass. 'Why, this belongs to me.'

The prisoner snatched it from his hand and held it against his chest. '*Capitán Hernando Cordova, Si?*'

The older man smiled at him. '*Si.*'

Remy felt a little flare of triumph. Good, they'd finally believed him.

The man stared at him intently, his eyes dark and intense. Slowly, he said, 'I remember you now. You were a seaman aboard my ship. You disappeared overboard about ... oh, eighteen months ago, or thereabouts?'

The prisoner remembered being on board a ship once, and the man talking to him seemed familiar. He thought he could trust him, but he wasn't sure. He nodded nevertheless. Anything seemed better than where he was now.

'He's been here a bit longer than that,' the guard said dubiously.

'Two years then. One tends to lose sense of time at sea, especially when engaged in battle. It was during the siege at Gibraltar ... a defeat Spain would rather forget.'

The guard spat on the floor. The captain followed suit. When Remy thought he'd better do likewise and managed to gather enough spit, the captain chuckled. 'Is that patriotic enough to convince you. It's obvious to me that this seaman has lost his wits. I'll take him back to the ship and deal with him there.'

'I don't know about that, sir. I'll have to get permission from the new governor when he arrives.'

The captain took a gold piece from his pocket. 'It's hard to get experienced crew and I'm sailing short-handed. He's a distant relative of mine. I thought him dead, and have just got wind of his survival, which is why I am here. His mother is a widow and I promised I'd look after him. I'll be back in her good graces if I can tell her he's safe.' He gave the guard a lewd wink.

The guard grinned at him and absently scratched his crotch.

A second gold piece was added to the first. 'Hand him over and lose his records, will you? I'll make it worth your while. The new governor won't even know he's been here.'

The guard gazed at the coins and hesitated. The captain added another coin and closed his hand around them. The guard nodded, lifted a key from a hook and released the manacles. 'If anyone asks I'll say he died.'

The prisoner felt light-headed as he shuffled towards the long boat after the captain. '*Capitán Hernando Cordova*,' he muttered.

The captain said. 'That's my name. Do you remember what yours is?'

'*Capitán Hernando*—'

The captain didn't turn round in case they

were being observed. 'You are Remy St Cyres, my English nephew.'

The prisoner appeared agitated and muttered. '*Capitán Hernando Cordova.*'

'It's obvious you're suffering from memory loss, and that suits my purposes nicely. As you will only talk in Spanish, you will be known as Hernando whilst you're on board. But you must drop the title of *Capitán*, for that belongs to me. My crew will not appreciate another calling himself by my name. They are superstitious and will think it will invite bad luck. Do you understand?'

Remy nodded, happy to go along with the arrangement. '*Si, Capitán, aim Hernando.*'

When they were out of sight the captain took Remy in a hug, tears pouring down his cheeks. 'My dearest nephew, I'm so glad I found you. We must get you back to your loved ones as soon as possible.'

Remy stood stiffly in the man's embrace. It wasn't manly to cry, but he didn't want to push him away in case he was sent back to the prison. Awkwardly, he patted his shoulder once or twice. Eventually, the man stopped, blew his nose on a large silk handkerchief and smiled at him before they resumed their walk to the ship.

A day or two later Remy was curled in a bunk, his stomach churning with the surfeit of food he'd bolted down. He wished he were back on dry land.

He made the crew feel uneasy. They closed their eyes and ears to his presence as they went about their work, but they crossed themselves each time they passed his doorway.

The fact that the *Capitán* had given up his cabin to this dirty and emaciated stranger gave rise to the rumour he was of political value, and very important indeed. Even so, they couldn't wait to get rid of him. It was obvious he was dying, and a stranger's soul left on board boded ill for the future.

El Julia was known as a lucky ship. The *Capitán* had got them out of many a scrape, and the crew had always received a share of any prize he might capture, legally or illegally.

So when the direction was given to set a course for England, they didn't even question it.

ELEVEN – SUMMER 1781

Dusk was closing in. Shadows crept darkly along the ground as the sun seared a hole in the horizon. The sky began to deepen into a violet haze.

Fleur gazed over the grounds of Rosehill with satisfaction. It had been a good summer. The wheat was a restless gold ocean, almost ready to harvest. She'd taken seriously the old earl's advice that the estate could maintain the family comfortably with good management if she didn't diversify too much. She'd given up the idea of a sheep flock in favour of cattle.

The practical gift of a bull from the earl had ensured the estate's small herd of cattle would increase in quality. The surplus would be slaughtered, some meat kept for victuals the rest sold at market or swapped for other goods. Fleur appreciated the thought behind the gift, despite grandmother Elmira's amusement.

At the beginning of the previous winter, her sheep had been taken, along with a litter of piglets, chickens, sacks of flour and stores of fruit. They'd been taken in the name of the King to provision a warship that had anchored in the bay for repairs.

Although she'd been furnished with a chit to claim cash back from the Admiralty, she'd understood that the treasury was so short of money the chit was practically worthless. The commandeering of the goods had set the household back, forcing them to stricter economies. Travelling to London to try and claim payment didn't seem worth the effort.

Fleur was well satisfied. The walled-in orchard, now tended by one of the two gardeners she'd hired, was fruiting well. Set up underneath the trees, hives had attracted swarming bees and were now producing honey. The kitchen gardens flourished and a full complement of servants gave the house the attention it deserved.

She had one niggling complaint. Sir Charles Boney had not yet returned the goods he'd cheated Remy out of. Fleur was negotiating through Simon Ackland, who visited on occasion and was acting on her behalf. The price seemed to go higher and higher with each visit.

Simon told her Charles had been taken under the Earl of Northhaven's wing after the man had become besotted with Catherine.

'I'd advise you to suspend negotiations until he's had a run of bad luck,' Simon had said the last time he'd visited. 'He'll be more eager to sell then. I'll keep my eye on the situation. You must understand though, I'm being excluded more and more from Charles' circle of friends now. He didn't like me taking Remy's side.'

'You're too good for him, Simon. Now tell me, how are your sisters? I believe you are to become an uncle shortly?'

His face lit up in a smile. 'I'm escorting my mother to London shortly, so she can attend the birth.'

As they chatted Fleur put her annoyance over the other matter aside. Sooner or later she would retrieve the missing treasures and restore them to their rightful places. If necessary, she'd ask her brothers to bring pressure on Charles, but not yet. They had their own lives to lead and she had to learn to manage without their support.

The infusion of money into the estate was beginning to produce results. Although Rosehill wasn't paying yet, Hamish McDuff had assured her the books would balance by the end of the season, despite the raid on her supplies by the navy. Next year the estate looked set to yield a small profit, which pleased her greatly.

She wheeled her horse around and cantered to the top of the hill. Remy's horse followed after her as he often did, with Gruff bringing up the rear. The gelding had allowed her to become more familiar with him now. He seemed to enjoy it when she fondled his ears and nose and spoke soft words to him. She hadn't attempted to ride him. He was a bundle of muscle and nervous energy, and easily spooked. Besides, he was kept exercised by Tom, who at the age of sixteen had become a strapping, handsome lad.

Still unable to quite believe Remy was dead, Fleur had almost abandoned the hope that he might be still alive. Something in her refused to let him die. She insisted his chamber be kept clean and aired, as if awaiting his return. There, her soul connected with an elusive something, an echo of himself Remy had left behind.

On the dresser was a silver backed hair-brush, a couple of dark, lustrous hairs still threaded through the bristles. There was a box containing tooth powder, a silver backed toothbrush and a scraper. His sandalwood soap had dried into fissures, but it remained in the dish. When she held the soap to her nose it exuded the faint, familiar scent of him – a scent imprinted in her memory.

Sometimes, she sat in the ordered quietness of the chamber with Gerard on her lap. As if Remy was in residence, she talked to him of their son's progress. She told him of Gerard's first tooth and of his first lurching steps, which had ended in disaster when he'd tripped over a rug and bitten through his lip.

Then there was the time Gerard escaped his nurse. They'd frantically searched the house before finding him fast asleep in a chair he'd climbed on to. She hoped her words reached Remy, wherever he was. Those of the staff who'd never known Remy pitied her those precious moments of comfort.

There was a breeze coming off the sea. Remy's horse turned his nose towards the horizon, his nostrils flared and he snickered. Gruff threw up his snout and gave a great baying bark, his tail flaying the wind.

Fleur laughed. 'I suppose we have time for a race along the water's edge before it gets dark.'

Her mare tossed her silky mane and they were off, clods of damp sand flying up behind them. Tail plumed aloft, Remy's gelding bucked and kicked with the sheer joy of it, like an exuberant child showing off.

As he always did, Gruff tripped over his legs several times trying to keep up. Falling behind, he barked ferociously until he ran out of breath, and then flopped on the sand, his tongue lolling out of his mouth. A movement caught his attention. Rising, he gazed out to sea, every sense alert.

On the return gallop Fleur noticed that Gruff was belly deep in water. His nose cast at the air. Hackles spread into a spectacular ruff, he turned his head towards her, growling deep in his throat.

'Good boy,' she whispered. 'I see it.'

A boat was drifting to shore. Apparently empty, except for a bundle of grey rags in the bottom, it rose and fell with the swell.

She peered into the gloom for the ship it came from, discovering it with sails furled, unobtrusively anchored in the shadows at the lee of the cliff. The ship seemed deserted, except the dark mouths of the gun ports yawned open. The breath caught in her throat as alarm crept stealthily up her spine.

She experienced a sudden sense of danger, and was about to flee when the boat hit a small outcropping of rock submerged under the water and was swamped by a wave. It turned over and a body rolled out.

For a moment the body floated face down, then the head lifted and the arms flailed ineffectually at the water. Whoever the man was he soon ran out of stamina, for his head went under again and stayed there.

Gruff glanced back at her, visibly agitated. He began to bark. Someone shouted something from the ship, but she couldn't quite catch the words. Still, she knew she couldn't leave the man to drown.

Throwing herself from her mare she waded waist-deep into the water, and turning the body on its back grasped it under the arms and dragged it up on to the sand. There, she let it fall. She placed a prudent distance between the body and herself.

Gruff stayed with the man, pawing and whining at the body. His tail whipped sand into the air.

'Come away,' she said in alarm, 'He might have a knife.' The dog ignored her.

There was a sudden heave of water, and the man began to cough. Remy's gelding fretted the sand with his forelegs as the man drew his knees up and began to retch. When it was over he rolled on to his back. He looked old, and thin to the point of starvation. Hair knotted and wild, his body was covered in sores and scabs. She wrinkled her nose at his odour.

She couldn't leave him here with the tide

coming in. It would only take one wave to wash over him and pull him back into the sea to drown. It was obvious he was spent. He needed nourishment and medical attention.

In the state he was in he posed her no danger. Kneeling by his side she said loudly, 'Are you conscious? We must get you to safety.'

His eyes opened. Dark and tortured, they were glazed by fever. He stared at her for a long time. Her tongue dried when she saw a tiny scar on his cheekbone. She traced over it with the tip of her finger, half-hoping, half-afraid. 'Who are you?'

His voice was a faint rasp of sound, like the wind brushing through dry summer grass. '*Hernando Cordova.*'

Oh God, oh God! It was Remy! Her prayers had been answered. She willed the wild, erratic beat of her heart to steady its pace. He didn't seem to recognize her. He fumbled inside his shirt, coming out with papers wrapped in an oilcloth pouch.

The thickest one she opened first. It was written in a language alien to her. The second was quaintly worded English

In a flourishing and elegant hand, she read.

Please to introduce, Viscount Remy St Cyres of Rosehill Estate, who no longer comprenders his former personage. Inform, if you please the Earl of Blessingham of his heir's survival. He will

222

justly reward you for your trouble. Go with God.

Hernando Cordova, Capitán, El Julia,

The nape of her neck prickled as she stared at the ship with its menacing open gun ports. Although it was flying a British flag, the ship was Spanish. There was a sense of watchfulness and waiting about it.

A faint movement caught her eye. Straining to see through the dying light, she made out the figure of a man. He stood on deck, watching her through an eyeglass. This was probably the seafaring uncle Remy had told Crispen about.

Grateful to the man for the safe return of her husband, she waved, wondering all the while how Remy had got into such a state. The figure lifted a hand in return, and then turned away. An order was shouted and men appeared from nowhere to swarm like fleas over the rigging.

As she stared at her husband in wonder, dusk pressed in, surrounding them in a soft cocoon. The ship readied herself for sea, heaving in the anchor and unfurling one white sail after another to capture the wind.

She looked beautiful as she headed for the open sea, like a graceful bird. Spanish or not, Fleur wished her God speed and a safe passage home before turning her attention back to Remy.

She wondered if she could get him on to the horse. 'Do you have the strength to stand up?' she asked, as the ship disappeared like a ghost into the gloom.

Remy tried, but was too weak to raise himself from the sand. When his eyes closed in exhaustion she used her lap as a soft pillow for his head. She wondered, should she leave him and go back to Rosehill for help, or wait until help came to her?

The wind strengthened, the waves crashed on to the shore and hissed up the sand, snatching at Remy's feet as if to pull him back in. Gradually, she dragged him across the sand, keeping him above the advancing tide.

As the night grew cool she cradled her husband's head in her arms and wept for all he'd lost. Gruff licked her face in sympathy, and then stretched out on the sand beside them. The horses leaned into each other, their eyes half-hooded and sleepy. They whickered softly to each other in the way horses did, touched noses and flicked their tails.

The stars appeared. The moon rose to send a pathway of pleated silk across a sea of amaranth. *El Julia* was nowhere to be seen. Silver edged clouds coiled in drifts across the incandescent orb of the moon. It was a beautiful night, she thought, content in its serenity. She was at one with the world. Remy had come home and they were healing together in its solitude.

It occurred to her that such a bright night

wasn't ideal for an enemy ship to anchor in the cove. It had taken courage for the captain to bring his ship here, and his departure had been timed to coincide beautifully with moonrise. When the hostilities were over she hoped to meet the courageous man who'd brought Remy back to her.

The staff would be looking for her now, checking the stables. She traced a finger over Remy's heated face, telling him fiercely. 'Only God knows what trials you've been through, but he's sent you back to me so understand this, I refuse to allow you to die.'

He muttered something fiercely unintelligible.

Before too long a flare appeared on the cliff top. 'Down here,' she called, drying her tears.

Remy didn't stir when Tom and McDuff carried him back to the house between them, and laid him like a bundle of worn out rags in his bed.

Mrs Firkins managed to smile through her copious tears. 'Master Remy's crawling with lice and he stinks like a sty full of hogs. He'll soon be his old self when he's had a good bath and we've fed him up, you mark my words.'

And Fleur, whose body inconveniently remembered how stimulating Remy's *old self* had been, blushed.

As soon as Macy received Fleur's message,

he dropped everything and sought out Leland.

Marguerite had recently presented his brother with a second healthy son. She was a tedious woman who made the most of the mildest of disorders. By her account she'd suffered from so many diseases, and had been snatched back from the jaws of death so many times that Macy's partner in the medical practice should be commended for the miracles he performed.

Leland ignored his wife's querulous complaints of being abandoned in favour of his sister once again. Macy didn't bother to contemplate why his brother spent more time with Sylvane Dumfries than he did with his wife. What was all too obvious was that Leland used Fleur as an excuse. He wondered if Fleur knew of Leland's infidelity or the existence of her two nieces. Somehow, he doubted it.

This time, Fleur's request couldn't be denied by either of them. Macy knew the visit would also present him with an excuse to visit his godson, plus spend some time with the boy's delightful nurse, Lucy Yates. The woman had occupied considerable time in his thoughts, of late, but had responded to his initial overtures with hardly any sign of encouragement at all. This had only served to whet his interest. This time, an opportunity to impress her might present itself.

When he and Leland were in the stables and about to depart, he sought his brother's advice. 'Do you think Lucy Yates might consider me as a suitor for her hand?'

'Lucy Yates? Is that the pert little blue-eyed nurse in Fleur's household? The one with the small waist and...' Leland cupped his hands against his chest, rolled his eyes and leered.

Macy scowled and punched him on the shoulder. 'You've noticed?'

'I've noticed you noticing her, brother. Your tongue hangs down to your knees every time you set eyes on her.'

'Well, what do you think? Would someone like her accept me or not?'

Leland grinned. 'Only if she were totally insane.'

A wrestling match ensued. They rolled around in the straw, laughing uproariously over nothing and scattering the horses in every direction. Finally, Macy pinned his brother down and sat astride his stomach. 'Give me a sensible answer or I'll knock your poxy teeth down your throat.'

Laughing, Leland opened his palms in a gesture of surrender. 'You have a splendid set of aristocratic balls going to waste. Of course she'll have you. I would, if I were a woman. Now get your fat arse off my stomach and let's be on our way before the groom thinks we're lovers.'

The pair arrived at Rosehill to be greeted by a harassed looking Fleur. 'Thank God you've come. Remy has a fever and is crawling with lice. He won't speak, hardly eats anything and refuses to get into a bath so I can clean him and tend to his sores.' There were tears in her eyes. 'He turns his face to the wall when I go near him.'

Macy smiled reassuringly at her as he took off his coat. 'I'll examine him first, and then we'll see what we can do about cleaning him up. Have a tub of warm water prepared.'

'I warn you, it will take more than one tub.'

Shocked by Remy's appearance, Macy tried not to let it show. He was used to sick room smells, but not so his brother. He grinned when Leland opened the window wide and held a handkerchief to his nose.

Remy's dull eyes gazed from one to the other. '*Hernando Cordova*,' he said wearily.

Macy held out his hand. 'We've met before. I'm Macy Russell. I'm a doctor, and I'm here to examine you. Do you understand?' Remy ignored the hand, and nodded.

As he examined his brother-in-law, servants carried in two tubs and began to fill them with water.

Apart from malnutrition, there were signs of physical abuse on Remy's body. Most of the sores were small burns that had refused to heal. Macy's mouth tightened. Powder flash burns! Remy's skin would be left permanently marked by those. Whip marks criss-crossed his back. At one stage a couple of his ribs had been broken and had healed. He'd been lucky his lung hadn't been punctured. Around his ankles and wrists, scabbed abrasions and calluses indicated he'd been manacled.

The lice were sucking him dry, and he probably had intestinal worms as well. No wonder he didn't want Fleur to tend to him, the shame he would feel would be unconscionable. It was not a task Macy would like Fleur to undertake.

Remy's state of mind worried Macy most. He had not recognised them and seemed unable to speak English. He certainly understood it, though.

Macy murmured, 'It seems to me that you've been subjected to torture. Can you remember your name?'

'*Hernando Cordova.*'

'That's the name of your uncle. You are Remy St Cyres, and that's the name you will be called here. Do you know where you are?'

Remy shook his head.

'You are at your home, which is Rosehill Estate in England. You are quite safe. No one will hurt you here ... understand?'

Remy stared at him for a moment, and then gave an uncertain nod.

'That's my brother, Leland by the window. We are going to clean you up to make you more comfortable. Do you need help in getting into the tub?'

'*Si.*'

The water was brown and scummed over when they finished. Macy carefully shaved the hair from Remy's entire body, pulling the crusts of weeping scabs away with it. Many of the wounds were flyblown and Macy grunted with satisfaction as he scraped out the wriggling maggots and the putrefaction they fed on. They would have prevented the onset of gangrene. Leyland gagged a couple of times and turned away.

When he finished his unpleasant task he rinsed Remy off in the second tub and began to apply ointment to the wounds. Remy's teeth began to chatter from shock and cold. So gaunt was he, he resembled a skeleton as Macy pulled a nightshirt over his head.

During his ministrations Macy had uncovered a scar and a hard lump on Remy's head. Once his patient had been laid in the clean bed, he examined the lump more closely. 'I'll be damned,' he muttered as his fingers delicately probed its outline. 'He seems to have a ball lodged in his head. It entered just behind the ear and travelled around the skull.'

'Can you remove it?'

'Not until his condition's improved. I don't know what's under it. It seems to have been there for a while, but there's some inflammation around the site. Judging by the appearance of the scar it's been lodged there for some time, so leaving it a bit longer won't harm him.'

The dirty bed linen was to be burned, along with Remy's hair and most of the lice. All were tied up in a sheet. There had been too many eggs to try and remove them by other means. The few who tried to escape were picked off and cracked between Macy's thumbnails.

Applying ointment to Remy's wounds, Macy said cheerfully, 'Once you're purged of worms, my friend, you should start improving. I'll dose you up with a decoction of hyssop boiled in honey for a few days. It's good for other ailments as well.'

'*Gracias*,' Remy said elegantly.

Leland chuckled. 'Thank him when his purges have you farting like an old cart horse.'

Macy threw his brother a grin. 'It will cleanse his other organs at the same time. I'm going to stay at Rosehill for a while so I can keep an eye on him.'

'Let me know when you intend to remove the slug from his head. You might need me to hold him down.'

'If the way you reacted to his treatment was any indication I doubt if you've got the stomach for surgery.'

Servants were summoned to remove the

tub. A nog of eggs beaten with milk and brandy was brought in. Remy had difficulty swallowing it, but Macy stood over him and insisted he drink every drop. Once it was down he was pleased to note it was retained by Remy's stomach.

Remy's eyes drifted shut and he fell into a fitful sleep.

Fleur was called in. Shocked by her husband's appearance, tears sprang to her eyes. 'He doesn't look like the Remy I knew.'

'He will, given time. He needs plenty of nourishment. Feed him egg nogs and broths at first, then introduce him to solids, much as you would an infant. I also need a decoction of hyssop and honey made for him, and I want someone with him until he's able to care for himself a bit.'

She nodded. 'I'll stay myself.'

His glance was faintly amused. 'Not you my dear. A manservant. Some lifting will be involved, and many of the duties are of a more personal nature. Remy has his share of pride. He'll not appreciate a woman in attendance until he feels more comfortable with himself.'

Fleur's expression plainly stated her opinion of male pride, but she didn't argue. 'It would be best if it's someone who knows how to keep his counsel. I'd not have Remy's return made public just yet. I've learned that he didn't go to be a soldier, but has been involved in something dangerous and secret.

What if the Earl of Northhaven visits to question him? Wouldn't it be better to keep his survival a secret until he's in full command of his strength and senses.'

Leland straightened up. 'Leave the matter to me. As Macy's skills make me feel a little inadequate it will give me something useful to do. His grandfather must be informed of Remy's survival so I'll ride over to Stragglemarsh Hall and ask him to lend you the services of a man of discretion.'

She placed a hand on his arm. 'The earl must be informed, of course, but I would rather inform him myself.'

'It will be as you say.'

Macy slid an arm round her shoulders. 'I'll impress the need for secrecy on your household and I'll stay until Remy is on the way to recovery. He has a slug imbedded in his skull. When he's stronger I intend to remove it.'

When she gasped, he smiled reassuringly at her. 'I can move it slightly between my finger and thumb, so it should take but a minute or two to remove it.'

'Will it hurt?'

'Laudanum will dull the pain. My main worry is that pus may have accumulated under the slug, which would account for the fever. If that's the case it will need to be poulticed and drained.' He shrugged, wishing he could have told her more gently.

'From what I've seen, he's been through much worse over the past couple of years.'

Crossing to the bed, Fleur stared down at her husband's skeletal face for a while. When he became restless she tenderly stroked his cheek until he quieted, the way she did with her infant son. 'Poor Remy,' she whispered. 'I will make a tonic to strengthen your blood.'

The brothers exchanged a wry glance. Fleur's blood tonic was guaranteed to raise blisters on boot leather.

'Better leave the dosing to Macy,' Leland suggested with a grin, then led her thoughts elsewhere. 'You must take me to see my nephew before we leave. No doubt he's growing into a fine lad.' Not only that, Leland wanted to cast his eyes over Macy's lady love. He grinned knowingly at his brother. He might even put in a good word for Macy whilst he was there.

'Tell Mrs Yates I'll visit Gerard when I've finished here and cleaned myself up,' Macy growled self-consciously.

'Gerard's growing into the image of his father.' The smile Fleur bestowed on the unconscious Remy was filled with love, as if she'd suddenly remembered her young son would not grow up fatherless.

Leland caught his breath. He'd never realized the extent of the affection he held for his sister, until now. He'd raised her well and she'd gained strength along the way.

Whatever life threw at her, Fleur would adapt and learn to cope with it.

He took her hand in his as they left the chamber. Raising it to his lips in a rare gesture of affection, he kissed her knuckles. 'You've got no idea how much I've missed you, Fleur. Thank God Remy prevented you from going to live with the bishop. I must have been mad to listen to Marguerite.'

She gave him a sideways look, her smile complacent. 'Believe it or not, I'm glad he did. I'm content with my lot.'

Leland could only wish *he* was content with his.

TWELVE

'Oh my dear, are you quite certain he will survive?'

'It would be too cruel to lie to you, grand-mother. He's in a disgusting condition and so ill he cannot remember his own name. Macy is of the opinion that good food and clean-liness will take care of the physical aspect. I need the services of a strong personal servant for him, if you have one to spare.'

Tears of joy glistened in the earl's eyes. 'I'm sure we can accommodate you. I thought nothing would make me happier than knowing you had given birth to Remy's son. Now I know I was wrong. We must celebrate.'

'No, we must not, at least, not yet, and the servant must be totally trustworthy and discreet. I beg of you both, keep this news close until Remy has recovered and regained his memory. I believe his life could be in danger if word gets out of his survival.'

The earl's eyes sharpened. 'What makes you think so?'

She handed him the oilskin pouch. 'Inside are some papers, which Remy handed over to me on the beach. There are several documents inside, all of which are written in Spanish, it seems. I know not what they contain, but I believe they'd be safer in your possession, than mine. If word gets back to Northhaven of Remy's survival and a search is made of Rosehill, I would rather they not be found, in case they incriminate him.'

The earl inclined his head. 'They'll be hidden safely away, and if Northhaven's men insist on searching Stragglemarsh Hall their efforts will be in vain. When Remy is fit and able he can read the contents.' He exchanged a meaningful glance with Elmira. 'We will send Noah to care for Remy.'

Fleur gave them both a hug. 'I must go now. My brother is waiting to escort me back home, where I'll do my utmost to nurse your grandson back to health. Leland asks me to offer you his felicitations.'

'And mine to him. Thank you for bringing the most gratifying news, Fleur,' he said. 'We're forever in your debt.'

Within days Remy's condition began to improve. Dark stubble spiked through his scalp, his eyes regained some of their former gloss. Noah was a silent and watchful figure. His servanting skills were barely adequate, but he was strong.

Fleur insisted on feeding Remy herself. One day he proved to be uncooperative. 'What is it, Remy?' she said. 'Do you feel unwell?'

He muttered something uncomplimentary sounding.

'You would sound more civilised if you spoke the King's English instead of that tongue-twisting outlandish lingo.'

In an instant her wrist was tightly gripped between his fingers. His eyes blazed into hers. Startled, she dropped the spoon. Immediately, he snatched it up and hurled at the wall. She placed the bowl of soup on a table next to the bed lest it was subject to the same violence.

He thumped his fist against his chest. '*You no soy un bebé.*'

The general meaning of which, she could guess at. 'What's the meaning of *bebé?*'

Dropping her wrist he cradled his arms and rocked them violently from side to side.

'*Bebé ...bebé!*'

What did a man who'd gone off to war, leaving her to give birth to his son alone, know about babies? He'd returned, half-dead, to an estate she'd slaved her fingers to the bone to save from ruin. If she hadn't treated him gently the living half of him would have perished by now. What ingratitude! Not one word of thanks, just a spoon thrown at the wall.

'*Si!* A baby,' he shouted.

Her eyes narrowed. At least she'd captured his attention, albeit a temperamental outburst. She could cope with that. Having been brought up by brothers she knew their bluster was often nothing but heated air.

She engaged his eyes in a challenge. 'So you *can* still speak English,' she muttered under her breath. 'Understand this, you heathen. I'm not going to tolerate any childish temper tantrums. If Macy says you have to be fed broth, that's what you get. If you don't like it you can go without.' Her lip curled. '*Comprener* that, my arrogant Lord.'

His hand pinned hers to the bed, the smile he gave her was a thinly disguised grimace. 'Am I, or am I not the master of this household?'

She was jubilant. At last, she'd goaded him into speaking. 'Yes but–'

His nostrils narrowed as he drew in a breath. His eyes were turbulent with a tem-

238

per he was trying hard to control. 'For days you have been patronizing in your approach to me. I will not be addressed so insolently, girl. You are dismissed from my service.'

Was she then? She tossed her head and laughed. 'I'm not your servant, Remy St Cyres.' And although tempted she managed to refrained from informing him of the true nature of their relationship. Macy had advised her it would be better if Remy remembered the past by himself.

They locked eyes in a silent battle of wills, one she was determined to win.

She smiled, saying softly. 'Did you hear what I said, master of Rosehill?'

After a while his eyes filled with anguish. His grip relaxed so she could have pulled her hand away if she wished. She left it there.

'Of course, I had forgotten. You are Macy's sister. Please forgive me,' he whispered. 'Sometimes people you consider to be friends turn out to be enemies. I have yet to determine whom I can trust.'

She slid on to the edge of the bed, touched by his admission. Her voice softened. 'Have I not demonstrated how much you can trust me, Remy?'

'Then it is not a trick. I'm no longer in that stinking prison?'

'Does this chamber look like a prison?'

'Sometimes, when I cannot see the sky,' he

murmured. 'Often I imagine I can hear the ocean, then I think I'm on a ship and feel ill from the motion sickness. Am I insane?'

'Would my brother leave me alone with you if he considered you were insane?' The sight of his weary face rapidly cooled the remnants of her temper and she felt ashamed of herself. Only God knew what he'd been though. 'As for the sensation of sickness. You were delivered back to us by ship and were near death. No, you are not mad, Remy. Just ill. You can hear the ocean because the sea is just over the rise.'

'The crew crossed themselves against me, but the captain was kind.'

'It was a Spanish ship, Remy. The captain was your uncle, I think. He risked his own life to bring you to safety.'

Alarm clouded his eyes. 'He gave me a packet of papers. I understood what was written but didn't know the meaning of them. He said they concerned family honour and it was important I kept them in a safe place.'

'They're safely hidden until you need them.'

He assimilated the information without comment, just nodded.

'If you would like to take the air, I'll ask my brother if he'll allow Noah to wrap you up warmly and carry you outside. It's a lovely day. You could sit in the shelter of the rose garden for a while. Perhaps the outing would do you good.'

Hope came and went in his eyes. 'You have my word. I will not try and escape.'

Her stomach knotted and tears filled her eyes. 'You are no longer a prisoner. This is your home, in which you may come and go as your heart dictates.'

Despite Macy's misgivings she decided to make a batch of blood tonic. The recipe had been given to her by a peasant women who'd been reputed to have the sight. Most of the ingredients could be found in the kitchen garden.

There was parsley and marigolds. She'd seen saxifrage growing in a boggy corner of the meadow and had a goodly amount of mustard seed to hand.

It was a little late for wild mushrooms but if she were lucky she'd find some growing in damp leaf litter in the woods. If Remy had been purged too harshly the blood tonic could only be of benefit.

She picked up the bowl again, coaxing. 'Come Remy, eat your broth before it cools, for you need it to regain your health. However, as you've pointed out, you're not an infant who needs to be spoon fed by his mama. From now on you can manage by yourself. If you eat it all I promise your next meal will be much improved.'

As he looked at her, his forehead wrinkled

in puzzlement. 'You are my mama?'

She pursed her lips. 'Your mama? Surely your brain is not quite so addled as that. How can I be you mama when it's perfectly obvious to all but a blind beggar that I'm younger than you?'

His laugh was totally unexpected. She gazed at him, uncertain. There was some wit left in him, after all. She managed a small grin in acknowledgement of the fact. Momentarily his fingers curled around her hand. He gently squeezed it, and then he released her.

Mindful of Charles Boney's threat, whenever Fleur took her son abroad a manservant went with them. Nothing untoward happened. After a while she came to the conclusion the threat had been an empty one and she became less vigilant.

After gathering together the ingredients for her blood tonic, she boiled them together over a fire in the kitchen. Nose wrinkling, Bessie threw open the door to drive out the foul fumes.

When all was rendered down she ground the ingredients into a paste with mortar and pestle, then added boiling water to the dark green sludge and left it to cool.

The next morning, bottle and spoon in hand she made her way to Remy. First shaking the contents of the bottle vigorously, she carefully measured out a dose.

Remy gazed suspiciously on. 'What is that?'

She smiled at him in reassurance. 'It's a blood tonic. I collected the ingredients myself and made it especially for you.'

His eyes hooded slightly. 'Ah, yes... Macy mentioned such a medicament, I believe.' He shook his head regretfully. 'He advised me against taking it, so I'd prefer not to swallow the concoction.'

A little persuasion was obviously in order. She held the spoon to his lips. 'You're being stubborn, Remy. Come, swallow it ... it will do you good.'

As soon as he opened his mouth to answer she tipped the tonic inside.

He spluttered. Some of the tonic dribbled from the side of his mouth and he made a strangled noise. It was an expected reaction, one almost exactly like her brothers had when they'd tasted it. However, he swallowed it, leaving her wondering why men made such a fuss over such things.

'There,' she said soothingly. 'That wasn't so bad.'

'I beg to differ!' Before she could step back he pulled her on to the bed, and placed his hand against her throat, effectively holding her down against the pillow.

She gave a squawk of protest, quickly suppressed when her eyes absorbed the ruthless intent in his. Reaching across her he thumbed the stopper from the bottle of tonic, then held the open neck to her lips. 'Drink it, Fleur!'

'I don't need a blood tonic.' Her nose wrinkled at the smell and she frantically tried to move her head to one side. Releasing her throat he took her nose between finger and thumb and applied pressure. Stubbornly, she kept her mouth clamped shut, making a sound like an angry wasp.

His eyes filled with laughter. 'Now who's being obdurate? Come, swallow it, Fleur,' he said all pleasantness. 'It will do you good.'

She frantically shook her head.

'Your eyes are beginning to bulge and your face is turning purple through lack of air ... a most unattractive colour.'

She couldn't deny her body the need for air. When she opened her mouth to breathe, he dribbled a little of the tonic inside. Instantly, her tongue and throat were afire. When she swooped in a deep, indignant breath some tonic went with it and she began to cough. It took a few moments to recover enough air to furiously berate him, and it wasn't until she ran out of suitable names to call him that she fell silent.

When he dared to laugh her eyes blazed into his. 'I should have left you to drown.'

He held the bottle up to the light, gazing into the murky green depths. 'It would be preferable to being fed this poison. It looks as though you've scraped it from the bottom of a pond.'

'It's not poison. It's a tonic to strengthen your blood.'

'It certainly has a warming effect,' he murmured, his gaze more intimate than was good for her. When he brushed a finger across her cheek her face heated even more. 'It has given you quite a blush ... or is it me who makes you agitated?'

'When you resemble a scarecrow plucked from a field by the wind? You're being impertinent, sir. Let me up, at once or–'

'Or you will what? Your threats are ineffective my Queen of Hearts. His palm pressed gently against her waist, keeping her there. 'It surprises me, the effect I seem to have on you.'

'It seems to me to be the other way around,' she hissed. 'I am going innocently about my business whilst you are acting like the unprincipled rogue you are.'

'It's because you make me feel that way. You have such a soft mouth.' Before she could summon the wit to stop him, he gently kissed her.

Immediately, her body evoked memories of him she'd tried to forget. When she gave a half-hearted murmur of protest he released her, and placing a finger across her lips for silence gazed down at her, seemingly perplexed. 'For my own good, I should not have done that.'

And for her own good, if the truth were to be told. She heard Macy's heavy tread coming up the stairs. 'My brother will be here in a moment. Unhand me.'

'It would not do for you to be found, thus compromised, would it?' He kissed her again, all to briefly, raising her to her feet afterwards. The grin he gave was a rueful. 'You will excuse this liberty I have taken, yes?'

Her heart thumped like a drum as she hastily tidied her skirts. 'On this occasion I will be forgiving, but you're much too sure of yourself.'

He wore an expression of puzzled introspection. 'And you are too sure of me; why is that, Fleur?'

She was saved from answering by Macy's arrival. Setting a tray covered by a linen towel on the table he gazed from one to the other. 'Hmmm,' he said, which when all was said and done, meant nothing.

But despite it meant nothing it brought the colour whipping to her face again. 'I've been dosing Remy with blood tonic,' she said unnecessarily.

Macy wiped his finger over her chin. 'It looks as though you've taken some yourself.'

She threw Remy a dark scowl as she furiously scrubbed it away. 'He was difficult to dose.'

Remy said casually, 'Your sister wished to

246

prove the tonic wasn't poison, so she took some herself.'

Macy turned an interested gaze on him. 'Did it taste like poison?'

'Undoubtedly.' He chuckled as he gazed at her. 'I shall not swallow another dose of it, and neither, I think, will she insist.'

Cheeks still heated she placed her hands against them. 'It's warm today.'

'I hadn't noticed.' Macy curled her a grin, one she studiously ignored. 'Did Remy tell you I'm going to remove the slug from his skull today.' He took a bottle from the tray and measured out a dose of laudanum. 'I need someone with a strong stomach and steady hand to assist me. Noah demurs at the thought of being assistant surgeon. Funny, I wouldn't have considered him to be a squeamish type.'

Fleur paled herself, unable to bear the thought of watching Remy being deliberately hurt. Drawing Macy aside, she whispered. 'Perhaps Lucy Yates would be better than me in this instance. She's the daughter of a barber surgeon, and in possession of considerable nursing skills.'

He smiled a little and patted her cheek. 'Mrs Yates is certainly a suitable choice then. Go and ask her. Make sure she's wearing a clean apron and tell her to wash her hands thoroughly.'

When Fleur left the room Macy handed Remy the laudanum. 'It's a strong dose and will dull the pain a little. Don't be surprised if you sleep for quite a while afterwards.'

Remy managed a faint, ironic smile. 'More sleep, and just when I'm beginning to know I'm alive. May I ask you something before I take the draught?'

Macy grinned at him. 'If you're going to ask me of the risk attached to this operation, it's negligible. Some pain is unavoidable, but as I explained to you before, the slug is just under the surface of the skin and you have the constitution of an ox. Judging by the state you were in when you arrived, you've been through much worse.'

For a moment, Remy's eyes assumed a haunted look. He shuddered. 'I wasn't going to enquire about the risk. It's more personal. I intended to ask if you would consider me as a suitor for your sister's hand.'

Macy nearly dropped the laudanum. 'It's obvious that you *are* feeling alive?' When he recovered from his surprise he gave a thin, satisfied smile. 'I'd consider you entirely suitable as a ... husband to Fleur. However, it is she you must ask. She does have a mind of her own.'

'Ah ... yes, I've noticed,' Remy said softly. 'That will be the challenge, of course, to persuade her to agree. She doesn't appear susceptible to flattery. Yet there is some air about her that gives me reason to believe she may not be immune to an approach.' He shrugged, and taking the narcotic from Macy's hand swallowed it in one gulp. 'Of course, I may be mistaken. Perhaps it is pity for the afflicted I see in her eyes.'

'I wouldn't count on it,' Macy whispered a little while later when Remy's eyes began to droop.

Somebody coughed behind him and he turned to see Lucy Yates. When her cornflower blue eyes gazed calmly into his, warmth spread through Macy's bones.

They'd exchanged such regard before, on several of his many visits to see his godson. He smiled at her, enjoying her frank and honest gaze, her lack of artificiality. 'Have you ever watched a ball being removed?'

'On occasion. And I nursed my husband when he was dying from the effects of not having one removed. It poisoned his blood.'

'A painful business ... where was the ball lodged?'

'In his stomach.'

'It would have ruptured his vitals and he wouldn't have survived it either way then.'

She nodded. 'I've sent Noah off to boil a kettle of water and bring up a bowl and some rags. He might as well feel as if he's doing something useful.'

Macy smiled and took off his coat. He rolled his shirt-sleeves up before opening his instrument case. He ignored the saws and larger knives, preferring to use A small folding knife. The handle fit comfortably into his palm whilst the blade extended the length of his finger. It provided a steady cut. He set it on the tray along with an ivory syringe to extract surplus blood and pus from the wound and a pair of blunt-nosed shears to probe for the bullet, in case his fingers proved inadequate.

He hesitated over the drill, and then pushed it aside. Remy displayed no chaotic brain symptoms so there was no need to subject him to the procedure of trepanation to facilitate the release of evil humours.

'I've brought you a clean apron to wear,' Lucy said, her breath tickling against his ear. It caused a delicious shiver to run down his spine.

'Thanks,' he grunted, inhaling the scent of lavender and acutely aware of her as he allowed her to tie it around his middle. He was too aware of her, so was forced to breathe in deeply in an effort to gain the concentration needed to work at his best.

Noah came in with a kettle of hot water, handing it over to Lucy before he hurriedly departed. 'I'll guard the door,' he murmured.

A bowl of water was placed at Macy's elbow, in which he would wash his hands and rinse his surgical instruments afterwards. Another was set aside and covered with a muslin cloth.

'I want you to hold his head still while I make the cut, then keep the blood clear of the wound.' He gazed at her, hoping she didn't have a fit of the vapours. 'The patient may jerk, so be ready for it.'

Calmly, she nodded.

'I won't jerk,' Remy said, his voice adopting a slur to rival that of the village drunk. 'But for pity's sake, get on with it.'

When Macy drew the blade over the swelling a thin red line appeared, then widened. Remy grunted and squeezed his eyes shut.

Within a few moments the slug was removed, along with a few minute splinters of bone that had been chipped from the skull. Removing a clot of blood cushioning the bullet Macy was relieved to discover there was no putrefaction. The skull bone, though dented, appeared to be intact. 'I always knew you were thickskulled,' Macy grunted.

Remy didn't make as sound when he closed the wound with a couple of stitches, but his jaws and fists were clenched and his neck muscles were rigid when Macy finished.

'The worst is over,' Macy said gently as he spread a tincture of St-John'sWort over the wound to keep infection at bay. He bandaged it with the clean muslin strips Lucy handed him, hoping the wound wouldn't become infected.

Remy's eyes opened a crack. 'When will I

251

recall my past?'

'It's difficult to say. Given time, you may remember everything. But then, you might not.' And before Remy suggested it, Macy reminded him, 'Try and remain patient. If you force things you may never remember. Now rest.'

When he turned away it was to discover his instruments had been washed in clean water, dried and replaced in their case.

'Thank you, Mrs Yates; you were a great help.'

'I found it interesting, Doctor Russell. You're fast as well as deft, which relieves the patient of much uneccessary suffering,' she said approvingly.

The compliment both pleased and surprised him, and he smiled at her. 'I was well trained at the John Hunter anatomical school ... and I insist that you call me Macy.'

'Then you must address me by my first name also.' An enchanting little smile flirted at her lips, which reminded Macy of his intentions with regard to this woman. He might as well broach the subject of whilst she was well disposed towards him.

'And you're a brave woman. You would be a good assistant for a doctor to have.' She was small waisted, her bosom was ample and her hips a wide span for child bearing. She'd ceased being wet nurse to Gerard, who'd been weaned on to solid food and goat's milk. Lucy Yates would be a warm armful in bed for a man ... but was she willing?

He grinned and came straight to the point. 'I'm seeking a wife who is intelligent, even-tempered, clean and capable – one who will keep my house and bear me children. I've had you in mind for some time, now, and if you have no objections I think we could deal together quite nicely.'

She coloured, and despite sounding slightly flustered didn't appear too put out by the proposal when she said, 'I ... I don't know quite how to answer, sir.'

'You need not answer at the moment. My sister will, no doubt, be pleased to inform you of my shortcomings. You might as well know the worst. It includes an overindulgence in wine at times.'

'A little overindulgence in a man is not too great a fault. Are you kind to women, sir? My late husband was disposed towards taking a rod to my back. I have no wish to experience such punishment again.'

Blood sang in Macy's veins and his eyes darkened at the thought of someone beating a fine woman like her. 'I've been told I'm a fool in my cups, but have never been violent towards children or the fair sex.' He grinned as memories of past conquests rushed in on him. 'I find women to be delightful creatures of grace and beauty, who were placed on earth to appeal to the eyes, ears and ... and finer attributes of a man.'

'*Finer attributes?*' She raised an eyebrow, but she was laughing.

He shrugged, and grinning at his near slip, raised her hand to his lips in as gallant a manner as he could. 'No doubt a good wife would keep me faithful.'

Lowering her eyes she curtseyed. 'Thank you for the honour of your proposal, Dr Russell, I will ask Lady Fleur for reference and convey my reply to you by the end of the week.'

Disappointment filled him when her hand was withdrawn. 'That's three days hence.'

'Patience cannot be counted amongst your virtues then?' The laugh she gave had a breathless quality. 'You are a man of little finesse, Macy Russell. In matters of the heart a woman requires a period of courtship. However, if we suit I see no reason why we should not wed ... in a year or so, perhaps.'

Macy considered he should take a leaf out of Remy's book. 'I see no reason to delay. Perhaps I'll throw you over my saddle and take me with you when I leave.'

'And perhaps I'll crack you over the head with a fire iron for your trouble.' She turned and strode away, her hips swinging in a slightly more provocative manner than they'd possessed when she'd arrived.

He rubbed his hands together, muttering, 'No finesse eh? We'll see about that, my

254

bonny. You're ripe for the plucking and I'll have you plucked within two weeks. Just you see if I don't.'

A strangled groan came from the bed. When Macy looked at his patient it was to find Remy was laughing. His eyes, glassy with the drug he'd been given, glittered darkly from under drooping eyelids.

Macy scratched his head. 'Don't you ever give in? The amount of laudanum I gave you should have felled an ox. You're just a man, so shut your cackle and go to sleep before I knock you unconscious!'

To his surprise, Remy did.

As he was about to leave the chamber, Fleur came rushing in, her eyes brimming with worry.

He answered the unspoken question in her eyes. 'He's fine and should sleep until morning. Tell his manservant to keep an eye on him and I'll drop in on him later.' He slid an arm around her. 'I'm going into town for a while. Tell me, Fleur, what do men give women for courting gifts?'

'Flowers, gloves, a book of poetry with a poem significant to the deep sentiment he holds for her marked, perhaps. Some men even write a heartfelt poem themselves,' she said, grinning at the thought of Macy doing so. Her expression sharpened and she smiled. 'Out with it, Macy, who has caught your fancy?'

Kissing her cheek he smiled and walked off without answering.

'Macy!' she said firmly.

He turned to smile at her. 'Remy asked me if I'd object to him as a suitor for you.'

Eyes huge with surprise, she stammered. 'I ... I beg your pardon. I didn't quite hear that?'

'I'm quite sure you did, Fleur. Remy thinks you would make him a suitable wife.'

'What did you answer?'

'It's not me he wants to wed. I told him to ask you himself, of course.' Macy was laughing to himself as he disappeared from her view. That would give her something to think about.

Had he stopped to look back he would have seen her stoop to tenderly kiss her husband, a smile on her lips.

THIRTEEN

Simon Ackland is dead?

The grief Fleur experienced as she read the note from his sister was heartfelt. Simon had been such a gentle man – a person who'd won her trust and respect in the months following Remy's disappearance.

She didn't tell Remy of Simon's death.

256

Time to do that when he remembered his friend. At the moment her husband was living quietly, slowly regaining his strength. She wanted nothing to set back his recovery.

Attending the funeral was out of the question. It was possible Charles might be there and she was hoping to avoid him. She sent a letter of condolence to Simon's parents and when next she was in Dorchester she called on them to offer her regrets in person whilst Hamish McDuff conducted some estate business.

'He was a good friend to my husband and we liked him enormously. I'm extremely sorry this has happened. I didn't realize he was ill.'

'Simon was murdered,' his father said quietly. 'He'd just left an alehouse in Poole when someone set about him and robbed him. His friend, Sir Charles Boney said he tried to stop the felon but was hit over the head himself and rendered unconscious. When he woke, Simon had been shot through the heart.'

A convenient blow for Charles, Fleur thought cynically.

Simon's mother and sister began to quietly sob. Lest she weep too, Fleur left them to their mourning.

She bought a holly wreath from market stall. The berries were brilliant beads of blood red against the glossy dark green of the prickled leaves.

On the way home McDuff detoured to the cemetery. Placing the wreath on Simon's grave she stifled a sob and said a prayer for his soul. He had not deserved to meet such an end.

Fed well and freed from the parasites that had plagued him, Remy made such rapid progress he was permitted to spend most of the day out of his bed.

Sometimes, he woke disoriented and with the smell of the prison in his nostrils. Then he knew moments of despair, of the thought of another day pitting the remnants of his will against that of his inquisitors.

They'd been cruel, torturing him with pain then offering him ease. But they'd gone too far. Eventually he'd forgotten what they'd wanted him to confess to. Pain had become a welcome friend who reminded him he was alive – who told him that deep inside him he had a strong will of his own. That will insisted he had to live.

Now he knew *why* he'd had to live. He was home where he belonged.

Today he had climbed the hill. The effort had tired him, but the battle to get here had been sweet. Spreading his arms he breathed deeply of the air. Beneath him spread a green landscape and the house in his dreams. His windows had no bars. His prison was the horizon, and beyond. His dream had become a reality. How he'd got from the prison to here, was hazy.

Fleur had told him he'd arrived on a ship. The ocean was over the hill. He could smell the salt and hear the waves pounding on the shore. Today he was too weak to make the short journey to see it. Tomorrow, he would be stronger and would conquer the world.

Power filled his limbs with a euphoric strength that he knew reality couldn't match at the moment. There was a need for his muscles to be worked and strengthened. There was a need to get to know the woman better. But right at this moment he was content to drift and to dream.

Lying on his back he stared up at the sky, watching the gulls wheel on the air currents. Here was freedom. The earth was solid beneath his back. The wind chased the clouds across the sky so the sun changed to shadows and back again. The horizon had no boundaries. It was early October, the air was growing chill. Brilliantly coloured leaves spun in a dance across the garden.

Melancholy filled him. When he was very young his father had lifted him to the saddle in front of him and brought him up here. He'd indicated the house with a sweep of his arm. 'All this will be yours one day, Remy.' He'd been too young to understand and had laughed, more enchanted by the flowing mane of his father's grey horse than the thought of property and title.

He could hear that laughter now, the high-pitched giggle of a young child. He raised himself to his elbow, his eyes seeking the source of the laughter. Lucy Yates was chasing a dark-haired child through the orchard. He smiled when she caught him under the arms, spun him round and gave him a hug.

The dark unmistakable hulk that was Macy detached himself from the trunk of a tree he'd been leaning against and took the child from her. They disappeared towards the house together, the child riding high on Macy's shoulders.

Remy knew Lucy was a widow, but hadn't realized she had a child. There was a lot he didn't know about people in his household, including himself. He thought it was about time he made it his business to find out.

His eyes widened. Hadn't he just recalled an incident from his childhood? Touching the wound on his head for luck, he gave a wide, jubilant smile. Standing, he hitched his baggy breeches higher, replace his hat and began to walk slowly back towards the house.

Fleur was waiting there for him on the terrace. Her gown was a tint of autumn colours her hair tied back with red ribbons. On her arm a basket of ripe chestnuts glowed. Her mouth was soft with smiles. He felt like kissing her when she said in a tone of tender accusation. 'You've been gone too a long a time and I was worried. I trust you've not tired yourself.'

'I'm afraid I have.' He picked an autumn leaf from her hair, feeling as if he'd won a contest. 'I remembered something.'

Her eyes glowed with the excitement she felt. 'Oh Remy, how wonderful. What was it?'

'My father took me on the hill when I was a child. We were on a grey horse.'

She looked slightly disappointed. 'Is that all you remembered?'

His smile faded. 'It's better than remembering nothing.'

'Of course it is.' She sounded ashamed as she confessed, 'I'm too impatient. Every night I pray you'll wake in the morning and remember everything.'

He stared down at her for a moment, the expression in his eyes teasing. 'Sometimes I wonder ... is there something specific you want me to remember?'

She avoided the question, saying instead, 'Lucy Yates has agreed to wed my brother. The marriage is to take place three months hence in the village church.'

So Macy did not have it all his own way, and a compromise had been reached.

His smile reflected the genuine pleasure he felt. 'They seem suited as a couple.'

'When she has children she will be a wonderful mother.'

'I thought she had a child. I saw her with a young boy today.'

She stared at him, silent for a moment. 'The steward, Hamish McDuff has children. I must introduce you to him. Now come into the drawing room and warm yourself by the fire. I will tell Mrs Firkins to bring us some tea.'

'The woman should be retired. She's too old to carry heavy trays.'

'She was your nurse when you were a child and remained loyal to you throughout the bad times. She regards serving you as her right. Would you deny her such a small pleasure?'

Remy didn't answer. He'd learned two things over the course of the previous few minutes. The boy he'd seen didn't belong to Lucy, and Mrs Firkins had known him longer than anybody.

He placed a detaining hand on her arm and caught her eye. Now was as good a time as any to ask. 'I have grown very fond of you, Fleur, and have spoken with Macy about the possibility of marriage between us. I seem to have a comfortable and thriving estate to offer you. How would you feel about such a union?'

He was surprised when tears filled her eyes. She blinked them away and touched his cheek in a small gesture of intimacy. 'You do me honour, Remy.'

'I would be the one honoured. Am I being presumptuous in thinking you regard me with warmth?'

The little grin she gave became mischievous, her manner flirtatious. 'Are you seeking compliments, My Lord?'

He chuckled and took the liberty of leaning forward to kiss her soft mouth. She spun away from him, laughing. 'You will have to be quicker than that. Away with you; I must order our refreshments.'

Whilst he warmed himself in the drawing room he gazed at the portrait of the woman and child hanging over the fireplace. The woman wore a gown the colour of lavender flowers, her face was framed by glossy dark hair. He felt a kinship with her.

Pressed against her knee, the boy's eyes were dark and mischievous. He thought the portrait might be of himself with his mother, but the child reminded him of the boy he'd seen with Lucy Yates. He wondered. Were they related? He allowed his mind to drift. Nothing but the prison came into it – but he instinctively knew his parents were dead.

Fleur came in carrying a platter of fruit tartlets, and followed by Mrs Firkins, who placed a tray containing a silver tea service on the table. The old woman moved stiffly, setting out cups and plates and humming tunelessly to herself.

His nurse, Fleur had said. He smiled at her, wishing he could remember her from when he was young. 'Do you recall the day the sketches were made for that portrait?'

Mrs Firkins nodded her head and grinned gummily. 'That I do, Master Remy. You wanted to go to the pond to fish for tadpoles that day. You had a right old tantrum when I wouldn't let you. In the end I threatened to put you over my knee and paddle the devil from the seat of your breeches with a stick.'

'Ah yes ... I remember it,' he said, and glanced at Fleur. She'd seen right through his manoeuvre and was frowning at him. He grinned and blew her a kiss. The way the colour heightened in her face was a delight.

After Mrs Firkins had gone, he asked her, 'Have our families known each other long?'

There was a slight hesitation in her voice and she lowered her glance to her lap. 'We knew each other as children. You visited Stratton House with your father on occasion.'

'I should remember that.'

'Should remember what?' Macy said, coming into the room.

'Visiting Stratton House as a child.'

'Why would you want to remember when Leland and I tried to hang you from the branch of a tree?'

Remy started and his tea slopped into the

saucer. He placed it on the table. 'My father was buying a horse from yours, wasn't he? And Fleur slid down the bannister to escape her nurse.'

Macy's guffaw rang to the ceiling. 'Yes to the first. As for Fleur sliding down the bannister, that wouldn't surprise me in the least. She always was a determined little brat. A pity her mother died. She would have benefited from a firm hand.'

Macy ducked when she threw a cushion at him. 'I'll remove those stitches from your head in the morning and will leave for Stratton House shortly afterwards. I have some other patients to attend to and should be back just before the wedding. No doubt Lucy will arrange things to her satisfaction. I will just do as I'm told.'

Disappointment filled Remy as he turned to Fleur. 'You didn't tell me you were leaving so soon.'

Fleur's mouth opened as if she'd been about to say something, then she closed it again. She exchanged a meaningful glance with her brother, who said slowly. 'With your permission, Fleur will be staying on. Someone has to look after you.'

'People will talk.'

There was an awkward pause then Macy shrugged. 'Will Lucy be an acceptable chaperone?'

Remy wanted nothing more than to keep

Fleur by his side, but he couldn't bear the thought of making her the centre of a scandal. 'I think not. Lucy is in my employ, I believe.'

'What about the sister of Sir Charles Boney? She lives locally.'

'Certainly not,' Fleur said, her face blanching. 'Catherine will not do. She cannot be trusted to keep Remy's survival a secret.'

Remy gazed from one to the other. 'Why should my survival be kept a secret?'

'We'd prefer you to recover your memory before its loss becomes public knowledge,' she said in desperation. 'Besides, I have heard that Catherine is in London.'

Remy's eyes sharpened. Something was odd about this evasiveness and he intended to get to the bottom of it. 'What is it you're you trying to protect me from?'

She would not meet his eyes, but twisted a ring nervously around her finger. He stared at it – at the ruby, which flashed with fire each time it caught the light.

'I have asked for your hand in marriage, Fleur. You have not answered.' His head was beginning to ache. 'Am I wed to another? Are you?'

'We are both married, Remy,' she blurted out, and gazed at Macy, who nodded. 'The truth is, I'm already your wife and this is my home. It has been for several years.'

'And you chose to keep the fact from me?'

The cup fell from his hand to break into shards on the floor. A pity, it was a pretty thing covered in roses. He rose, embarrassed and dizzy from the anger he felt towards her.

Macy stepped between them. 'It was on my advice, Remy. Being fed such information is not the same as remembering it. If you were fed false facts in your state you might believe it to be the truth.'

Feeling cheated, Remy's vision began to blur. The room canted sideways. Fleur gave a cry of alarm and someone caught him before everything faded.

He woke later. The boy from the portrait was standing by his bed. They observed each other for a few moments, then somebody whispered, 'What are you doing in here, Gerard? Come away now.' The child giggled and scampered from his sight.

Remy smiled, wondering if it was an apparition he'd seen. When he woke the following morning to find a lead soldier on his pillow, he knew the boy had been real.

He thought about the child a lot over the next few days, and he thought about his wife. After a while, he reached certain conclusion.

With Macy gone Fleur did her best to follow her usual routine.

One day, when she was about to exercise

her horse, Remy came into the stables. Without hesitation he made for his own horse. It had begun to move about, restless and eager for exercise, when he'd seen her arrive.

'How did you know the gelding was your usual mount?'

'Is it?' He smiled at her for the first time since Macy had left. 'I hope I can remember how to ride him.'

'Be careful, Remy. He's strong willed and can out run the wind when given his head.' She called Tom over to saddle him.

'I've noticed he follows after you like a faithful dog.'

'He's missed you.' She rubbed her mare's velvety nose. 'He likes our company, I think, but he won't let me ride him. He bucks without warning.'

'Thank you, I'll be prepared for it.' He came to where she stood and gazed down at her. 'I imagine you're wondering if I'm strong enough to ride, my sweet.'

The unexpected endearment, when coupled with his closeness, both disturbed and excited. All she'd felt for him in the past was returning in an arousing combination of senses. She nodded.

'I will not know that until I try, of course. Now seems the right time, when you are with me to pick up the pieces again. Perhaps I should have taken your blood tonic, after all.'

'Perhaps.' She couldn't hold back her

laughter. 'I admit it. It was vile, and you are regaining your strength and health every day without it.'

'To whom does the boy belong?' he asked directly, taking her by surprise.

Fleur considered lying, then decided not to. Their son wasn't a memory because Remy had never known about him. To lie to him when there was so much hope in his eyes seemed cruel.

Her glance engaged his. 'He is our son. He was born when you were abroad and I named him Gerard.'

'After my estranged grandfather?'

So he remembered him as well. 'The earl is no longer hostile towards you and our son also bears your name. When I was informed of your demise I attempted to heal the breach by using your grandfather's name. I needed to ensure our son's future, and wanted him to hear only good things of his father, so he could be proud. The earl is almost housebound now.'

'Do I have a grandmother?'

'Elmira. She is well, but she suffers from stiffness and aching bones in the cool months and cannot get around very well. When you are strong enough we must visit Stragglemarsh with our son. Your grandparents are longing to see you, and they will appreciate being reunited with their great-grandson again.'

'You seem to have kept faith in my survival? Why?'

'I prayed a mistake had been made, and that you were alive and would eventually come back to us.'

'It seems your prayers were answered.' Cupping her face between his hands he kissed her slowly and tenderly, robbing her of the will to move. 'For that I thank you, Fleur. Your words have touched my heart. When we've ridden together I would like to be properly introduced to my son.'

She laid her head against his shoulder. 'I'm sorry I didn't acquaint you with the truth of our relationship.'

Tipping her face up he grinned, whispering. 'The truth of our relationship is still a mystery to me. Perhaps we should become better acquainted later. Our chambers adjoin, do they not?'

She gave a gurgle of laughter as she looked him up and down. His hair had grown into short, tight curls, the lines of his face were sharp blades under the skin.

'Were we well suited?' His expression was intimately personal, bringing a warm bloom to her cheeks.

'You were ... quite the man, Remy. We must do something to help you regain your strength before we...' She shrugged, out of her depth.

He grinned. 'What do you suggest?'

'From now on you must eat everything put in front of you, and you must get adequate rest during the day. Gruff is growing fat on your leftovers.'

Remy's horse thrust its head over his shoulder. Nostrils flaring and teeth bared the gelding snickered loudly. Remy's long fingers folded over its snout. 'Hush, we'll be off soon, so no loutish behaviour in front of the ladies.'

Remy's mount behaved skittishly as it followed after hers. He tried a couple of tricks but Remy was ready for them and brought him easily back under his control. After a while the horse seemed to settle down and it became obvious Remy hadn't forgotten any of his riding skills.

Fleur led them over the hill and along the beach. The tide was out, revealing an expanse of damp, rippled sand. The dinghy Remy had arrived home in must have been carried out to sea, for there was no sign of it now.

On the horizon a ship scooped the wind into its sails, canting to one side with the weight. It seemed odd that something as light and invisible as air could summon up enough strength to disturbed the ocean, drown a ship and blow down the strongest trees.

Accompanied by wheeling seagulls, the ship seemed to be coming nearer. Fleur hoped it wasn't the Royal Navy coming to rob them of livestock again.

Gruff barked impatiently. He had an expectant look on his face and his tail threshed at the air.

She glanced over at Remy. He was watching the ship, his eyes intent. When it turned side on he relaxed. 'It poses no danger, the gun ports are closed.'

She shivered, recalling the Spanish ship which had brought him home, and the menace of those dark, open ports. 'Did you expect it to attack us?'

He shrugged. 'I forgot where I was for a moment,' and although he smiled, the expression in his eyes was troubled when he turned to gaze at her. 'Did I have a telescope with me when I arrived?'

'It's in the library, where you used to keep it before.'

'And where was that?'

'On the bureau in a wooden stand.'

The dog barked again and Remy fondled his ear. 'What is it, Gruff?'

'We usually race along the beach. He never wins, but he enjoys the chase.'

Remy's smile was so much like his old one that she remembered the past too vividly. So much warmth flooded through her she forgot to caution him when he said, 'Then let's do so. My body is restless with the lack of exercise.' He had gone before she could stop him.

Remy had already begun to tire when she caught him up halfway along the beach. With

her mare at full gallop and at considerable risk to herself, she reach out and grabbed his mount's rein, gradually slowing the pace to a halt. She tried not to let her anger show. 'Your strength must be conserved and built on, not expended in one rush.'

He leaned forward to catch his breath, muttering, 'I shouldn't have given the damned animal its head. The loss of my strength is frustrating. Noah has devised some exercises to improve it, but I haven't practised enough for them to take effect.'

She wouldn't allow him to feel sorry for himself. 'Be glad you have your life. You are not long out of your bed. Only time will heal you now.'

'And my mind?'

'You remember more things each day.'

'But they're of no significance. They are fragments sent to tantalize ... of people, of places, smells and names. They mean nothing to me. All I can remember clearly is being in the prison.'

She led them up over the dune into the hills where the wind was less boisterous. There, where a ridge of chalk divided the coarse skin of coastal grass, she dismounted. 'Come, we will sit in the lea of this stone and you will tell me of the prison.'

Remy dismounted and angled himself to the ground, knees and elbows stark shapes under his topcoat. He stared at the house

for a long time, his eyes bleak and retrospective. She didn't interrupt his thoughts, just watched the play of emotions come and go on his face.

Eventually he said, 'At first it was hard. My cell was four paces wide and six paces long. I shared it with five others at first. They tortured us on a regular basis. The others died from their injuries. They left one of the corpses in the cell until the stench became unbearable.'

She shuddered wanting to block her ears from the horror with her hands. But instinctively she knew he needed to unburden himself.

'The other prisoners were British marines. The guards were never sure whether I was Spanish or not, which might have caused my punishment to be a little more lenient. I was wearing a British uniform jacket when I was captured.'

'What were you doing there?'

'Carrying information back to the fleet. I'd be put ashore with the Spanish exchange prisoners, collect information about troop numbers or gun positions, or anything else that seemed useful to us, then I'd strip a uniform from one of the British dead and smuggle myself back with the next exchange.'

'You were a spy?'

A smile touched his mouth. 'The word sounds too heroic for what I actually did.' He

hesitated, sucking in a deep breath. 'The last thing I remember of my life before prison was of standing on a beach at the *rendezvous* waiting to be picked up. There were bodies all around me. One of them stood up and shot me.' His forehead furrowed. 'I knew the man.'

'Who was he, Remy?'

'That, I cannot remember. When I woke I was in the cell. Time seemed to stand still. By day I broke rocks in a quarry. I was nobody, an object of the guards' derision. They set out to break me. I knew if I told them the truth it would be the end, so I spoke and thought only in Spanish. Then I forgot the truth and it became easier. I didn't know what I was doing there, who I was or whether I was Spanish or not. Eventually someone came to claim me.'

When he fell silent she took his hands in hers. They were cold. 'What kept you alive?'

'A vision used to come to me, of a house set in a green hill. I didn't know where it was, but I knew I belonged there.'

'And now you're here.'

'And have found more than I dreamed of.'

She lifted one of his hands, turning it palm inward so she could kiss it. He pulled her against him so she was nestled on his chest. His chin rested on the top of her head and his breath stirred through her hair. 'You were right, Fleur. I should feel grateful to have my life back intact, for it has never seemed so important to me as it does now.'

Gruff came to flop beside them. His shaggy head rested in Remy's lap, his tail thumped on Fleur's thighs. When she placed a hand over the rope of hair to stop its movement the dog gave her a reproachful look followed by a resigned sigh.

They cuddled together in a comfortable silence, until Remy gave a shiver. 'I'm growing cold, but I think I've built up enough strength to convey myself home.'

She rose and pulled him to his feet. 'When we reach the house you will rest and refresh yourself before I bring Gerard to see you.' When he smiled and looked as though he was about to argue, she placed a finger across his lips. 'You're a stranger to our son. I need time to prepare him.'

Later, she said to Gerard, 'Remember the times I took you to your papa's room and told you he might come home one day.'

Gerard nodded, his dark, solemn eyes gazing into hers.

'Your Papa is here now, resting in that chamber I showed you. Later, I will take you to visit him for he's eager to see you.'

'Papa?' His mouth lifted in a smile and he giggled, saying imperiously, 'Put me down, mama.' He scampered off to snatch up a toy horse he'd been playing with.

She discovered Lucy explaining Gerard's schedule to the new nursery maid, a comfortably built woman who'd been employed by Hamish McDuff. The steward had told her that Rose came with good references. Fleur had not quite taken to her as yet.

'How are you getting on with my son, Rose?'

She bobbed a curtsey. 'He's a lively little lad, My Lady, but a good boy for all that.'

'I'll be taking him to visit his papa in an hour or so.'

The woman looked shocked. 'I understood your husband to be dead.'

Fleur blessed her staff for keeping her secret so well. 'He was badly wounded, and it turned out he was being held prisoner by the Spanish. Now he's home and being nursed back to health. You would oblige me by not mentioning the fact outside of these walls, for his memory of the past is impaired and he needs to regain it before he ventures abroad.'

Rose lowered her eyes. 'As you wish, My Lady.'

'Make sure Gerard wears a clean woollen smock over his dress for the visit, and his hair is tidied.'

'That I will, My Lady. But now it's time for his rest.'

But Gerard had gone, making use of the turned backs to escape the nursery. 'Come back,' Fleur called as she saw his small figure turn a corner at the end of a corridor. For a small boy he could run remarkably fast.

His laughter floated back to her. Picking up her skirts she chased after him. He reached Remy's chamber before she did. Both hands grasped the knob and turned it. The door swung open.

'*Papa!*' he yelled and giving her a triumphant look, disappeared through the door.

'Gerard?' There was a catch in Remy's voice, a sense of wonder, '*My son!*'

When she reached the scene it was to see Gerard leap into Remy's outstretched arms. She held her breath as Gerard examined his father's face. His small hands touched Remy's cheeks, his nose and his lips. Remy's hair was patted. '*Papa, papa, papa,*' Gerard whispered, as if tasting the word on his tongue. He was smiling.

So was Remy.

The two profiles looked exactly alike. Two dark heads regarded the other. Then the foreheads came together and they turned towards her cheek to cheek. Two slow smiles, so alike, brought tears to her eyes and a choking sensation to her throat.

'Thank you for this, most precious of gifts, Fleur. You have given me a future to live for.'

The love she experienced reached out to

surround them, but all she could do was scold them through her tears. 'Don't either of you ever do what you're told? You're both supposed to be resting.'

FOURTEEN

Could this laughing man in uniform really be her younger brother? Fleur thought wonderingly. He was taller and broader than Macy and Leland, and twice as handsome.

'Cris,' she exclaimed. 'I hardly recognized you!' She threw herself into his arms, hugging him tight and scolding him all the while. 'How dare you run off to sea without telling me? I swear I'll never forgive you, you with your weak chest and hardly out of the sickbed. I hope the Admiralty has been looking after you or I'll have something to say to them.'

Running out of breath and stopping to replenish it, she stepped back and took a good look at him. She was astonished by the change in him. 'You look so handsome in that uniform, Cris. I wager women must fall at your feet every time you step ashore. Be careful not to associate with those women who frequent the waterfront bars. They are not to be trusted.'

His grin spread from ear to ear. 'I most certainly will be careful.'

She gave him a sharp look. 'I swear, you have turned out to be as incorrigible as your two brothers. Are you happy?'

He laughed. 'As happy as a bilge rat. And what of you, Fleur?'

'What a horribly vulgar expression.' She couldn't help but smile, though. 'Did you know I have a son?'

His face was deeply tanned from the sea air, his eyes crinkled at the corners when he smiled. 'Yes. There was a letter waiting for me from Leland when I stepped ashore. He said Marguerite is expecting another child.'

'So soon? Marguerite has not long been delivered of their second son.'

'Leland said he has enough heirs now, and if this one's born healthy it will be their last.'

She opened her mouth and shut it again. The thought of Marguerite being wed only for breeding was abhorrent. Women had very little say in the matter. It was a matter of luck if one acquired a husband of good nature and sensitivity. She wondered if her sister-in-law had ever had dreams of love, and sighed.

'What is it, Fleur?'

'Nothing, Cris. Just womanly thinking. It's nice to have a child to love. Perhaps they'll have a daughter this time.' She hooked her arm through his, leading him into the house. 'Are you staying for Macy's wedding?'

'Macy's getting married?' He whistled. 'I'll be damned ... who's the heroine brave enough to take him on?'

'A woman of my household called Lucy Yates. I'll introduce you to her later.'

Drawn by the commotion Remy came into the hall. His eyes narrowed in thought for a moment. The name seemed to be dredged from the depths of his mind, shook free with a toss of his head and triumphant glance. 'Crispen?'

Crispen appeared stunned. 'You got back all right then? Thank God! I heard you'd taken a slug in the head. I came to offer Fleur my condolences.' A broad grin split Crispen's face and he slapped Remy on the shoulder. 'You damned fraud, Remy. I wasted time saying prayers for your soul when the Devil would have the stronger case for possession of it.'

Remy's laugh sounded a trifle reluctant. 'It seems the Devil didn't want it either. For that I'm grateful. Now I'm home each new day is so very precious to me.'

'We'll have to celebrate your escape over a bottle of wine and talk about old times.'

Remy fingered the scar on his head. 'I did stop a bullet. Macy dug it out, but I can't remember much. He said my memory might return one day.'

'*Lucifer's oath!* You allowed my brother to butcher you?' Crispen chuckled. 'I watched him dissect a rabbit when I was a child. It ended up with more bones than it started with.' Pity coloured his eyes. 'Perhaps you'll allow me to remind you of some of what's gone before.'

Fleur gave an imperceptible shake of her head. 'Macy said–'

'Enough!' Remy's eyes flicked her way, bland and impenetrable. 'Crispen is hardly likely to fill my mind with false memories, is he? And I think I'm well enough to make decisions about my own welfare now.'

Infuriating creature! 'You might be well enough, but do you think you're old enough?' she said tartly. Gathering her skirts together she swept past him, the dignity of her exit ruined by his hand descending on her backside on the way past. When she rounded on him, his smile was so warm and personal her breath hissed in her throat and she instantly forgot what she'd been about to say.

'Behave yourself, woman,' he said with soft menace. 'Go and tell a servant to bring some refreshment for our guest. We'll be in the library.'

'He isn't a guest he's my brother.'

'All the more reason to attend to his needs then.' Stooping a little he kissed her mouth, then turned her round and sent her on her way.

Knowing he had a family seemed to give

Remy purpose. Every day he grew stronger and healthier, until he was almost back to his old self – except for his lack of memory and his habit of retiring early and falling straight to sleep.

As a result they'd not attempted to resume their personal relationship. Knowing he needed rest more than anything else, Fleur didn't do anything to encourage the resumption of their physical relationship either. But her body was surging with long dormant urges, and the yearning to hold another child against her breast was not the least of them.

Crispen spent a week with them before leaving for Stratton House. He intended to return with Leland for Macy's wedding, after which he'd rejoin his ship, which was undergoing repair in Poole.

What had passed between her husband and brother on the day of their reunion was not divulged to her. But Remy was pensive for some time after Cris departed.

She and Remy fell into the habit of an early morning ride together. Afterwards Remy spent some of the day with Hamish McDuff. Although he didn't discuss it with her, she knew Hamish was keeping him fully informed about estate matters, and teaching him as much as he could absorb.

In the late afternoons Remy joined her in the company of their son. Gerard thrived on the attention and cried bitterly when they left him. Of late, he'd displayed some bruising on his body.

Fleur wondered about this. Eventually she brought it to the attention of Lucy. They had always been closer than mistress and servant. Now, with her wedding to Macy drawing near Lucy had become more of a friend than an employee.

Lucy's chamber was a small room off the nursery. It was lent privacy by a curtain suspended across the doorway. The room had a high set window and was furnished with a narrow bed, a small chest of drawers and a rack on which to hang her gowns.

Two gowns hung there. They were old. One grey and one blue, both faded and patched. Lucy was wearing her best gown today, a faded brown taffeta with a pleated frill at the sleeves. Surely she was not going to be wed in it. A white apron was tied over a top – something that had prevented her from noticing Lucy's shabbiness.

Perhaps she couldn't afford another gown. Fleur frowned at the thought, but brought her mind back to Gerard's bruises. 'Does Rose physically chastise him?'

'I've not observed any ill-treatment from her towards him, though she's impatient when he misbehaves. She's aloof towards the rest of the household staff and not very popular.'

'But you rub along with her all right?'

Lucy shrugged. 'She questions my authority at times, when she displays an insolent manner. I believe she'll be happy to see the back of me so she can have sole charge of Gerard. There is something about her I cannot quite put my finger on.' Lucy slowly shook her head. 'Perhaps I'm too critical because I must hand Gerard over into her care. Still, she doesn't seem suited to her employment.'

'How does my son like her?'

'He's resentful with her, but it's not entirely her fault. Gerard has been with me since he was an infant. He's used to me and is being difficult because he knows I'm leaving.' Her eyes took on a tearful expression. 'Truly, I'm going to miss him.'

Fleur gave her a fond hug. 'And we will miss you, Lucy. I expect Macy will command all of your attention. He is not a man to allow himself to be overlooked, nor will he take no for an answer unless he wants no for an answer. His ardour towards you has surprised me. Hardly a week passes without some token of his regard being delivered.'

The colour in Lucy's face deepened, but she managed a grin. 'He's sent me enough gloves and lace handkerchiefs to last a lifetime, ribbons and feathers to trim the hundred hats I do not possess, and poetry books enough to start a school. He's so sweet. Listen to this.'

Sweet! Fleur thought, as Lucy slipped her hand inside her bodice and came out with a sheet of paper tied in a red ribbon. Surely Lucy's opinion of him must be coloured by affection if she carries it so close to her heart.

Lucy cleared her throat and giggled. 'Macy wrote this himself.'

Hush, through the window flies the dove.
Coming to thee, my sweetest love.
Around thee, folds his snowy wing.
Peace, my angel. Let me sing.

'He equates himself with a dove?' Fleur laughed. 'My brother is as unsubtle as a mule is stubborn, but he's determined to stand high in your regard. I warn you though, you will regret it if you allow him to sing one note.'

'He has always stood high in my regard. I liked him the first time we met, and my affection for him grew over time. I was a little taken aback when he asked me to wed him because I thought him socially too far above me. His behaviour toward me has always been more than circumspect. I was honoured he regarded me as a suitable companion, but I do not fool myself that he's in love with me.'

'You think not? You have my brother running around in circles. You're perfect for him and I'm so glad you are going to become part of my family.'

Lucy gave a little smile. 'I'm looking forward to becoming his wife. This afternoon I'm going into Dorchester to pick up the marriage gift I bought for him. It's being engraved.'

'What is this gift?'

'A watch and pair case.' She bit her lip. 'It's similar to one he took a fancy to. I couldn't afford the more expensive one so I hope he likes it.'

'Macy will love it. He's never craved riches or power so will appreciate only the thought behind the gift.' She beamed a smile at her. 'What of your gown, Lucy? Do you have one suitable to be wed in?'

She shrugged. 'The watch was a little more expensive than I expected, and I cannot afford a new one. I thought ... perhaps I could buy something suitable from a market stall.'

Fleur nodded, but her gaze quickly ran over her son's nurse. Lucy was larger in the bosom and hips, but they were about the same height. Now was as good a time as any to purchase a wedding gift for the couple. She could do better than allow her beloved Lucy to wear another's cast-offs, even her own. She intended to have a word with Macy about the state of his future wife's wardrobe, for such domestic detail wouldn't enter his head, and Lucy was not the type to ask for anything.

'Meet me in the drawing room in half an

hour. We'll take the cart and go shopping together. Macy's abode lacks everything but the basics for his own needs and I've decided to buy a dinner service for you both. You shall choose the design.'

Clothed in a worn brown cloak, Lucy presented herself on time.

'You won't object if I accompany you,' Remy drawled from the doorway. 'It's about time my survival was made public. I've told Tom his services will not be required. Noah has business in town and will accompany us.'

When their eyes met she smiled at the challenge in his. 'My Lord, your company will be most welcome, but only if you can stand patiently whilst we women dither over our purchases. We shall need a strong pair of arms to lift the many boxes into the cart.'

A faint smile acknowledged her mischief. 'Ride with me a little way Fleur. Lucy can take the reins of the cart.'

So they set out on a fine, but cold day, with herself seated sideways on the horse in front of him, Lucy going on ahead and the taciturn Noah astride a horse at the rear. Remy's proximity was disconcerting, as was his smile.

'You're looking almost like your old self, Remy.'

'I must admit, I'm pleased my clothing now fits and my hair has grown some length. I fatigue too easily still, and regret the need to fall asleep so quickly.' His mouth quirked into a smile and his eyes held hers as he murmured, 'Sometimes I dream you're in my bed, then I wake with an urgent need to discover you are not.'

She couldn't fail to grasp the invitation in his words, but remained offhand. 'If you're patient, perhaps one day you'll find me there. But not at the moment for your health is of paramount importance. It's obvious nature intends you to sleep.'

He raised an eyebrow. 'And if I cannot be patient?'

'You must learn to be. Perhaps you should romance me with soft words, gifts and stolen kisses,' she cooed, her smile provocative as she recalled Macy's contribution to romancing Lucy.

He chuckled. His glance went to her mouth, lingering there as he murmured, 'You're the very devil of a woman to deal with, Fleur.'

'I know. Had you taken my blood tonic you might not have needed to sleep so much.' Lifting her chin so her mouth was an inviting inch away from his she was rewarded with the most ardent of kisses, and a nip to her bottom lip that sent an arrow of desire to her core.

When he murmured, 'Have I always been in love with you like this?' she amended her earlier decision to make him wait.

The marketplace was bustling. People stared at Remy, but although they respectfully doffed their hats before gathering in little bunches to gossip, nobody addressed him directly.

'I expected attention, but why are they staring so?' he muttered, beads of sweat breaking out on his forehead despite the coolness of the day. His face showed the strain of the unwelcome attention and she realized how much courage he'd needed to come here this day.

'It's because you're back from the dead. See how they smile and nod when we pass. They mean you no harm, so stop glowering and smile in return. The novelty of seeing you back from the dead will soon wear off and someone will talk to you.'

'Then you'd better stay by my side, for the faces are unknown to me.'

The first to speak was Farmer Blaggs, who removed his cap and held respectfully against his chest. 'If I may be so bold, My Lord. It be nice to see you back amongst us hale and hearty.'

'Thank you.' Remy sent her a desperate look.

'Bessie sends her best wishes, Mr Blaggs. Your grandson, Tom, said to tell you not to bother entering your pig in the spring fair because the one he's preparing is being fed on his mother's cooking, and is unbeatable.'

'Is it now?' Blaggs shook his head and grinned. 'The cocky young varmint. I'll give him pig when I see him at the fair, you see if I don't. My pig is an aristocrat and descended from a prize sow belonging to the earl hisself. Infirm as he is at the moment, his lordship is sending me instructions on how to feed the porker.'

Remy gave him an interested look. 'Is he indeed. What are these instructions?'

'I can't say, My Lord. The old earl sent me a message via his steward. Now don't you go telling anyone, he says. If it wins I'll give you a guinea.'

'But I'm his grandson. He didn't mean me.'

Blaggs grinned. 'Good reasoning, My Lord, but I wasn't born yesterday. If you want to place a wager on the outcome, Rob's the one to see.'

'G'day, Mr Blaggs,' Remy said, smiling to himself as they moved on. They weaved through the market towards the shops, with only the occasional cue needed. Remy picked up on them quickly, so there were no awkward gaps in introductions or any explaining to do.

Whilst Lucy entered a small jewellers and Remy decided to explore a book shop, Fleur headed for a dressmaking establishment. From the small selection of assembled gowns on display she selected a pretty design of blue flowered brocade. To wear with it, a coat of deeper blue velvet edged with rabbit fur. There was a matching muff to complete the ensemble.

Carrying the box she went in search of Remy, only to be brought to a halt by the sight of Charles and Catherine Boney. Although in full view of them, their backs were turned as they gazed into the jeweller's window. Fleur prayed Lucy would not call to her as she backed hurriedly away.

Remy chose that moment to emerge from the bookshop. He smiled when he saw her, called her name and hurried across the road.

Charles and Catherine saw him at the same time, and turned to intercept him. Obviously not recognizing them, Remy sidestepped the pair and came to where she stood, relieving her of her burden.

Charles and Catherine hurried after him. Charles gave a strained chuckle while Catherine's lips were pulled into a fixed smile. 'Remy, old friend. We'd heard of your survival and were about to call on you. We'd also been told that you'd lost your memory, Catherine has decided not to feel slighted at being ignored.'

'I beg your pardon.' Remy gazed with uncertainty from one to the other. He gave a slight start and the colour drained from his face. His fingers strayed to the scar on his head.

Fleur slid a supporting hand under his elbow. She knew he'd recognized Charles but his reaction had startled her. Charles seemed to have noticed nothing untoward.

Strangely, Noah lingered nearby, staring into a milliner's window, where hats were on display. His hand was inside his coat and she caught the glimpse of metal. A pistol? A chill ran through her as it took her a moment to realize he was watching their reflections in the window. Had Noah been sent by the earl to watch over Remy, or did he mean him harm?

She slid between him and her husband and caught his eye. He gave her a faint smile, putting her mind at rest.

Remy's eyes narrowed slightly and his natural charm asserted itself when Fleur didn't introduce them. He smiled. 'Alas, my memory is a little faulty. Perhaps you'd introduce us, Fleur.'

He'd recognized them, she knew it. So why was he denying it?

Reluctantly, Fleur did as asked, saving a glower for Catherine when she smiled sweetly at Remy and trilled, 'I'm so glad you're back amongst us. Life has been extremely dull without our regular little social gatherings.'

'My health has not recovered enough for

me to entertain in the evenings, as yet, I'm afraid.'

Hah! At least he hadn't fallen for that obvious ruse.

Fleur's triumph was short-lived when Remy lifted Catherine's gloved hand to his lips and bestowed a kiss upon it. 'For me, life has been anything but dull of late, but you must call on us one afternoon to remind me of these things. My mind is a blank page eager to be written upon where the past is concerned.'

No! Fleur wanted to scream out. This is the man who threatened our son. Instead, she asked Charles pointedly, 'How did you learn of Remy's return and his memory loss?'

For a moment he gazed at her obviously nonplussed, then his eyes narrowed in a most unfriendly manner. 'Much as you try to keep these things secret, people will talk and word eventually gets out. Had I known of his predicament sooner I could have called on him and filled in some gaps.' His cold eyes held a warning. 'Or were you worried in case I did, dearest Fleur?'

A glance towards Noah showed him still vigilant.

'Of course she was worried,' Remy said. 'My doctor advised otherwise, lest false memory be fed to me.'

Charles sniffed. 'Since we've been friends since before your marriage, who but the three of us could judge whether the memories be true or false?'

He had forgotten Simon Ackland.

'And to suggest we would feed you with falsity when Fleur is well aware we were friends long before you wed her, suggests she has something to hide. Who was this doctor ... her brother Macy?'

'It was Macy,' Remy said, his jaw tightening as if displeased by the implied criticism. 'I think very highly of his skill and count him as a particular friend of mine.'

Two pairs of grey eyes flicked accusingly her way.

She smiled thinly at them. 'I'm sure my brother would prefer to answer any charges you wish to bring against him personally.'

Catherine's lip curled. 'After the beating he subjected my brother to?'

'I noticed you did not mention Simon Ackland as part of your earlier circle,' Fleur murmured. 'Have you forgotten him so soon? I believe you played a heroic part in Simon's death, Charles.'

Catherine exchanged a glance with her brother, then dabbed a handkerchief to the corner of her eyes, 'Poor, dear Simon. His death was such a shock I asked Charles not to mention his name in my presence. The dreadful event occurred just as we were about to become engaged.'

'Strange ... Simon did not mention such

news the last time I saw him. In fact, he indicated you were *involved* with the Earl of Northhaven.'

Charles slid his hand inside his jacket. Metal glinted.

Beside her, Remy's arm twitched as he flexed his fingers. Noah stepped forward and relieved her of her packages, forming a barrier between herself and the pair.

Fleur let out a breath when Charles consulted a silver pocket watch. She couldn't help wondering whom he'd cheated it out of.

Catherine looked openly hostile. 'One should not listen to gossip. We were socially acquainted, that's all.'

'One would not have to if another did not spread falsehoods,' Fleur said sweetly.

Charles gazed meanly into her eyes. 'Simon's death was most unfortunate, my dear. No doubt his poor mother grieves for her only son. She doted on him, so will be inconsolable in her loss, I expect.'

Just as she knew this was a threat, she knew with certainty that Charles had murdered Simon Ackland. Fear sprang into her heart as she thought of Gerard ... and how could she warn Remy to beware?

She gently squeezed her husband's hand when Lucy emerged from the shop, thankful for a reason to make an escape. 'You must excuse us now, we have to choose a wedding gift for my brother and his bride before we return home.'

To her relief the pair immediately took their leave. Noah moved away.

Remy had missed nothing. 'You dislike each other. Why is that?'

Fleur snorted. She could give him a thousand reasons why they didn't like each other. Each would sound irrational and she didn't want to burden him with worry. Instead, she told him. 'Charles is a gambler and opportunist. You nearly lost Rosehill to him once and you told me you vowed never to take a wager from him again.' She didn't tell him of her own unfortunate wager with Charles, even though the outcome had been resolved before any harm had been done.

'And you fear I might break that vow.'

'Yes, but only because you're unaware of making it.'

'Now you've reminded me, I promise to keep it.' He lifted her hand to his lips and smiled. 'Is that all?'

She engaged his eyes. 'Why did you pretend you didn't recognize them?'

'Was it that obvious? I remembered they were opportunists in the past. It seems I was very young then.'

'And Simon, do you remember him?'

Pain filled his eyes. 'How did he die?'

'He was shot through the head. Charles was with him at the time. I believe he may have been involved in his death.' Anxious now, she gazed into his eyes. 'Instinct tells me we cannot trust the man. You will take all care, won't you, my Remy?'

'My dearest Fleur,' and his smile was a tender caress, 'I beg you not to worry about me. It seems I have Noah to protect me.'

So he'd noticed that too. But she knew she would worry, despite that.

Later that night, Fleur snuffed the candle and slipped into bed beside her husband. Lying on his back in a deep sleep, his breath was an even whisper of sound.

She settled herself comfortably against his warmth, her arm across his chest, and snuggled her head against his shoulder.

Soon, she slept as deeply as him. The clock struck midnight. The moon moved into the frame of the window, sending a beam of light to shine across their faces. Remy turned towards her. She snuggled closer, her silk chemise sliding between their bodies like the caress of warm water.

Gradually, awareness came to her. The warm smell of their flesh tantalised her nostrils. His was spiced with warm sandalwood. Her breasts began to tingle, as sensitised beyond measure they brushed against his chest. Sensing the increase of tension in his body she knew he'd woken too.

Pressure increased against the apex of her thighs and she grew moist. She allowed her hand to drift down between them. Her fingers brushed against the silky skin of his rampant maleness in a teasing way, bringing it to nudge hard and pulsing against her palm.

When he swooped in a jagged breath she opened her eyes and smiled, the seductive power inside her a potent and powerful force that would not be denied.

A shaft of moonlight held them in its powerful aura. His eyes were liquid dark, absorbing her thoughts. They gazed at each other for a long time, hardly breathing, their bodies separating into thousands of tiny cravings. She made a tiny mew of supplication in her throat.

His smile was an enigma, his eyes turbulent with the urgency of his passion. A finger drifted over the curve of her mouth, making her tremble.

Tangling a fist in her hair he eased her head back and his tongue sought the hollow at the base of her throat.

FIFTEEN

On the day of Macy and Lucy's wedding the sky was overcast. The only people of the household not attending were Mrs Firkins, Rose Hardwick and Gerard.

Bessie had created a splendid feast of cold meats, pies and pastries, which surpassed those of Christmas and New Year. It was laid out and ready in the dining hall.

The dining hall had been made festive for the occasion with garlands of ivy and holly. Fires burned in the main rooms and were stoked up with a large, fragrant logs added just before they left for the church.

The onset of severely cold and wet weather had driven Mrs Firkins to her bed with an attack of rheumatism so severe her joints creaked when she tried to move.

Rose had informed Fleur earlier that day that Gerard was suffering from a mild fever. She suggested he was sickening for a cold.

'He'll be better off left in the warmth of the nursery than taken to some draughty church,' she said. 'The dust will irritate his throat and make him cough.'

Fleur surprised a sly look on her face. When she gazed sharply at her, the woman dropped her eyes. She decided to check on Gerard's condition for herself. When she saw the red patches on his cheeks and the tears gleaming in his eyes she was inclined to agree with Rose. He seemed lethargic and sleepy.

She hugged him tight, telling him to be good and promising they'd be back in a little while. When he snivelled and said he didn't like Rose, Fleur decided she might get rid of the woman and find someone more motherly to take charge of her son.

The church was small and half-filled with only immediate family, servants and some of Macy's acquaintances. Lucy had nobody but herself to invite. The bridal pair hadn't wanted a fuss made, preferring a simple celebration.

Fleur's three brothers stood side-by-side, tall, well built and handsome. Just seeing them altogether like this filled Fleur's heart full of pride.

Crispen drew the eye in his uniform. Leland was splendid in a blue striped jacket and dark blue breeches. Macy wore a new suit in his usual black. The red and black striped waistcoat under his cutaway jacket was triumphantly flamboyant for him.

Macy was completely relaxed. It was Leland who seemed preoccupied as he shuffled from one foot to the other.

Fleur blew her brothers a kiss then blinked back her tears when they all smiled at the same time. She slipped into a pew next to Marguerite, who looked pale and pinch-faced sour.

Remy escorted Lucy to the altar, glowing, and beautiful in her blue ensemble. Macy's face lit up at the sight of her and Leland grinned as he caught her eye. My big, tough brother is in love, Fleur thought, and bubbled with joy for them both.

When Remy joined her they exchanged a

301

smile of new awareness and entwined hands. Marguerite sniffed and cried throughout the service. Instinctively, Fleur knew she was crying for herself instead of the beautiful emotion evoked by the exchange of wedding vows.

Afterwards, she drew Margeurite aside, concern on her face. 'What's amiss, Marguerite. Are you feeling unwell?'

Bitterly, she said. 'I've just learned my husband has a mistress.'

Shock hit Fleur like a wave crashing over her. She floundered her way to the top. 'Surely you are mistaken.'

'Why is it that the Russell family support each other come what may? You never see any wrong in each other, do you? I saw them with my own eyes, Fleur. The trollop has a house in Dorchester where she entertains my husband. Don't tell me you didn't know about it?'

'It's not a subject Leland would discuss with me. Oh, Marguerite, are you quite certain it wasn't something totally innocent you saw?'

'There's nothing innocent about my husband kissing a woman on the mouth in public. There's nothing innocent about two daughters who call him papa. Besides, he admitted it when I charged him with it.'

'Admitted it? He has daughters?' Fleur didn't know which surprised her most.

'He said he knew her before he wed me – that the woman and her children were none of my business. He said I'd have to be content with being the mother of his heirs, and if I didn't like it I could go back to live with my family. Oh, the humiliation of it. And to think I've been jealous of *you* all these years.'

Fleur's eyes widened. 'Why would you be jealous of me?'

'Oh, don't play the innocent with me,' Margeurite hissed loudly. 'Leland dotes on you. Crook your little finger and he goes running to your side. All your brothers do. However, you're not entirely to blame for his constant absences. Between you and *her*, I'm left with the crumbs.'

'I'm sure that's not true.'

Her voice rose. 'Not true! Leland offers me no endearment, makes no pretence of affection. I thought things would improve between us once I'd persuaded him to send you away, but you put down roots within a comfortable distance for him to reach.'

Margeurite glanced at Remy, the expression in her eyes surprisingly malicious. 'I wouldn't be at all surprised if the abduction was arranged between you. There's still lots of talk about your marriage, and it's started again since Remy showed himself in public. Some say the marriage wasn't legal,' Margeurite flung at her. 'That you're little more than his mistress.'

The ground seemed to shake beneath Fleur's feet, leaving her knees trembling and weak. Appalled, she whispered, 'I beg of you, keep your voice down. Of course it was legal. Our uncle, who is an ordained bishop, conducted the marriage between us.'

Marguerite smirked. 'But it didn't take place in a church, did it? I believe marriages must be performed in a church to be considered legal.'

Marguerite stopped talking when Leland emerged from the church and gave her a hard stare. His dislike for his wife was all too apparent. Fleur's pity for her was replaced by the beginnings of a similar dislike. The woman was full of bitterness. She soured everything she touched. But if Marguerite was right, Gerard was an illegitimate child who had no claim to anything – not even his father's name.

Leland came to where they stood, his glance raking over her ashen face. She was trembling, but whether from cold or shock she couldn't tell.

'What's she been saying to you?'

Marguerite's lips pursed. 'I've told her the truth, that her marriage is a sham.'

Leland's fingers closed around his wife's arm. In a low voice, he said, 'I swear. If I hear you repeat any more malicious gossip I'll petition for a divorce. Fleur's had enough to cope with of late.'

'And do you think I haven't, learning about that sow you service and her two bastards?' Marguerite said shrilly. 'When I find out who she is I'll confront her with her sins.'

'I will not allow you to spoil my brother's wedding.' Set faced, Leland grasped his wife by the elbow and marched her towards the carriage. In a moment she was shut inside and the vehicle was on its way back to Stratton House.

'How much of what she said is true?' Fleur whispered, when he returned to her side.

He didn't bother to lie. 'It's true ... I do have a mistress. I have known her a long time and over the years she has become more than that to me. Her name is Sylvane Dumfries.' He gave a tender smile. 'We have two daughters. One of them is the image of you.'

Shocked though she was, Fleur took his tense hands in hers. 'I should like to meet my nieces. How much do you care for this woman, Leland?'

'More than my life.' He shrugged. 'I should have ignored her lack of social standing and wed her in the first place. To hell with the scandal.'

She trembled at the thought of her own status. 'What of my marriage to Remy ... was it legal?'

'I don't know. I insisted it be recorded in the parish register.' He appeared troubled. 'I

305

intend to find out. The next time I go to London I'll call on our uncle and discuss it with him. I'm sure it will be a simple matter to put things right and bring an end to the gossip.'

She glanced at Remy, who was was emerging from the church followed by Noah. A lump settled in her throat, followed by an irrational burst of fear. She whispered. 'What if ... he doesn't want to wed me when he finds out?'

Leland's face set in a stubborn mould. 'Intuition tells me he's a man of honour. If not...'

She placed a hand on his arm. 'Please don't go any further. I don't want an unhappy marriage like yours. I love Remy. He's never questioned the validity of our marriage, and he may never discover it's illegal. I want him to care for me in the same way I care for him. He has said he loves me, but when driven by desire men's declarations are often suited to the occasion.'

Leland smiled. 'Why would a husband tell his wife he loved her if he didn't mean it?'

He heart gave a little lift. 'Still, I would rather remain his mistress than do anything to jeopardise our relationship, or his peace of mind.'

His hand gently cupped her face. 'With tongues like Marguerite's wagging in the district how long do you think he'll remain in ignorance?' He lowered his voice as Remy started towards them. 'He has the responsibility of estate and will one day be The Earl of Blessingham. You must make sure your son is legitimised else he'll have no claim.'

'Promise me you'll do nothing. Trust your instinct about him.'

'I'll promise to trust my instinct,' Leland growled, all bristles and menace. 'But the day of reckoning will come if he fails you, of that you can be sure.'

Damn you, Leland! She thought as he brushed past Remy with a curt nod and headed towards the bridal pair. Why can't you leave well alone?

She retracted the notion as soon as they reached the house. As they walked through the door Lucy gave a cry and ran towards the bottom of the staircase. Macy was not long after her.

They stood around anxiously as Macy examined Mrs Firkins. Blood matted her hair and her breathing bubbled and frothed. She was alive, but only just.

'Master Remy,' she whispered, and when he bent to catch her words, said just one name.

'Charles Boney? What of him?'

Fear punched Fleur in the midriff. 'Gerard!' she cried out, and pushing through them raced up the stairs to the nursery floor. The nursery was empty; the fireplace contained a heap of cold ashes. Throwing open a cupboard she saw Rose's bag and belongings gone. Ashen-faced and trembling she made her way back to the top of the stairs, gazing at Remy in despair. She hardly recognized her own voice when she choked out. 'Charles has taken our son. Rose Hardwick must have been in league with him.'

Remy's expression remained surprisingly calm as he joined her, and then drew her down the stairs to be comforted by Lucy. 'Try and make Mrs Firkins comfortable. They threw her down the stairs and she's in great pain. Macy has given her a large dose of laudanum, but that is all he can do for her. He said she'll not survive for long.'

Striding into the library he returned with a pair of pistols shoved into his belt. 'I'm going after Charles. Noah, you must stay with my wife in case Charles comes back.'

Fleur's three brothers were readying themselves to support him. 'You're not going after him alone,' Macy growled.

It was her husband Fleur went to for mutual comfort. 'He has a head start. The nursery fire is cold so they must have planned it and left some time ago. Take care please, Remy. I don't want to lose you again.'

When he stooped to kiss her she slid the ring he'd given her from her finger to his. 'Wear this, it will bring you luck.'

'The lord of gems,' he whispered. 'It was a birthday gift. My mother said it would protect me from misfortune. How come you by it?'

'You gave it to me on our wedding day.'

He looked at the ring then back at her, his face suddenly remote. 'I remember it now. I wronged you.'Tenderly, he kissed her mouth. 'I will find our son and bring him home to you, Fleur. This I promise.' Then he was gone, her three brothers flanking him as they strode off towards the stables.

She turned to Mrs Firkins, and with tears in her eyes fell to her knees and gathered the woman's head into her lap. How could anyone be so cruel as to throw a frail creature like this down the stairs.

'I tried to stop them,' Mrs Firkins whispered.

Fleur smoothed the matted grey hair back from her forehead. 'Hush, my dear. It was not your fault and you mustn't torture yourself.'

'Master Remy will get him back, you'll see. He'll not let you down.'

'I know he won't. Sleep now,' Fleur soothed.

Mrs Firkins clutched her wrist with surprising strength. 'I want to be buried in my best gown, the one with the lace collar. And I want you to place my silver cross in my hands so the good Lord knows I'm not a sinner.'

'Don't agitate yourself, Mrs Firkins. Try to sleep.'

'It's time to sleep when God's angel comes to claim me. Odd, but I feel no pain now. Promise you will not bury me looking like this. I want to look my best in case little Gerard comes to me. He won't be scared with old Mrs Firkins waiting to greet him at the gate.'

Fleur choked back a sob at the thought. 'I'll lay you out myself, and will carry out your wishes.'

The woman's grip relaxed. 'Ah, but you're a good girl, my bonny. I knowed it as soon as I set my eyes on you.' A few moments later Mrs Firkins breathed her last rattle and her body relaxed.

She seemed to weigh nothing as a couple of the footmen carried her away and laid her on a trestle in a room adjoining the servants' parlour.

Fleur sent one of them off with a message to the undertaker, and another scurrying upstairs to find Mrs Firkins' best gown. Between them, Fleur and Bessie washed and dressed the old women. They placed a sheet under her body and a pillow at her head. Folding her palms together in an attitude of prayer Fleur wound the chain about her hands to keep them in position and placed the silver cross between them. With the strain gone from the housekeeper's face she looked younger and at peace.

'Bless her dear old soul, she looks as if she

be asleep,' Bessie whispered in an awed voice.

They buried her the next morning. Fleur was tired after a night spent without sleep. Worry about Gerard was like a black shroud about her shoulders. The men hadn't returned.

It was drizzling. The trees dripped moisture on to a carpet of mouldering brown leaves. Mist drifted between the trees, settling in the hollows in clammy patches. The smell of decay and dampness was depressing.

Anger kept Fleur warm. Mrs Firkins hadn't deserved to come to such an undignified end. She hoped Remy made Charles Boney pay for that, as well as stealing her son.

Fear attacked her in terrified little spurts. What if Charles killed Gerard? What if he became ill with cold, or was mistreated by Rose? If they ever came face to face again she would kill Rose Hardwick herself.

Lucy gave a wretched sob now and again, and dabbed at her weeping eyes with a handkerchief. Fleur gave her a hug. Lucy's wedding day was one neither of them would ever forget and in years to come the anniversary of it would remind them of the horror as well as the joy.

Arms around each other's waists the pair found comfort as they walked back to the house, followed by a quiet group of servants.

The men had searched Charles Boney's

house the night before, finding no one but a trembling Catherine, who had hidden herself in a closet when she'd heard them approach.

Remy's fist closed around her bodice and he jerked her out of her hiding place. Chivalry cast aside he shook her until her teeth rattled in her head.

'Where's my son?' he roared. 'And where can I find your cowardly brother?'

'He ain't my brother, My Lord,' Catherine blubbered, every trace of her fine accent obliterated. 'His name is Charlie Hardwick, and he was a servant to the Earl of North-haven. I was an actress with a travelling theatre when we met. We joined up.'

'Then where's the real master of this house?'

'The inheritance was going beggin' so Northhaven fixed it so Charlie could have it. He knew Charlie was good with the cards, and wanted him ter ruin you. This place was to be a reward for services rendered. I posed as his sister. It was a real lark while it lasted, hobnobbing with the toffs and all. Charlie would've made a good stage actor. I didn't expect it to go this far. Honest to God.'

Remy's hand whipped across her face, making her cry out. 'I'm not interested in your life story. Where's he taken my son?'

'London, most like. He intends to go abroad and is short of cash. London is full of stupid, bleedin' toffs willing to lose at cards.'

He threw her away from him on to the couch. His eyes sought out those of Leland. 'You deal with her. I'll try and catch them up.'

'I'll tell you something useful if yer pays me,' Catherine whined when he began to walk away.

Leland's hand shot out. He grabbed her upright by her throat, applying pressure until her eyes bulged. Softly, he suggested, 'You'll tell him something useful from the goodness of your heart, yes?'

Frantically she nodded. When his hand relaxed she croaked. 'Charlie ain't gone by road; the highways are closed by floods up past Poole. He and his bitch of a sister got a coach to the quay and took a ship. Had it all planned, they did.'

'Rose Hardwick is his sister?'

'She runs a bawdy house near Covent Garden. If she takes the boy there he'll never surface till he's been trained in thievery, sold to a sweep, or used as entertainment for the worst of her clients.'

'If my son is not found alive and well, you'll die as painfully as Charles. This I promise.'

The chill in Remy's voice made the Russell brothers exchange a swift glance.

'If you're quick you might catch the ship before it sails,' Catherine said, trembling fearfully.

They left at once, detouring to the magis-

313

trate. When he learned of their mission he promptly made out arrest warrants for Catherine, Charles and Rose. Even if she fled, Catherine would not get very far.

It started to rain heavily. Horses and riders struggled through thick mud. When they reached Poole midnight was a memory, they were soaked through and Charles was already more than half a day ahead.

They battered at the door of the blacksmith until he rose to see what the ruckus was about, his face as dark as thunder. Impressed by the threatening quality of his customers and the coinage pressed into his hand, he accepted custody of the horses and led the bedraggled creatures into a warm stable, promising to treat them as lovingly as he would his own children.

Charles had sailed several hours before. Dismayed, the four men stared at each other. Crispen smiled when he caught sight of a fishing boat. 'Follow me.'

The young lad on watch was fast asleep. Crispen hauled him upright, dangling him with his feet just off the deck. 'I requisition this ship in the service of the King. Hoist the sail and let's get under way. Make hearty now.'

His eyes on Crispen's uniform the lad pulled himself smartly to attention when he was lowered to his feet. 'Aye aye, Captain.'

Grinning, Macy cuffed Crispen around the ear. 'Less of the sea prattle, just get us there, Admiral.'

'Couldn't you have picked something a little more comfortable and less smelly,' Leland grumbled as the vessel slid past the dark shape of Brownsea Island.

Crispen laughed. 'If you think this is uncomfortable, wait until we clear the harbour. With this wind it will be a bit choppy out there.'

This brought Remy a recollection of something he wasn't really comfortable with. He'd learned to his cost that he was a bad sailor. However, with Gerard's life at stake, he had no choice but to use any means of reaching London as was available.

Soon, his stomach began to churn. Miserably he took a seat at the stern, where he hugged his stomach and swallowed his rising nausea. Only Crispen and the lad were unaffected by the uncomfortable journey.

Remy was a man with a mission, and seasickness wasn't going to keep him from finding his son. As soon as they berthed he was out of the boat and on the run before it tied up, his legs unsteady, but gaining strength with every stride.

'I'm looking for a couple with a small child,' he shouted, tossing a coin at a sailor who was carrying barrels on to a merchant ship. 'They would have boarded at Poole.'

The sailor scratched his head. 'A hard-faced cow, she was. The man made out he was some sort of toff, till he got sick. Then he hung over the side and cursed fit to bust. The kid was as quiet as a titmouse. Poor little bugger.'

Alarm filled Remy's eyes. 'Was he injured in any way?'

'Just cold. His teeth were chattering. I put a couple of sacks under him and makes him a little bed between some straw bales so he was sheltered from the wind, cuddling him up nice and cosy and warm in my sea jacket. Now don't you be afeared none, old Jackie will keep watch over you, I says to him, and I secured a line round his waist and tied the other end to a hatch so he couldn't wander off and fall over the side. He soon fell asleep.'

A lump rose to Remy's throat at the thought of the man's kindness towards his son. 'Which way did they go?'

'Off towards Covent Garden.'

'My thanks.' And they came straight from his heart.

'After him,' Leland called out to his brothers when Remy took off at the run. 'He'll need us if he's going into Seven Dials.'

Leland wished he had a weapon. At least Macy had had the foresight to snatch a whip from the Rosehill stables. Cris had his uniform sword and he'd be surprised if his younger brother didn't know how to wield

316

it. He grabbed up a chunk of wood, which was heavy enough to serve as handy cudgel. It slapped solidly against his palm. It would have to do.

Catherine had spent the night making her plans. She was in no hurry. Remy and his companions had not gone back to Rosehill to inform Fleur. They'd rushed off to London like the hotheads they were. All the same, she didn't envy Charlie when they caught up with him. It served him right. He'd got too greedy and had outsmarted himself.

She'd heard there was a troupe of players at Salisbury. If she made it there she could join them – and once they reached London she could contact the Earl of Northhaven. The old fool, though almost past it as a lover, liked to fumble and had offered to set her up in a house in Italy. She could hide there indefinitely. With cosmetic enhancement, a wig and a change of name, she'd never be discovered. But first she must set the groundwork in case she ever needed to return and act the innocent victim.

Gathering together every item her partner in deception had cheated Remy St Cyres out of, she placed them on the cart. She intended to take the haul to the meadow adjoining Rosehill, where she'd leave it to be found. If she did get caught, she hoped this act might stand in her favour.

She was tempted to take the horse, but decided against it. The beast belonged to the Boney estate and horse stealing was not treated lightly. She suddenly shivered, remembering the death of Simon Ackland with some regret. She'd liked Simon, and the slaying had been unexpected.

Charlie had bragged about it. Simon had sided against him with Fleur St Cyres, he'd said. Charlie had designs on the woman himself – an eye to the bigger prize. The fool! The bitch had seen right through him from the beginning.

Catherine intended to keep her mouth shut from now on, and quietly disappear.

She turned the horse loose and set off towards the forest. To her surprise she was apprehended just after she entered it. The stable hand from Rosehill had seen her dump the loot, and had informed their steward. The pair had detoured around the meadow and waited for her.

The youth's gaze lingered on her breasts. He was a big, handsome lad. She deliberately shifted her glance down his body, lingering on his thighs. She smiled when he reacted positively. If he'd been alone she'd have been tempted to show the young stud a thing or two.

But perhaps she'd get a chance later. She pushed her breast against his hand when he grasped her arm and he flushed when she whispered mockingly against his ear, 'If we're ever alone I'll teach you what a real woman is like.'

Tom, who'd already made that important discovery with his grandfather's milkmaid, reckoned that nevertheless, there was lots of things a woman like her might be able to teach him.

Catherine was defiant when she faced Fleur. She'd really fancied Remy St Cyres, and if this green-eyed bitch hadn't reached the inn five minutes before her she'd have been mistress of Rosehill now. She and Charlie had timed it. It wouldn't have been too hard to keep up the pretence of being a toff. It was almost second nature to her now.

She shrugged, and knowing Fleur wasn't going to believe a word she said, she placed her hands on her hips. 'I was returning Remy's goods, Lady high and mighty, Fleur. And if you think I'm frightened of the likes of you, think again. You can't have me arrested for returning something he lost at cards. And I didn't have a hand in kidnapping your whey-faced brat.'

'Remember my housekeeper, Mrs Firkins? She was thrown down the stairs and killed – a hanging offence. I hope you can furnish the magistrates with proof of your innocence.'

'I didn't have anything to do with that.'

Fleur's pitying smile whipped fear into Catherine's heart, especially when Fleur murmured to the two men. 'Wait outside. After I've finished with her you can take her to the stables and lock her in the tack room for the night.'

Tom smiled to himself, hoping the mistress wouldn't leave her too badly damaged. He reckoned she'd be prepared to do anything if she thought she might be set free.

Catherine hadn't seen the riding crop held against Fleur's gown. She didn't see it until Fleur raised it and examined the tip. Her eyes widened and her mouth fell open. 'Here, what the hell are you going to do?'

'Remember the last time you came here? I said I'd take a riding crop to you if you set foot on Rosehill land again.'

'You wouldn't dare.'

'Wouldn't I? You have a lot to learn about me.'

Fleur demonstrated exactly what she'd dare. The crop came down so swiftly on Catherine's back she didn't see it coming, just felt its agonizing sting.

'Did you hear something?' Tom murmured when a prolonged scream rang out.

Hamish McDuff slowly shook his head.

Tom grinned and scratched his crotch. 'Neither did I.'

SIXTEEN

The area known as Seven Dials was the cesspit of London.

Here, the cut-throats, pickpockets and prostitutes surfaced at night like scum on a pot of rotting vegetables. They preyed on the wary, the unwary, and each other. The dim alleyways stank of human waste, vomit and the putrefying flesh of animals used for sport. Shadows moved stealthily, disappearing into other shadows or sometimes erupting in a violent flurry of movement. Moisture oozed, bubbled and slimed on the surface of the street. Doorways guarded watchers in their dark recesses.

Remy and his companions were not in the mood to be stopped and their size was intimidating to even the most hardened of criminals. The shadows retreated before them as they strode purposefully through the dark night.

Remy refused to rap on any door to enquire the whereabouts of Rose Hardwick. The seaman's instructions were sufficient. When they reached the darkened establishment he earned the admiration of the Russell brothers when he ripped a hitching post from the ground and used it as a battering ram to splinter open the door to the whores' dwelling.

The darkness inside was suddenly filled with shapes, cursing and scrambling. A flint was struck several times before the tender caught and a wick began to burn. A candle was held aloft. 'Who the hell are you and what do yer want?'

'Rose Hardwick and her brother.'

'Never 'eard of 'em.'

There was a crunch of fist against bone. A squawk. The candle changed hands and Remy headed for the stairs.

He was nearly knocked aside by a half-naked man, who charged past clutching his breeches in front of him. As the man skittled past Macy out into the street, his bare arse bobbed in the darkness like two skinny white moons.

A chamber pot was thrown from an upstairs window and a raucous voice shrieked. 'Hey, you 'avent paid me you thieving cove.'

A woman at the top of the stairs cursed when she saw Remy. She turned on her heel and began to run. Remy took the stairs three at a time, his fist bunched the fabric of her shift and he jerked her to a halt. 'Where's my son, you raddled old hag?'

'Charlie's got 'im. We weren't going to ask for much, honest.' Rose Hardwick's voice became an ingratiating whine. 'I could tell you where he is. All I wants it something for me old age. I'll give yer a toss into the bargain, luvvy.'

Remy gazed down at this piece of scum who'd stolen his son. The very thought of her corrupt hands touching his flesh was totally abhorrent to him. He wanted to choke the foul breath from her body, very slowly.

He gave a mirthless smile. 'There are three men downstairs. They are Gerard's uncles. Every one of them would take great pleasure in beating you to death. Personally, I'd rather not soil my hands on filth like you but if I have to I'll pull your entrails from your body and choke you with them. Now ... I will ask you once more, and only once. Where is my son?'

The menace of his voice was all the more noticeable, because of its softness. Rose Hardwick had no doubt her former employer would do exactly as he threatened and felt a moment of terror. Teeth chattering, she contemplated lying, then thought better of it. 'There's an undertaker down near the river. Charlie 'as him holed up there.'

He threw a skirt at her. 'Cover yourself. You're going to show us the way.'

Her fists went belligerently to her hips. 'And what if don't?'

'You'll freeze to death, because it's cold outside and I'm giving you no choice.'

'Why should I show you the way? What's

in it fer me?'

He did something he'd learned to do well as a prisoner of the Spanish. Lied. 'Once I've got my son back, and only then. I'll release you.'

'Trustworthy cove, ain't yer?' she said, glaring at him.

He placed the business end of a pistol against her ear. 'Shut your mouth and cover yourself or I'll not waste any more time on you.'

Rose scrambled into her skirt and bodice, and then slid her dirt-encrusted feet into a pair of kid slippers he'd last seen in Fleur's dressing room. The woman's fat ankles bulged over the top. He burned when he saw how badly soiled they were.

They were downstairs a few moments later. 'There's a crowd gathering,' Cris told him.

The woman smiled as she knotted a grubby shawl around her shoulders. 'Don't think gentry like you can walk into these parts and do what yer like. They'll have yer watches, yer purses and the clothes off yer back before they tear you limb from limb.'

'They can try.' Remy pulled a pistol from under his cloak, strode outside and confronted the group of creatures who'd been attracted to the ruckus. All of them had their eye on the main chance.

'Rose Hardwick and her brother have stolen my son. I intend to get him back. I've

324

got no time to waste on niceties, so be warned. If any one of you tries to stop me I'll shoot to kill and my companions will take over if I miss.' He took aim at the largest of the men.

When Macy's whip cracked through the breath vapouring above the mob's heads, to reinforce his words. They cowered back.

A voice came from behind them. 'And me and my shipmates will crack the skulls of the rest of you buggers.'

Boos and hisses went through the small mob as the old salt from the ship pushed through them with a complement of tough looking crew members. Most of them brandished belaying pins. 'Shift it, you murdering bastards,' the seaman shouted, and walloped a couple of heads to show he meant business.

Remy grinned at him, grateful for the support.

'God blind me, I think it's the bleedin' pressmen,' someone yelled out. Some of the mob melted into the shadows, the rest circled like hungry curs then sidled towards Rose's house.

Suddenly catching on to what they were about, Rose squealed, 'The thieving bastards are after my goods.'

'You've been putting your poxy 'ands in our pockets for years, you fat old floozie,' someone shouted out.

'And in our crotches,' someone else shouted.

Leland choked on a laugh. 'You won't need anything where you're going, anyway.'

Rose tried to make a break for it but Remy seized her by the scruff of the neck and pushed her in front of him at arm's length. 'Lead the way or by Christ, I'll disembowel you just like I said.'

'Better let me do that,' Macy said pleasantly, 'It's a messy business and I've had more experience.'

The beginnings of a clammy fog began to drift through the alleyways as the small band of rescuers made its way towards the river. Remy picked up the pace and hoped it wouldn't thicken. The fog in his mind had cleared when Fleur had slipped the ruby ring on to his finger. His memory had returned with a vengeance.

He recalled how ruthless Charles could be. It had been Charles who had shot him on the beach, which meant Charles was also in the pay of Northhaven.

That fact made things worse since Remy had learned from Hernando Cordova that Northhaven had been responsible for the death of his parents. He'd brought back with him a written account signed by a witness, the agent who'd enticed Northhaven to become a traitor to his country. Now he remembered what the contents signified, he hoped Fleur had concealed it well.

Remy's father had asked his wife to act as an interpreter for a highly secret meeting with Spanish government representatives on the day of the murder. She had learned too much for her own safety – knowledge with which his father had charged Northhaven. The Cordova family honour demanded revenge.

He thought of Mrs Firkins, and the notion of his son at the mercy of his former companion horrified him. He wondered, how could he have allowed himself to be duped?

Memories crowded in – memories which both shamed and horrified him. The man he'd been and the man he'd now become seemed like two separate beings. He didn't hold much admiration for the former, and had a great deal to put right before his pride could be restored.

The fog grew denser as they neared the river. Rose Hardwick's breath laboured in her chest as he pushed her relentlessly in front of him. She slowed to a halt, her hand splayed against her bosom, panting, 'It's over there.'

They stopped as one. The fog pressed in suffocatingly on their ears. Remy twitched when a childlike cry rang out, then everyone jumped as a couple of cats exploded from beneath their feet, spitting and snarling in a fury as they fought for possession of the carcass of a rat. The rat obligingly parted company with its rear and the two protagonists slunk off in different directions, trailing entrails behind them.

When a couple of the sailors nervously laughed Remy held up his hand for silence. Before them was a solid brick building with a stout wooden door. Above it, and creaking slightly as it moved back and forth was a painted sign depicting a coffin, *George Crivens. Undertaker. Established since 1756*, it stated, looking slightly sinister in the mist.

On exploration, behind the building they discovered a pathway wide enough to take a horse and the rough cart that doubled as a hearse. The pathway led to a wooden stable building. On the river's edge was a wooden landing, a boat tied to it by a long rope to accommodate the tide. The tide was in; the river was a dark flow of water, the surface just visible under the greasy fog. There was no way into the building as far as Remy could see.

Remy shuddered, George Crivens obviously did more than undertake. He fished bodies from the river for a fee. He eased out a breath as he stared at the windows, sensing they were being watched. There was a patter of feet as Rose Hardwick took advantage of the situation to make good her escape.

Most of the sailors took off after her with whoops and shouts. He'd noticed one of two of them eyeing her, and guessed she'd be in for a rough time of it when she was caught. He didn't much care.

'No matter,' he said when his companions swore. 'If the crew doesn't catch her the authorities will, and as soon as I post a reward.'

Striding to the door he tested his strength against it. Finding it too solid to shoulder open he thumped on it with his fist. 'Come out, Charles, and bring my son with you.'

A window opened and a head poked out. 'Wot's going on? You're making enough noise to raise the bloody dead.'

'I want Charlie Hardwick and my son.'

'Charlie Hardwick?' The man sounded genuinely puzzled. 'He used to hang around here but I ain't seen him in years.'

'Then you won't object to us coming in and taking a look. Either open the door or I'll kick in a window.'

There was a sound of cursing, and then the window banged shut. A few moments later they saw the glow of a candle as it was lit. A wavering light made its way downstairs. There was a noise as a bolt was drawn back, then another. The door creaked open. Behind the man stood a scared-looking woman and two young boys. Neither of them was Gerard.

'I swear to you, sirs, Charlie Hardwick ain't here. Take the candle and have a look for yerselves.'

Remy searched every nook and cranny of the undertaker's abode, including the stables, where two rough wooden coffins were set on trestles. One cradled the body of a woman. She didn't quite fit, so her ankles had been broken and her feet folded under her.

'I don't get paid much for floaters fished from the river, and she was a tall one,' Crivens said apologetically when Remy shuddered.

A weary-looking horse munched on some oats, gazed mournfully at them and pocked a hoof at the floor. They were about to leave when a noise came from underfoot.

The sailor kicked some stinking straw aside. 'There's a trapdoor here, My Lord.' He yanked it open.

Beneath the stable was a cellar. The wooden walls dripped with black slimy moss and pinpoint eyes gleamed in the candle-light. The place was alive with river rats. As Remy dropped through the hole into the darkness they scattered in every direction, giving high-pitched squeaks as they disappeared into the ceiling rafters or through another trapdoor in the floor. It was open and big enough for a man to drop through.

Macy handed him down the candle. As Remy stepped forward to investigate he heard Macy follow him through the trapdoor, landing on the balls of his feet with hardly a sound. For a big man, he was light on his feet.

Rotting sacks were piled up in a corner. A stack of crates had toppled, which accounted for the noise. Remy could almost smell his prey now, and could sense the fear of his son.

'I know you're in here, Charles. Show yourself.'

'Papa?' The small, whimpering voice came from out of the darkness and set his heart beating at a fast pace, 'I don't like it in here.'

'Take one more step and he's gone.'

Remy's muscles froze him to the spot. Charles had Gerard by the scruff of the neck and was dangling him over the trapdoor. Water frothed and eddied around it like a small whirlpool.

'Name your price?' he said, fear strangling his voice.

'The satisfaction of seeing you die,' Charles drawled, and he lifted a pistol and took aim.

'Is everything all right?' Leland called down through the trapdoor.

'Tell him yes, and send him away,' Charles growled. His arm was beginning to droop, so he was obviously tiring with the weight of Gerard. Remy's tongue clove to the roof of his mouth. Charles had only to open his fingers.

At that moment Charles could have asked anything of him and he'd gladly have forfeited it for his son. Estate, title ... his life? Yes, he was willing to sacrifice that for Gerard.

'You can have me, Charles. Just hand my son over first. His mother is worried out of her wits.' To his left, he could hear Macy inching forward. He raised his voice to cover any noise Macy might inadvertently make and set the candle on a box so both of his hands were free. 'For the love of God. Give me back my son. I'll give you a stake and help smuggle you abroad.'

Charles sniggered nervously. 'I'm not that stupid. I know I'm done for if I'm caught. You know about Northhaven, don't you? He underestimated you, which is why he sent me to finish you off.'

'And overestimated your prowess with a pistol. Even up close your aim was inaccurate, making it obvious you were never in the army.'

'I fooled everyone posing as a toff though – everyone but that bitch you plucked from the road. I wasn't good enough for the likes of her. She turned Simon against me too but she nearly clawed me to shreds when I approached her.'

Remy managed a tight smile. Fleur had kept that particular snippet to herself.

'She sent for her precious infant and flaunted him. Remy's son, the heir to Rosehill, she said, as if the rest of us was dirt beneath her feet. She certainly knew how to stiffen your spine, Remy. Now we'll see how she likes losing the brat you fathered on her.'

His fingers opened.

A whip suddenly cracked. It snaked across the room in an instant and coiled tightly around Gerard's body. The boy was jerked forward.

Gerard gave a shrill scream as the water snatched at his legs. As he began to slip under, his small fingers scrabbled desperately for a hold on the edge of the trapdoor. In an instant Macy twisted and rolled sideways, jerking him from the water like a fish on the end of a hook. The child slithered across the filthy floor into Macy's arms.

His face contorted with rage, Charles fired his pistol. He missed Remy despite the close proximity, his shaking hands sending the shot wide. He was not so courageous without the element of surprise.

Two strides and Remy had Charles face down on the floor, his face pressed into the dirt. His brain was as clear as ice and he had no intention of showing him any mercy.

Dragging Charles across to the hole, Remy's fingers closed around the back of his neck. The ruby on his finger glowed red as it caught the candlelight. He gazed at Gerard whose eyes were round with fright, and jerked his head towards the trapdoor. Macy calmly nodded and handed Gerard up to Leland. He exchanged a significant glance with his brothers before joining them.

The small band of men was quiet. There

was no noise from below, no struggle – just a momentary sucking noise as the river stole the breath from a man

Remy emerged after a short while, and taking his shivering son into his arms tucked him under his coat.

'Papa,' Gerard whispered, and, snuggling into the safety of his father's body he clung on tight. Tears filled Remy's eyes as he hugged him.

The undertaker shuffled from one foot to the other. 'I didn't know he was down there, honest, My Lord, and I wouldn't have 'ad no hand in takin' that there lad from you. I got two precious young-uns of my own. Charlie must have come up through the trap when the tide was low.'

Remy stared at him for a long time, inclined to believe the man when his eyes met his honestly and without wavering. This man scratched a living the hard way. He couldn't see him being drawn into anything that could earn him a dance on the rope.

Satisfied the man was telling the truth, he shrugged. 'He probably went out the same way, but you'd better get your story straight in case the authorities decide to pay you a visit.'

The man shrugged. 'River's on the turn and it has a mighty powerful pull. If Charlie tried to escape arrest that way I wouldn't be at all surprised if he hasn't drowned, then.'

'Neither would I.' Remy tossed him a coin, and, turning on his heel he strolled from the house to emerge into the first light of morning. The sailors sent up a cheer when they saw Gerard.

'Where's Charlie?' The captured and dishevelled Rose said sullenly.

'I don't know,' Remy said truthfully. If anyone had bothered to take a good look at the river they'd have seen something resembling a man's body floating on the tide with the rest of the rubbish.

The sailors were rewarded with the contents of Leland's purse for their trouble, and then went on board their ship to face the wrath of their captain.

Crispen decided to take the fishing boat back to Poole, where he was due to rejoin his ship. Macy was eager to start his married life. He elected to trust his safety to the impressive seamanship skills displayed by his younger brother, threatening Crispen with a boot in the seat of his fancy breeches if he didn't provide a smoother journey than the one on the way up.

Leland indicated he had some business to attend to in London before he returned home. Remy said he had the same, and confided what the thrust of that business was to the brothers. He had to sort out his personal life for the sake of Fleur and his child. The problem of Northhaven could wait until he was in possession of the proof.

'That'll save us taking a whip to you again,' Leland said, and promptly gave him a letter of recommendation to his legal representative.

The five of them breakfasted at an inn on the wharf. Gerard was wide-eyed with wonder and clinging on to his father for dear life. He drank the milk and sops he was fed, and then cadged tidbits from the plates of his father and uncles until he was full to the brim, and sleepy.

'Young Gerard has a man-sized appetite. You should insist he be breeched early,' Leland advised. 'Their mothers keep them in baby skirts for too long. It didn't do Cris any harm to be put into breeches.'

Macy nudged Leland gently in the ribs. 'Up until then we couldn't tell the difference between him and Fleur, could we? Many's the time I threw him over my knee and discovered it was Fleur. Cris was such a pretty lad. He still is, come to that.'

Cris grinned. 'Try and put me over your knee now, Aunt Macy. I'll knock the heads of you and Mama Leland together.'

They laughed and jostled, ruffling up Crispen's curls. Remy thought it might end up as a free-for-all, but a serving wench arrived with a jug of ale, which claimed their attention.

The four of them talked as they ate. When the boy fell asleep, Remy wrapped him in his cloak, laying him carefully on the seat whilst he called for the landlord to bring him parchment and quill.

'You'll be lucky if Fleur speaks to you again for keeping her son from her,' said Leland with a laugh.

'She will, and she'll forgive me for this. Trust me.' He gazed around at his three companions, a lump forming in his throat. 'I don't know quite how to thank you all. You've been true brothers to me. I'll never forget it.'

'Aw, cease that palaver,' Macy said. 'You can pay for breakfast. That will be thanks enough. I'll have another slice of that ham and crusty bread, and another jug of ale to wash it down with. I need something to chuck over the side of the boat on the way home.'

They all gave embarrassed grins, aimed a few punches his way and then at each other, dismissing the emotional pull of the moment.

'This is outrageous. He can't do this to me.' Fleur screwed up the letter, dashed it to the ground and stamped on it. 'The arrogance of him, I will not be abandoned like some errant servant. How dare he keep my son from me?'

Macy smiled. 'Remy said to tell you not to

worry. He'll personally select a new nurse for the boy ... and he said he'll check her references thoroughly.'

'As if Hamish McDuff didn't. Can I help it if Rose Hardwick and her referees conspired to deceive? Gerard was *my* son before he was Remy's,' she said irrationally. 'I carried him inside me, suffered pain to birth him and nursed him through all his illnesses. Whilst Remy St Cyres occupies my house in Hanover Square and enjoys himself in London I am to be imprisoned here.'

Macy kissed her. 'Stop being so melodramatic. Remy has some urgent business he needs to conduct. I offered to bring Gerard back but he said he's seen so little of the boy he welcomed the opportunity to spend some time with him. He is the boy's father, after all. He risked his life to save him. He was quite prepared to die for him.' The expression in Macy's eyes retreated into retrospect. 'Remy was impressive. You have a man who commands all of our respect, despite his fancy looks.'

Fleur seated herself again, gazing at him with glowing eyes. 'Tell me of his deeds again. Was he very heroic?'

Macy exchanged a wry glance with Lucy, who managed a small smile that promised much. 'As I've already told you the full story twice and the hour is late, I beg to remind you that I'd like to spend some time alone

with my wife. If you recall, I parted with her on the steps of the church.'

Fleur looked horrified. 'You should have reminded me sooner, Macy. I'm being selfish and I wouldn't blame you if you both hated me.' Jumping to her feet she hugged one after the other. 'I will retire to my chamber at once and you shall hear no more from me until the morrow, when we part company.'

Fleur slid into bed longing to feel Remy's arms around her. Thoughts shifted through her head in a never-ending succession. Why hadn't he come back to her? Perhaps Macy wasn't telling her everything. Had he been hurt? She sat up in bed, saying out loud. 'What if it's Gerard who's been hurt?'

Gruff's tail thumped against the floor at the sound of her voice. He gave a small huff.

She was being foolish. Macy wouldn't have kept that from her. She subsided back on to her pillow and was nearly asleep when someone shook her awake again. It was her maid.

'What is it, Mary?' she said crossly.

'It's the coachman from Stratton House, My Lady. The Countess, Marguerite has been taken poorly. Her doctor says you need to come quickly.'

'Send my husband's servant to rouse my brother and his wife. Tell Noah to be discreet. Then pack a small trunk. I may need to stay for a few days.'

Within the hour they were on the road, Macy on horseback whilst she and Lucy occupied the carriage. Dawn was breaking as they entered the gates of Stratton House. The sky was overcast, heavy with rain. Mist rose from the ground to hover at knee height. A couple of crows wheeled over the house, cawing harshly.

To Fleur, it no longer felt like her home when she entered. There was an air of un-happiness about the place, as if Marguerite's misery had chased the laughter from the walls. Fleur shivered as she handed her cloak to the housekeeper.

'How is the countess, Mrs Bates?'

'Lost the baby and bleedin' real bad, poor soul. You've got here just in time, Lady Fleur. The physic says the countess will be lucky if she lasts another hour.'

But Marguerite had never attracted luck. Dismissing the others and beckoning Fleur forward she whispered something so wicked and shocking in her ear that Fleur gasped and took a step back. Marguerite managed a small triumphant smile, and then expelled her very last breath.

'May God forgive you,' Fleur whispered, and giving an anguished cry ran into dressing room where she found a sharp piece of cane. It was bloodied at one end. Hearing Macy's tread behind her she tossed it hastily on to the fire.

Her action came too late. Gazing at the burning instrument of evil Macy said slowly, 'Marguerite displayed early symptoms of black melancholy, but I never thought she'd do anything so desperate. Leland has been forced to bear much responsibility on his shoulders from too young an age. He deserves to be happy so I sincerely hope this will be the last sad event he must bear.'

'Marguerite told me to tell Leland what she'd done. Oh Macy. How could she be so wicked? We must never tell him of this. Never!'

Together, they crossed to the bed and stared down at Marguerite, pale from loss of blood but peaceful now the discontent had fled from her face.

Fleur turned her face into her brother's shoulder and wept for the soul of her poor unhappy sister-in-law. In her heart she could only rejoice that the woman was finally at peace and Leland was free of her.

SEVENTEEN – SPRING 1782

Easter. The service began as a sombre affair with three recent graves to remind them all of their human folly and frailty. The resurrection story, narrated with simple conviction by the priest was an uplifting experience.

Spring had arrived late. It had been worth the wait, all the spring flowers emerging in a joyous chorus of colour. In the church grounds daffodils formed a glorious carpet of gold and yellow trumpets interspersed with fiery red and pink easter flowers and pale primroses. The blackthorn blossoms formed dense and fragrant lace caps on the boughs.

With Remy and her son still resident in London, Fleur had sent Noah back to Stragglemarsh Hall. Fleur remained at Stratton House, unable to bring herself to abandon Leland or his two sons, who filled the gap in her arms vacated by her own son. The youngest was hardly out of infancy. They were their father's sons, with hardly anything in their features to remind Fleur of Marguerite.

They didn't seem to miss their mother, which was sad. They greeted their father with boisterous and obvious delight when he visited them each evening before bedtime. This was to the chagrin of their nurse, because Leland played and romped with them for an hour before handing them over to be settled into bed – an almost impossible task when they were so excited by the games.

'It's of no consequence if they don't sleep at a given time,' Leland said when Fleur mentioned it, 'I want them to know me as a father rather than a dispenser of justice. I

342

always found the late earl, our father, to be a figure to be feared rather than regarded with affection. He's remembered by both Macy and myself for his beatings.'

She kissed his cheek then, noticing for the first time that his temples were greying. 'Dearest Leland, you were a most wonderfully affectionate example to me when I was growing up. I love you dearly and so will your children. This however, reminds me of something I'm determined to ask you. Am I to meet your daughters whilst I am here?'

His hand closed over hers. 'It's too close to Marguerite's death to invite them here, but I'll see what can be arranged.'

Macy and Lucy had joined them at Stratton for Easter. Due to Leland's recent bereavement and to satisfy convention, it was to be a quiet family affair. The pair looked supremely happy, the reason for which was confided to Fleur by a smiling Lucy after the church service to celebrate Christ's resurrection.

Fleur gave her a hug. 'I'm so pleased. I have no need to ask if you and my brother are happy together. Your smiles tell me so.'

Lucy's smile was almost smug with contentment. 'Your brother is a bear without claws, but don't tell him I said so.'

Fleur grinned when Macy looked across Leland's head to catch her eye. He looked twice as tall and twice as proud as usual. A bear without claws, she thought. How apt, and how well Lucy knew him. She blew him a kiss, knowing he'd make a wonderful father.

Leland had a surprise in store for her. As they followed him from the church she noticed an elegant looking woman with two young girls. Macy nodded pleasantly to them as he passed her and strolled on ahead.

The woman stood to one side. When the congregation had thinned and she and Leland were about to depart, Leland said quietly. 'Fleur, may I introduce someone special to you?'

She knew then who the woman was. When she nodded, Leland beckoned the woman forward. 'My sister, Lady St Cyres, has expressed a desire to meet you. Fleur, may I present Sylvane Dumfries and her daughters, Constance and Elizabeth.'

Sylvane's smile was slightly hesitant when she gazed at Leland, who grinned reassuringly at her. The three of them, eyes modestly lowered, curtseyed. But the eyes of one of the girls flickered upwards to regard her with curiosity for a moment.

Sylvane had an air of serenity about her. Dark hair framed a high cheekboned face that contained light grey eyes and a handsomely curved mouth. A grey cloak trimmed with dark fur gave a glimpse of wine-coloured velvet underneath. Her two daughters were young ladies emerging from childhood. They shone with the dew of youth.

She slanted Leland a glance. All this time she'd taken her brother's love for granted. She'd never known the depth of Leland or imagined he'd had secrets or longings he'd kept from her. She could see the anxiety in his eyes now, and knew how much the outcome of this meeting meant to him.

Sylvane met her eyes openly, but a little warily.

Fleur smiled warmly, trying to put her at ease. 'I'm glad we've met. Your daughters are charming.' She smiled upon the pair, recognizing in Constance the resemblance to herself Leland had spoken of, whilst Elizabeth was a petite image of her mother, '*My nieces*, are lovely. I hope to see more of them, and of you in the future. Perhaps you'd allow me to call on you the next time I'm in Dorchester.'

Fleur heard her breath softly expel in relief. 'I'd be honoured, My Lady.'

There was a smile in Leland's voice when he turned her way. 'Perhaps you wouldn't mind catching Macy up whilst I have a private word with Sylvane.'

Gently, Fleur kissed the two girls on the cheek. 'You're a wonderful Easter surprise for me. I hope we'll become friends.'

'Thank you, My Lady,' they both chorused, and curtseyed. Constance handed her a daffodil. Then their eyes turned towards their father for approval. The giggles they gave were delightful, because Leland was grinning at them so proudly.

How often she had sought that same approval from him when she'd been growing into womanhood. How readily he'd given it.

As she walked off to rejoin Macy one of the girls whispered, 'Where's the handkerchief we embroidered for our papa. Let's give it to him now.'

As Fleur walked off smiling, the sun came out from behind a cloud. When she looked back the quartet was standing in shafts of gentle, golden light pouring through the tender spring greenery of a beech tree. Leland's expression was filled with such affection for the trio Fleur felt humbled as she slipped her hand into Macy's and squeezed it.

Despite Lucy's good news, Fleur was sad. Playing with Godwin reminded her forcibly of her own son. Though she tried to fill her days she now felt out of place in her childhood home. She grew increasingly despondent waiting for word from Remy. Her heart belonged with him and her son. She would have disobeyed Remy's instructions and undertaken the dangerous journey to London to see them if the weather hadn't taken an unseasonable and ferocious turn for the worse.

As fierce gales battered the coast and rain pelted from the sky there was news of ships foundering on the rocks and of whole villages being swept away by floodwater.

The roads became a morass. Finally the storms abated. A week later they had dried enough to allow a messenger through with letters for them.

Leland was out inspecting the estate for damage with his steward, and Fleur was in a fever of impatience by the time he returned.

When he disappeared into his study she wandered into the drawing room, where she plucked a few discordant notes from the harpsichord. An embroidery frame stood disconsolately by the window. It held an unfinished tapestry of the Russell coat of arms. The needle was still stuck into the canvas where Marguerite had left it, threaded with grey silk.

Poor, troubled Marguerite, she'd soon be forgotten, Fleur thought. Her position in the house would be filled by another, less worthy by social standards perhaps, but a more suitable wife for Leland in many ways. A few minutes later, when a servant came to fetch her, she ordered the embroidery to be removed and stored with the rest of Marguerite's personal goods.

Fleur hurried across the hall into the study. Here, in the oak panelled room with its familiar odour of ancient leather and tobacco smoke, Leland was very much the head of the family. His hounds thumped their tails when she entered, and one gave her a friendly growl and rolled on his back so she could rub his stomach with her foot. She wondered if Gruff was lonely without her companionship.

From the wall behind him, a portrait of their father, George Russell, kept vigil with splendid and haughty indifference. Leland was like him in looks, but not in his ways. Responsibility had been thrust on her elder brother's shoulders early in life. With the support of Macy he'd coped wonderfully well. The love she felt for him nearly overwhelmed her.

As was her habit from childhood, in this masculine room that they'd always referred to as the Earl's Lair, Fleur showed him the deference due to his position by dropping into a curtsey. Sinking into the worn leather chair he indicated she gazed at him in silence, waiting for him to speak. His face was grave as he cleared his throat.

'I haven't thanked you for acknowledging Sylvane. Your acceptance of her pleased me greatly. She was touched by your attention and friendliness.'

'My dearest, Leland. How can I fail to like such a charming woman? I'm looking forward to seeing her again and will call on her as soon as I'm able. You will not mind that, I hope.'

'Since I'm determined to legalise our

relationship as soon as convention allows, I'd be grateful on her behalf for your continuing friendship towards her. She will need your support if she's to gain acceptance in the position she must fill.'

'Sylvane will be given all my support. Your happiness means much to me, Leland.'

'And yours to me.' His palm flattened a square of paper against the desk. 'I have bad news. I've received a letter from my attorney in London. Remy has been arrested for crimes against the state and is awaiting trial in Newgate prison.'

'Newgate?' She was glad for the support of the chair under her when her knees seemed to crumble. Yet her brain refused to absorb the seriousness of the situation and caused her tongue to engage in triviality. 'I thought Newgate had been looted and fired by a mob.'

Leland traced a calloused finger over the scarred surface of a desk. It had served several earls and would probably serve a few more. He answered her automatically. 'Restoration has taken place and Newgate has recently been reopened.' His eyes slowly came up to hers. 'You do understand how serious this charge is?'

'Yes,' she whispered the colour ebbing from her cheek as the information was accepted. Alarm stabbed her. She didn't want to think of Remy in danger again, not when she'd just got him back from the dead. She didn't want to lose him again, either. How could she survive another period of that awful, deadening grief – grief that had made her feel only half alive?

There was an urge to hide. She wanted to curl into a ball like a threatened hedgehog, snug herself safely into her prickles and keep the pain of living at bay. She allowed herself to remember her son. Her eyes flew open as fear consumed her in one bite. Was he alone amongst strangers? 'What's happened to Gerard? Surely he's not in Newgate prison, too?'

'I've been informed he's being safely looked after by the nurse Remy engaged.'

'Thank God! Oh Leland!' Her hastily erected defence crumbled beneath her in an onslaught of grief. She rushed into his arms and began to weep. 'I must go to them, this instant. I must!'

He stroked her hair in comfort, leaving it in disarray when they parted. 'We'll leave as soon as we can ready ourselves. We'll take the horses and buy passage on board a ship at Poole. Dress warmly. I'll send the messenger on ahead to inform Macy of developments. He can meet us on the quayside.' He pressed a paper into her hand. 'This note was enclosed for you. It's from Remy.'

It was short.

My dearest Fleur,
Heed me. You must collect Gerard from the
London residence and make all haste to Straggle-
marsh Hall, where my grandparents will be ex-
pecting you. Oblige me by delivering to my
grandfather the eyeglass, which, as you may
remember is a family heirloom. Above all, do not
worry about me.
Remy St Cyres

'The eyeglass?' Her eyes glinted indignantly.
'Truly, Remy is an enigma to me. He's accused of treason and all he can think of is an
eyeglass.' Her shoulders slumped a little.
'Newgate of all places. Do you suppose he
has money to feed himself? The sooner we
can get there the better and I will certainly
not go back to Stragglemarsh.'

'For once, do as he instructs,' Leland said.
'He has enough trouble on his shoulders
without worrying about your safety.' Wearily,
he shook his head. 'There's something afoot
– something which could put you in danger.
That's why he wants you to stay at Stragglemarsh Hall. The Earl of Blessingham may be
old, but he has many powerful friends, and
Northhaven won't dare touch him directly.'

'Yet he accuses Remy of being a traitor,'
she snapped. 'Northhaven is a liar. He told
me himself that Remy was mentioned in
dispatches, so why should anyone believe
he's a traitor? I think he's seeking to destroy

Remy because he has information which may prove he had something to do with the death of Remy's parents.'

Leland started. 'What do you know of the affair?'

'Remy had papers on him. They were written in Spanish. He was anxious about them when he began to recover, but told me he didn't understand the meaning of them.'

'You have those papers?'

'I gave them to his grandfather to conceal.'

'Good girl.'

The colour rushed back into her face with a vengeance. 'I never did trust that man. He has a sly way about him, and his conversation is double-edged.' She gazed apologetically at him. 'I'm sorry you're being obliged to spend so much time away from your estate.'

He shrugged, as if it were of no consequence. 'You are my family. I must go to London anyway. The lawyer has also discovered that Sarah Boney is still alive. Presently she is residing in Bethlehem Hospital in Southwark.'

'Bedlam,' Fleur whispered, her hand fluttering to her chest. 'The poor woman. Is she insane then?'

'Her mind wanders a little, I believe. She has told my lawyer she was secretly married at Gretna Green in Scotland. When her brother found out he had her husband murdered. Her child was taken from her immediately after birth and left at the foundling hospital, she believes. Enquiries are being made. If the information is more than just wild fancy, eventually the manor will have a lawful owner. Sarah Boney is not violent so perhaps she'll be able to return to her home if a proper companion can be found for her.'

Forgetting her own troubles for a moment Fleur managed a sympathetic smile for the poor unfortunate woman. 'We must make sure she has one.' Which brought Catherine into her mind. 'I believe Catherine was sentenced to the stocks and a public caning for her deception. Then she is to be sent to the West Indies for nine years. She is with child.'

'A convenient excuse,' Leland growled. 'It has prevented her from being sentenced to death and following Rose Hardwick on to the gallows.'

'Would you punish an unborn infant for the sin of the mother, then Leland?' she asked softly. 'Although I disliked Catherine I'm convinced she was unaware of the plan to kidnap Gerard. She would not have stayed to get caught, but would have fled with Charles and Rose Hardwick.'

'The world is overflowing with bastards,' he growled. Then it seemed he remembered his two daughters for he gave a wry grin, turned her round and pushed her towards the door. 'I spoke from anger not from the heart. Of course children should not be penalized for the sins of the parents. She did return the goods Charles robbed Remy of. All I can do on her behalf is send a note to the magistrate and beg for leniency as regard to the caning and the stocks. As for the West Indies ... with her looks and artifice she will probably marry a plantation owner and do well for herself. Now, go and ready yourself. We've wasted enough time and I want to reach the harbour before night falls. We have much travelling to do over the next few days.'

They found a ship's master willing to take them on board after ten minutes of hard bartering.

Offered a small, but evil smelling cabin to share, they were thrown this way and that as soon as they left the shelter of harbour. The journey was a nightmare of heaving swells that washed over the deck above and continually dripped on their head and shoulders through several leaks in the caulking. The floor beneath them was constantly awash.

The sails and rigging sang an eerie song as they took the strain and everything creaked and shivered. Fleur prayed for a safe passage. Although she managed to weather the journey without feeling queasy, even to the extent of enjoying the buffeting a little, Leland and Macy were whey-faced and staggering when they stepped ashore in the middle of the night.

'I don't know how you and Cris remain unaffected,' Macy muttered, gulping in a breath or two of unhealthy London air to recover.

'I enjoy it and can understand why Cris does. If I were a man I think I'd go to sea too.'

This remark was followed by a short bark of laughter from Macy. 'It wasn't long ago you blamed Remy for sending your baby brother away.'

'I was wrong.'

'Wrong?' He stared at her in complete amazement. 'I thought I'd never live to hear you admit to such a thing.'

She punched him lightly on the shoulder and grinned. 'I didn't think Cris was fit enough at the time. However, the sea air strengthened his lungs and he looks so strong and healthy I must have been wrong. That doesn't mean Remy was right.' She slowly shook her head, saying darkly as her mood plunged again. 'Why does that man attract so much trouble?'

When they reached Hanover Square, Leland pounded on the door until a light appeared in an attic window above. Thrown open, a voice wavered. 'It's the middle of the night when decent people are abed. What do you want?'

Leland clicked his tongue impatiently. 'It's the Earl of Stratton with your mistress. Open the door, man, Lady Fleur is chilled and damp.'

Not long afterwards they sat by a roaring fire sipping hot chocolate – but not for long. As soon as the warmth returned to her fingers Fleur announced her attention to visit Gerard.

'Wake Gerard's nurse and tell her his mama will be up to see him,' she told the manservant who attended them. 'She need not dress herself and she need not wake her charge. You understand? I just want to look upon his face.'

The nursery was warm, the embers of a fire still glowing in the grate. A night light flickered in a shallow dish of water, a comforting glow on the table. The nurse had been seated when they entered. She sprang to her feet, lit a candle from the night light and bobbed a curtsey.

Past her youth, she was not old, and although she was slender, she was not thin. She was plain, but not ugly. Her expression was respectful, but contained no subservience. Fleur liked the look of her. Remy would have been thorough when hiring her, but still she determined to interview her all over again.

The nurse didn't have to wake her son. As soon as Fleur gazed down at Gerard's dear face it was as if he sensed her presence. Liquid eyes opened to gaze at her. Despite

their sleepiness they were intense and un-
blinking – an expression borrowed straight
from Remy.

'*Mama?*' A small smile came and went,
followed by a wide, unbelieving one. Scrambling upright he flung himself into her arms,
buried his head in her neck and hugged her
tight.

Tears filled her eyes as she inhaled his familiar scent. 'Oh, my dearest love, I've missed
you so much.' She covered his face in kisses
then smiled at the nurse.

'I'm sorry I roused you from your sleep,'
she choked out, and, fumbling in her pocket
found a handkerchief with which to dry her
eyes. 'I just couldn't wait until morning to
see him.'

'To be sure, it's no trouble. The young
master is a well-behaved little man. He'll
soon settle down again and he'll sleep
through the night with dreams of his mama
to keep him content, won't you, my darlin'?'

Thumb jammed in his mouth, Gerard
smiled at her and nodded. His dark eyelashes
were already fanning his cheeks.

As Fleur laid him back on his pillow the
nurse began to croon a lullaby in a lilting
Irish accent. 'What's your name?' she en-
quired after giving Gerard one last, lingering
kiss.

'Maura Gallagher, My Lady.'

'We'll talk on the morrow then, Maura,'

she said, and deciding she liked this Irish woman, gave her a smile before she headed for the cold comfort of her bedchamber.

Newgate prison was a dank, cold place. Remy was isolated from the other prisoners and held in a condemned cell, which was sparsely furnished with a rough wooden bench and table.

Perhaps he was held there to save moving him after the trial, because the penalty for treason was death, Fleur thought with a sudden chill. A sturdy looking public gallows had been erected outside of the prison as a warning to people.

Remy looked pale, but at the sight of them his eyes lit up, a glow that was immediately extinguished when he glanced at Leland. 'You shouldn't have brought her here.'

'I would have come whether he'd brought me or not,' she said with determination. 'Why is it as soon as you are gone from my sight you attract trouble? It would please me greatly if you would furnish me with a plausible explanation of how you came to be in this predicament.'

'Would it, be damned?' he spluttered. 'I'm not a child to be talked to in this manner.'

Leland found it hard not to grin when his sister snorted, 'If you don't I'll be forced to confront the Earl of Northhaven, who once employed you and now stands to accuse you. He's a slimy rat and I'll batter down his door and cut off his tail to find the truth, if need be.'

'You will do no such thing. You will take our son to Stragglemarsh Hall as I instructed, and you will stay there until you are told differently. Don't forget to give the eyeglass to my grandfather.'

Blood sang in her ears. 'You are the most infuriating and obdurate of men, Remy St Cyres. I'll not be ordered about like some scullery maid, and would point out that you're in no position to compel me to do anything. As you seem incapable of extricating yourself from this mess I intend to stay and petition on your behalf.'

'You will go,' he insisted furiously.

'I most certainly will not! If you go to the gallows I'll be left a widow. Having been in that bereft state already on your behalf, I have no intention of making a habit out of mourning you.'

'You were never a widow, our union was not blessed by the church,' he said cruelly. 'You are not my wife. You never have been.'

Her heart plunged as she hissed. 'So, you low bellied snake ... you were lying when you told me you loved me?'

'I cannot recall saying such a foolish thing to you and when I'm released you will end up over my knee for your impertinence.'

Her voice rose a fraction. 'Let me refresh

your suspiciously inconvenient memory, then. The first time was at the Duke of Warrington's ball, just before you disappeared from my life to get yourself killed for the first time. The second was more recent, on the day we went to market and you asked me to ride with you. You said...' She glared at Macy, who was grinning slightly. 'Well, never mind the exact words.'

'You're talking nonsense, Fleur.'

'Hah! You are the one talking nonsense. And dare to lay one stroke of the cane on my rear and I'll command my brothers to finalise the punishment you attracted when you snatched me from their care.' Hands on hips she glared at him, her eyes alert for his reaction.

A pulse beating in his jaw was the only thing alive in his face. The remainder appeared to be carved from stone. 'The abduction was merely a means to an end,' he drawled.

They stared at each other. Remy's eyes were dark and cold, keeping her at a distance. Did he consider her lacking in intelligence when she'd been raised by men? She'd get past that facade of his if she killed him in the attempt.

He didn't flinch when she whipped the back of her hand across his face, leaving a red welt. Behind her, Leland sucked in a tightly controlled breath when she hissed,

'Never lie to me again, Remy. I can have no respect for a man who stoops to deceit.'

She turned on her heel and was about to leave when he drew in a ragged breath. 'If you stay you'll be in danger. Take our son and go, I beg of you, Fleur. Make sure the eyeglass is delivered.'

She turned, and observing a moment of naked misery in his eyes her breath caught in her throat. Thank God her instincts had been true.

'First,' she said, her voice hesitant and uncertain, 'Tell me you didn't mean what you said.'

He knew exactly what she referred to. When he held out his arms to her she rushed into them and covered the face she'd just hit with kisses.

The brothers moved to the barred window and stared out, smiling at each other as they allowed the pair a moment of intimacy.

Leland thought. Fleur is a cunning little vixen, always has been. Thank God Remy hasn't got the measure of her yet.

EIGHTEEN

Their return to Rosehill was swift.

Hamish McDuff was relieved to see them. The house had been thoroughly searched in her absence by soldiers.

According to Hamish, nothing of value had been taken, but documents and books had been strewn around and a couple of items broken.

The note that Remy had given her on the beach, written by the hand of Hernando Cordova, was missing.

The three of them made all haste to Stragglemarsh Hall; where the situation was discussed at length. Her input was taken into account by the old earl.

'I will need those papers I gave you for safe-keeping,' Fleur told him. 'And for the sake of safety, Gerard and his nurse must stay here with you. Whatever Remy's instructions, I'm returning to London. I cannot abandon him.'

They didn't bother to argue. In fact, Gerard's great-grandfather heartily approved of her loyalty. 'The boy will be safe here with us. I'll set two of my stoutest footmen to guard him night and day. No doubt your brothers will act for you, if needed.'

He thought for a long moment then smiled. 'Northhaven is bound to subject you to a search now. To have those papers on your person would be extremely foolhardy, and dangerous for Remy.'

'I will send my man to London by road. He will carry the papers and a message for a colleague of mine, who has been useful in the past. Even if you recognize him do not approach the man unless it's strictly necessary. God keep you safe.'

'I must inform you of something,' she said hesitantly, and glancing at her brothers for support. 'It has come to light that the marriage between Remy and myself may be invalid.'

The earl gently kissed her. 'In my mind and heart you are the beloved wife of my heir, and the mother of my great grandson. This, I conveyed in a letter to Remy when he voiced his concerns.'

'He's told you?'

'I received a letter a little while back. He'd just regained his memory in full, and wrote to ask for my pardon for past wrongs. He informed me he was staying in London to petition the King. He wanted his marriage recognized and his heir to be declared legitimate. He was doing this for you, as well as the child, Fleur. It was to be his gift for you, he said.'

Fleur felt weepy, and a little humbled.

'Remy also remembered he had an important mission to conclude. He said he'd been entrusted with a document that named a network of people plotting to overthrow George and install his son on the throne as regent. He was waiting for an audience with the Prime Minister so he could inform him of the plot against the King. Then I received news of Northhaven's accusation and Remy's arrest.'

Unease flushed through her. 'So, the Earl of Northhaven cannot be trusted. I knew he was behind this. But why?'

'The spider has ever been an opportunist. He wormed his way into the King's confidence by pandering to his ... strange fantasies.' He gazed at Elmira, smiling as he took her hand. 'Forgive us, but we took the precaution of having Remy's papers translated.'

Elmira nodded. 'Tell her, Gerard.'

'The affair concerns Remy's parents and the need for the Cordova family to avenge his mother's death. It is a matter of honour for them, not politics, as it is with us. Remy has been given the task of exposing Northhaven and bringing him to justice.'

Elmira made an impatient noise deep in her throat. 'Our son had an important position in court. Northhaven was jealous of that and incensed when Julia Cordova spurned his advances.'

364

Fleur sucked in a shocked breath.

The earl murmured. 'Julia had a flirtatious manner.'

'Completely misunderstood,' Elmira said, throwing him a dark look. 'She loved William.'

'Quite so,' the earl said hastily. 'Julia overheard two envoys from Spain discussing confidential information received from Northhaven. William charged the man with it. The accusation was denied of course. Northhaven was about to be dismissed from his post when William and Julia were assassinated.'

Elmira had tears in her eyes. 'The papers are a deathbed confession by one of those envoys. The man was distantly related to the Cordova family, and was shocked by the killings. Although Northhaven wasn't directly involved in the deed, he did give the order.'

'Remy was only a child. Why is he being made to pay for what was his parents' business?'

'Northhaven has never been sure if William left an account of what Julia overheard that day.'

'Did he?'

'Julia did. She sent a missive to her family. They could not act on it because the two envoys were agents for Spain. To do so would have been treasonable. That letter is included with the papers.'

'So Northhaven recruited Remy and arranged for him to be killed abroad as a precaution,' Leland finished.

'The man is dangerous because he feels cornered,' Fleur said with an apprehensive shiver.

'Which puts you in danger too my dear. I shouldn't be surprised if Northhaven's name doesn't feature on the list Remy has.'

The eyeglass, and Remy's insistence it be given to his grandfather suddenly took on a greater significance. She smiled and holding it out to him, said. 'I believe I know where that list is hidden, grandfather.'

London society had snubbed her. Not one card or invitation had arrived and backs were turned at her approach in the street.

'Slut,' somebody shouted from the safety of a window. 'You and your bastard son should be ashamed to show your faces round here.'

Excrement was left of her doorstep and one night the kitchen cat was skewered through the guts and hung by a hook from their door. It was still writhing when Macy put it out of its misery.

Half her staff had found other appointments, the rest were sullen, grumbling about the extra work even though she recompensed them. Fleur went about her business, her head held high and flanked by her ever-vigilant brothers.

Chief amongst the business was visiting Remy. She paid the guards to keep him adequately fed and to provide him with extra comforts such as water with which to wash, a warm blanket and books to read. He was not allowed to mix with the other prisoners awaiting trial, but seemed content with his own company nevertheless.

'I've been in worse places,' he said, 'And my own thoughts are company enough.'

They were never left alone. With a vigilant guard always in attendance they had to be careful not to relax too much, lest their conversation give away information that might be reported.

It was an agony being near Remy, knowing he suffered and being unable to help him or comfort him.

'Did you discover the whereabouts of the eyeglass you mislaid?' he said casually one day.

Her glance tangled with his. 'It was left behind when I last visited your grandfather. He has taken quite a fancy to it and tells me he has cleared the blockage and can see quite clearly through it now.'

His smile was breathtaking. He leaned forward and took her hands in his. 'Why didn't you stay in the country when you were told? You have no idea how much I worry about you.'

'Leland and Macy are with me constantly.'

Her smile faltered. 'This waiting is so frustrating,' she burst out. 'How can I best be of help to you?'

'By being patient, my love.' He took her hands in his and raised them to his lips. 'There are no circumstances under which I'd betray my King and country.'

'How can you be so calm?'

'It's Northhaven's word against mine. There is no proof that brands me a traitor. I'm innocent, and when this goes to trial I'm confident of the verdict.'

She hugged him tight. 'I love you,' she whispered against his ear. 'I wish the guard would give us a little privacy.'

Remy grinned, then tipped up her chin and tenderly kissed her. 'So do I, but the fellow has a job to do and he does it well.'

'Time's up,' the guard said, smiling a little at the compliment. He liked the viscount, who was unfailingly polite and uncomplaining towards him.

He considered. He might just find some excuse to step outside the next time for a small consideration. A man deserved a little comfort from time to time, and the woman was a tasty piece.

Fleur arrived back at Hanover Square to discover her house being ransacked by several soldiers. A small crowd of their neighbours had formed outside. She was hissed and spat at as they pushed their way through.

The Earl of Northhaven lounged in a chair, a glass and decanter of wine on the table beside him.

'Ah, we meet again my dear, Lady Fleur ... gentlemen?' His hand waved over the table. 'Do please join me in some refreshment.'

'Do you have to do this to her?' Leland ground out, annoyed by the knowledge he was powerless to stop it.

'My dear sir, I would be remiss in my duty if I did not.'

'What is it you're after?' She cried out, outraged by the vandalism taking place.

The man's smile faded, and any pretence of pleasantness fled. 'Anything that will incriminate your husband ... *or clear his name.* The right piece of paper might set him free. Have you seen one?'

Vehemently, she shook her head.

His smile appeared; thin and dry like the mouth on the face of a lizard. 'Oh, I keep forgetting, the viscount is not your husband is he? How unfortunate he managed to force his bastard into you. Or was it force? Some women, even those of noble birth will accommodate a man's lust given only the slightest encouragement.'

She put a restraining hand of Macy's arm, which was rigid. 'Do not allow him to provoke you,' she whispered.

'The unfortunate liaison must have quite

spoiled your chances of making a decent marriage. No man wants a soiled woman for a wife.'

'Finish your business, then get out,' Leland growled at Northhaven. 'In the meantime keep your foul thoughts to yourself or I'll cut out your tongue.'

Northhaven's eyes narrowed. 'Be careful, My Lord. You are not out of reach of the King's might.'

'And a spider is not beyond being trampled underfoot, however fast he thinks he can run,' Fleur warned him. 'Will you be long about your business? I'm tired.'

It seemed hours before they left. She could have wept at the damage they left behind them. Mattresses and hangings had been slashed, paintings dragged from the walls and ornaments and china smashed into shards whilst they all gazed impotently on.

She sat in the middle of it all afterwards, shrugging when Macy and Leland tried to comfort her. 'He can pull the house down around my ears brick by brick. He can torture me, bury me alive and drown me in a bathtub. Nothing will make me betray Remy.'

'We must pray that the Earl of Blessingham has everything in hand. Whilst I act as a decoy it might delay Northhaven's thoughts from going in that direction.'

The next day she was taken to the local

watchhouse and questioned about the note from Hernando Cordova.

Her brothers were left fuming outside as Fleur was subject to a personal search. Northhaven was thorough. His hands pinched and squeezed her breasts. They lingered under her skirts where they forced apart her thighs to fumble at her most private of parts with a loathsome and brutal familiarity.

'It's surprising where women keep things hidden,' he said, breathing heavily.

She dug her nails into the palm of her hand as the insulting intimacy continued, wondering where it would stop.

It was a violation of her body without the intimate incursion, for one glance showed him lacking the ultimate potency to react in a truly manly way. He was flushed of face when he finished, but his eyes displayed the shame of his failure.

Although she longed to taunt, Fleur kept her counsel. Northhaven was vindictive enough to hand her over to the guards should she point out his shortcomings as a man.

The questioning began. His voice was loud and harsh, as if to regain his belief in his own potency as a man.

'Where did the note come from?'

She told the truth. 'It was on my husband when he was washed ashore. He was almost dead and without memory.'

'Who is Hernando Cordova?'

'He's my husband's uncle on his mother's side.' She gazed calmly into his eyes and moved as close to an accusation as she dared go. 'A fact of which you're well aware, for you were once acquainted with William and Julia St Cyres, were you not?'

He flinched. 'Remy St Cyres is not your husband. You are, in fact, his mistress, a state that brings shame upon your family. Bishop Chalmers has signed a statement saying he was compelled at sword point to wed you to Remy St Cyres.'

Her lips tightened but she said nothing. She was determined to remain calm and allow no threats of imprisonment, accusations or insults to penetrate her armour or panic her into an admission.

'Who brought him ashore?'

She hesitated slightly, choosing her words with care. If she mentioned the Spanish ship she would be arrested for not reporting it to the authorities. 'I did. He was in a small dinghy that hit a rock and overturned. I waded into the sea and dragged him ashore before he drowned.'

His eyes were hard against hers. She didn't bother to hide her disdain because she had neither the inclination nor artifice to waste on pretence.

'Did he say anything of significance?'

She smiled slightly. 'The viscount was near

death, starving and had a bullet lodged in his skull. He was too weak to stand and had no recollection of his name or his past. He recognized no one and was covered in scars from many months of being tortured by the Spanish.' She leant forward, her expression accusatory. 'No, My Lord, he said nothing of significance, unless…?'

Northhaven leaned forward, his face intent. 'What is it he said?'

'He asked me if I was an angel. Perhaps he thought he'd died and gone to heaven. Wouldn't that indicate his conscience was clear? If he'd been guilty of betraying his country he would have expected to go to hell, wouldn't he?'

'You're being blasphemous?'

'Not at all, My Lord. I'm merely pointing out the fact that evil-doers ultimately answer for their sins. If not in this life, certainly in the next.'

He stared hard at her, but she was saved further questioning when an officer came into the room and whispered something in his ear.

He smiled and flapped a dismissive hand at her. 'I've been summoned to the palace by one of the King's chief advisors. I will put Remy St Cyres case before him and set a date for trial. However, I will not recommend clemency.' He looked her up and down. 'You should reconsider the offer I made regarding marriage to my wife's cousin. He's in need of a wife of means, and one healthy enough to bear his children.'

'As you indicated, My Lord...' Fleur curtseyed, mocking him, for she knew the old earl's messenger had got through with the papers, and Northhaven was about to experience the bite of the St Cyres snake. 'My reputation is sullied beyond repair. No man of decency would want me for a wife now.'

She felt exhausted when she left, her head held high.

Leland and Macy were waiting anxiously outside for her. Both of them had been questioned rigorously. She smiled reassuringly at them, for nothing would make her reveal the insulting personal search Northhaven had inflicted on her body.

Shaking her head when they tried to lead her away, she said. 'Let's find a doorway and wait for a moment or two. I have a feeling the spider is about to be snared in his own web.'

Within a short time Northhaven emerged and strode off up the street. Two officers came out after him and signalled to a man who was slumped against a wall opposite. The man straightened, then followed after them. As he passed, he caught her eye and smiled. Fleur's breath hissed in her throat. It was Noah.

Though she would have rushed straight to

the prison, Leland stopped her. 'It could be some time before he's released. Someone is bound to want to question him. Macy and I will escort you home, then we'll try and find out what's happening.'

It was a long wait. When dawn was breaking she finally heard a single set of footsteps approaching the house. Pushing open the window she stared out into the cold, grey light. 'Remy, thank God you're free,' she whispered, and warmed by his smile, gathered her robe about her and raced downstairs to let him inside.

She was in his arms in an instant, covering his face with kisses. He pushed her to arm's length, his eyes hungrily consuming every inch of her. 'I'm here only to reassure you of my safety and to bathe and change my clothing. I'm expected back at the palace in a little while.'

'Oh, Remy. Can you not stay with me?'

He tipped up her chin and gazed into her eyes, his expression serious. 'I have an audience with the King. I love you, Fleur. I want our marriage declared legal and my heir legitimate. Nothing must stand in the way of that.'

She rang a bell, summoning a maid of all work whose job it was to rise early and light the fires before the other servants appeared. 'Rouse a manservant and tell him to prepare the master's bath and make sure his clothes are fitting to wear at an audience with the King,' she ordered, with more than a little pride.

When the girl scuttled off to do her bidding she took Remy's hand and led him towards the stairs, smiling a little. 'It will take a little while. In the meantime we'll rest together and I'll tell you how much I love you.'

'Perhaps it would be better if you demonstrated,' he whispered in her ear.

It was a satisfied man who left the house later. Feeling happily lethargic, Fleur sank back into the pillows, smiling to herself. When Remy returned from the palace she'd be legally married to him, for the King was bound to reward him in some way for his services.

Then she would insist they go back to Rosehill. With that thought uppermost in her mind she drifted off to sleep.

It was not to be.

'The King has denied my petition,' Remy whispered in her ear upon his return.

'How dare he do such a thing!' Propping herself on one elbow Fleur gazed with consternation through her dishevelled hair at him. 'I will have words with him myself.'

Remy's laugh rang out. 'There is no need for you to take him to task. His Majesty tells me he hasn't the power to change the law. But he'll declare our son as my legitimate heir if I meet certain conditions.'

'Which are?'

'We are to be wed in his presence in the chapel of St James's palace in four weeks hence. After which, we will be guests of honour at a ball. He said it will take everyone's minds off the Americans.'

She laughed, and stretched herself like a lazy cat. 'I'll need a new gown for the occasion and I will wear the diamonds your grandfather gave me.'

He smiled approvingly at her, and his fingers trailed across her lips. 'There's another condition. We must not see each other in that time.'

'He *is* mad!' she gasped.

Remy chuckled. 'Take care woman, it may be an offence to say so.'

'But I cannot live another moment without seeing you.'

'You'll have to.' Remy's kiss was passionate with promise. 'However, I have an hour or two to spare, so we must make the most of it.'

So they did.

EPILOGUE - SPRING 1783

A daughter had been born to Fleur and Remy at Rosehill in the late winter. Today she'd been christened.

Julianna was named for her two grandmothers. The child would grow up to be a beauty with her dark Spanish eyes and sable hair.

Her parents and older brother adored her ... and each other. Leland had never known another couple that shared such a closeness of heart and mind.

Leland's glance moved on to Macy. His brother, who had never done things by halves, was inclined to favour his own daughters. He'd surpassed himself with the twins. Lucinda and Marigold had arrived six months previously with eyes as blue as cornflowers and soft golden curls. Their smiles melted the heart.

Macy had admitted he didn't know which one he adored the most. Like Leland, Macy could never tell which twin was which – although he wouldn't admit to it to their mother.

Leland gazed with pride on his own brood. His daughters were cooing over the newly christened infant, held in the arms of their beloved Aunt Fleur. Over to his left, and watched over by two vigilant nursery maids, a pack of small boys romped and tumbled like unruly puppies amongst the daffodils.

Amongst them was Gerard, who was pleased he had a cousin almost his own age to do boy things with occasionally.

Leland took Sylvane's hand and gave her a smile. Today she'd become Godmother to Fleur's infant daughter – an honour that had set the seal of respectability on her. Soon, Sylvane would become his countess. Today was the day he'd chosen to let the world know it by having the banns called.

The church had been crowded, but not for the christening. People were curious to see Sylvane.

Also, word had got around about the arrival of the new squire, so some had come to run an eye over Sara Boney and her son.

At fourteen years, Tarshish was small for his age. For most of his life he'd been boarded in the family of a soldier. His foster mother had found him to be quick and clever, so she'd taught him his letters and numbers. As a result, the young squire was reasonably educated and was now being tutored for entrance to Cambridge and a possible career as an attorney.

At the moment he was awkwardly conversing with the Earl and Countess of Blessingham, both of whom who kept glancing at Remy with fond smiles.

There would be plenty of gossip next market day. Young Tom had just trounced the old earl and his grandfather, farmer Blaggs, winning the prize for the fattest pig at the spring fair.

'Young varmint,' Blaggs was saying to anyone who would listen, his ruddy face beaming with pride.

Then there was Crispen. Leland gazed at his young brother and smiled as he saw the dreams still in his eyes – of horizons he'd yet to explore and of exotic women he'd yet to meet, no doubt.

The child Leland had always known was still there – the adventurer in him. Crispen had grown into a fine young man, one with courage and integrity. Leland experienced a feeling of extreme satisfaction. Not because a task well done was over, but because another had started with his own children.

Fleur was looking at Crispen too. She couldn't believe the change in him and wondered when she would see him again.

'He will be all right,' Remy whispered against her ear.

How well her husband knew her ... and how well she knew him.

'Something is on your mind. What is it, Remy?'

'Northhaven has been executed.'

'So Cordova honour has finally been satisfied.' Her eyes searched the darkness in his. 'Charles Boney has never been apprehended. Did you kill him?'

He gave a swift intake of breath. Her brothers would not have informed her of what took place. 'What makes you ask?'

'Part of you will always be Spanish.' She slipped an arm through his and gently kissed his cheek. 'You need not answer, Remy. Just know that I love you.'

Watching them all, but standing a little apart, Lieutenant Crispen Russell beamed benevolently on them. His eyes absorbed the scene and imprinted it on his memory.

Soon, his ship was to set sail for the Southern Ocean, a taxing and dangerous journey of several thousand miles, at the end of which they would chart the reefs and shoreline of the great continent claimed for Britain by his hero, Captain James Cook.

Although he looked forward to the adventure of it, there would be hardship and danger and it would be many months before he set eyes again on his family again.

But ties of kin were never broken. They would live in his memory and one day he would return to them – his own man.

This Large Print Book, for people
who cannot read normal print,
is published under the auspices of

THE ULVERSCROFT FOUNDATION

... we hope you have enjoyed this book.
Please think for a moment about those
who have worse eyesight than you ...
and are unable to even read or enjoy
Large Print without great difficulty.

You can help them by sending a
donation, large or small, to:

**The Ulverscroft Foundation,
1, The Green, Bradgate Road,
Anstey, Leicestershire, LE7 7FU,
England.**
or request a copy of our brochure for
more details.

The Foundation will use all donations
to assist those people who are visually
impaired and need special attention
with medical research, diagnosis
and treatment.

Thank you very much for your help.